Praise for

pamela klaffke

and *Snapped*

"Klaffke's debut is a delicious guilty pleasure
full of hilarious, irreverent moments…
A dark, comic absurdity peppers every page."
—*Publishers Weekly*

"Profane, painfully honest and savagely funny,
Klaffke's debut novel is a coming-of-middle-age story
sure to evoke terror in the under-40 set and
reminiscent smiles in those who have already crossed over."
—*RT Book Reviews* (4 stars)

"*Snapped* had me laughing
and wondering what was going to happen next…
Klaffke's writing was so brilliant."
—*Kansas City Literature Examiner*

D1515536

Also available from MIRA Books and Pamela Klaffke

SNAPPED

every little thing

pamela klaffke

MIRA®

MIRA®

Recycling programs
for this product may
not exist in your area.

ISBN-13: 978-0-7783-2923-7

EVERY LITTLE THING

Copyright © 2011 by Pamela Klaffke

For questions and comments about the quality of this book please contact us
at Customer_eCare@Harlequin.ca.

www.MIRABooks.com

Printed in U.S.A.

every

little

thing

REUNION

The apartment my mother shared with Ron is possibly the tackiest I've seen. Everywhere, there are mirrors and furry rugs. The lights are off and the curtains drawn. Lit candles cover every surface and there is a giant photograph of my mother above the fireplace. It's the photo that accompanied her column. It's at least twenty years old and her lipstick is magenta.

Seth pushes a glass of champagne into my hand. The bar is open; we missed the service thanks to the wake-up call I forgot to book at the hotel. I hear someone say something about a pagan priestess and down my drink too fast and the bubbles stick in my head, fizzy needles pricking at my brain. "She's here," Seth says in a whisper.

"Who?"

"Your mother."

"Not funny."

"I'm serious, Mason. She's in the bedroom. She's wearing

fur. And big earrings that look like diamonds but they're so big, they might just be—"

"They're real," I say. I know the ones. My father gave them to her before I was born, when she was his mistress and the scandal whore of San Francisco. I edge through the crowded living room, my head down and Seth a pace behind me. I have no idea where Janet is, but I need another drink more than I need to find her. I order a vodka from the tuxedoed bartender and he pours me an ounce over ice. It is not nearly enough. He pours another careful ounce and now this is tedious, so I take the bottle from him and pour until the vodka is flush with the rim of the glass. "There," I say and take a sip. Half burns down my throat while the rest dribbles down my chin. Seth gets a napkin and dabs at my dress. I swat him away. I don't care. It will dry.

I'm wearing a black dress and heels. My blond roots are showing but I have the pearls my mother gave me for my eighteenth birthday clasped around my neck. I bring my hand to my throat to make sure they're still there, that they haven't fallen off and already been pawned. That's surely what she'd expect. She'd call it typical and then write about it in her column.

We find Janet in the bedroom, talking with Ron, who is crying, but his face is perfectly still. He may have had more work done than my mother.

"Mason! Thank God you're here!" Ron pulls me into a hug and weeps onto my dress. He kisses my cheek and his fluffy mustache tickles my skin. I've met him only once before, about five years ago, when he and my mother came to visit me in Canmore shortly after I started working at the bookstore and was living with Neil. The trip was a disaster. Neil and I split up a week after my mother and Ron left. He said the timing was a coincidence but he wasn't a good liar, and I added him to the list of things my mother has fucked up for me. The list is in a spiral notebook in the bottom of my suitcase back at the hotel. I started it when I was fifteen. It has three hundred pages and is nearly full.

"I just feel like it's my fault," Ron is saying, "that I shouldn't have bought her the gift, but that's what she wanted, she really did, Mason. And you know there was no way to stop Britt from getting what she wants—you know that, right? But I can't help thinking that it's my fault."

Ron is blubbering and he keeps trying to touch me. I think he's right: it *is* his fault. He's the one who bought her the stupid vaginal rejuvenation surgery. It was a gift for her sixtieth birthday, which would have been next week. As much as I'm sure she's pissed about this whole situation in whichever afterlife she believed in lately, she's undoubtedly glad she is forever fifty-nine because it sounds so much better than sixty.

Ron is a tacky asshole with a cheesy mustache and he killed my mother, whose body is laid out on the double-king four-poster bed, dressed in fur and diamonds just like Seth said. Her eyes are closed, her makeup is perfect and in the forgiving candlelight she looks almost as young as she did in her twenty-year-old column photo. I wish I had a magenta lipstick so I could smear it on her lips—then she'd be perfect. But I only have red.

Two men are staring at me from across the living room. They're young—well, *youngish*. I'd say they were in their thirties, like me. They're impeccably dressed in tailored black suits and polished leather shoes that even from a distance I can tell are too expensive for them to be writers or arts people.

"Who is *that?*" Seth asks, pointing to the taller of the men. Seth has never been known for his subtlety.

"Stop pointing," I say.

"Do you know him?"

I turn my head to the side, and pick imaginary lint off my shoulder. I squint and focus. "I don't think so," I say. I really do need to get glasses.

"You don't think what?" Janet asks as she joins us.

"That she knows those yummy guys over there," Seth says.

"Which guys?"

"Never mind," I say.

"The ones in the good suits?" Janet asks.

"Yes, the ones in the good suits," I say. Can we please change the subject? I'm trying to mourn.

"The ones who are walking over here?" Janet asks.

"What?" I spin around and sure enough, there they are.

"Mason, I'm so sorry about your mother," the shorter man says. He knows my name. "She was always my favorite, you know."

"Favorite what?" I take the bait, though I know where this is headed: your mom was great, *your mom was funny, I loved her column, you're so lucky.* He looks like someone I know, or maybe someone on TV. He's grinning and staring at me like he's highly amused.

He looks puzzled. "My favorite stepmother."

My mouth falls open. I look at him. It's Aaron. I remember the dimples, those bright blue eyes. I look at the other man, the taller one. God, it's got to be Edgar. My mother was married to their father when I was—what, five, maybe six at the most? He was a widower and we lived in a big house on his vineyard in Sonoma. We were only there for a year.

Edgar leans in and hugs me. "It is so wonderful to see you after all this time," he says. "I just wish it was under better circumstances." I look up at him. He's awfully tall. "You look great, by the way." He smiles down at me. Edgar, I suspect, is also a good liar. I push my long black bangs out of my eyes. I wish I had had time to touch up my blond roots before I came, before I had to drop everything and jump on a plane, after Ron called and told me my mother was dead.

"Are you still in the city?" Aaron asks. He's a year younger than me. Edgar and I are the same age.

I shake my head. "I live in Canada," I say. This always throws people off; they never know quite how to react.

"That must be very nice," Edgar says.

"It is," I say, and it's true. It is very nice, my quiet life in Canmore, the small Canadian mountain town where I work at the bookstore and everyone thinks I'm some sort of witch because I wear black and dye my hair. "And you?" I feel like we're reading from a script at a modern etiquette class that teaches you how to deal with awkward situations like running into your ex-stepbrothers at your mother's funeral reception surrounded by animal print furniture and rugs.

"I have a studio in SoMa," Aaron says.

"He's a painter," Edgar adds.

Aaron blushes. "I try."

"What about *you?*" Seth asks Edgar. The look on his face is carnivorous. I step to my left and my arm grazes Seth's. I take my free hand and pinch him hard on the forearm, through his jacket. "Ow!" he yelps. Aaron and Edgar look alarmed. I notice my black polish is chipped and slide one hand into the front pocket of my faded black cotton dress and drop my drinking hand down, holding the glass behind me in hopes that no one will notice my nails.

"I'm Janet—and this is Seth." Janet shakes Aaron's hand, then Edgar's. Leave it to her to know exactly what to do in an uncomfortable situation like this. She's got a sixth sense for these kinds of things. *She* should be running modern etiquette classes. She could write books, be on TV—she would make a fortune.

"Looks like everyone could use another cocktail," Edgar says. With introductions done, Janet shuffles the five of us off to a corner that's freed up. I sit on the sofa, between her and Seth. I kick off the cheap, low-heeled pumps I bought yesterday at an outlet store. But my black toenail polish is chipped, too, so I shove my feet back into the ugly discount shoes.

"Just bring a bottle," I say to Edgar, only half joking.

"Maybe you should take it easy," Janet whispers to me. I scowl. I have no intention of *taking it easy*. Janet is out of line, telling me what to do. *She's not my mother,* I think, but the moment that thought hits my head I want it gone. I close my eyes in an effort to keep the bigger truth down. *She's not my mother.* No one is.

"Mason, are you okay?" I hear Aaron's voice and open my eyes. He's kneeling across from me, a long glass coffee table between us.

"I'm—" What am I? I blink back the tears I can feel rising. Janet rubs my back. "I'm—" I look up and see Edgar, an ice bucket under one arm and a full bottle of premium vodka in the other. I laugh and smile. "I'm fine."

I have no idea what Aaron and Edgar are talking about, but I nod and laugh in all the right places and stuff myself with grapes and cubes of cheese. They're reminiscing, telling stories about the silly games we played as kids, the times we got away with things and the times we got caught and in big trouble. Most of it I can't remember. Before middle school, there are only flashes and faces, moving boxes, new schools and new classmates, but no complete stories. And everything I do remember I hardly trust, since most of the information about my earlier childhood I got from reading my mother's

"Are you sure you don't want to freshen up first?"

"What's that supposed to mean?"

I lean over until my mouth is at her ear. "You smell like sex."

Janet gasps and clutches at her chest. She's never been one for melodrama, so this makes her behavior especially hilarious. "I do not."

"You do."

"Shit. I'll be right back." She stands up and turns to go—to the bathroom, I expect—but I grab her arm and pull her back.

"I'm kidding. You're fine."

"Then how did you—"

"Flushed, fidgety, cagey, nervous, *Oakland*—take your pick." I know her too well, even if I have been away for eight years.

"Okay, fine. You win."

"Who is he?"

"Just a guy. You'd like him."

"Who is he?"

"Actually, I think you may have met him—a long time ago."

"Name, please."

"Victor Durrell!" Seth says, startling both Janet and me. He's standing behind us. "It's Victor Durrell! What do I win?"

"Sorry, wrong answer—better luck next time," I say.

"No, seriously, Mason. It's Victor Durrell," Seth says as he takes a seat.

"You don't even know what we're talking about. Why don't you go get us some drinks?"

"Nuh-uh, no way. I wouldn't miss this," Seth says, crossing his arms and leaning back in his chair. I notice Janet biting her bottom lip. She's looking down and she's awfully quiet. Oh. *Ew.*

"You've *got* to be kidding," I say. "*Victor Durrell?* I'm sorry, Janet, but *gross.*"

"He is not *gross,*" she says.

"He is sorta sexy in a certain kind of way," Seth says.

"In what? A gross old man kind of way? I can't believe you didn't tell me about this." I hit Seth on the arm.

He shrugs and gestures to Janet. "She wanted to tell you herself."

"He is not *old* or *gross,*" Janet says. She sounds wounded and looks as if she might cry.

"Okay, he's not old or gross," I say, even though he is. It was fifteen years ago when I first met him and I'm quite confident in my assumption that he has not reversed the aging process, nor has he somehow, miraculously, become *less gross.* He was friends with my mother, when she was married to David, the English painter, and Victor Durrell was one of David's friends. We lived on the top floor of a giant warehouse. It was all exposed brick and concrete floors and David smoked a lot of pot. Victor would come by for drinks and to talk about art. "How old is Victor? He must be—"

"He's not sixty until January," Janet snaps.

Good God. *Extra gross.* Is his skin all loose and flappy? Can he still get it up? I guess that's what Viagra is for. I shudder and hope Janet doesn't notice. I rub the sleeves of my jacket in an attempt to cover, just in case. "It's cold in here. Aren't you cold?"

"He's very talented—and smart," Janet says.

"He is," I say. He could be—I know he gets a lot of press. He's a sculptor—or a painter.

"His work has been chosen for the Venice Biennale next year." Janet is doing the hard sell.

"I'm sure it's great, I'm sure he's great, I'm just surprised. He doesn't seem like your type," I say.

"And what do you know about *my type,* Mason?"

"He just seems—"

"Old? Gross?" Seth does nothing to ease the tension.

"No—I meant short. Isn't Victor shorter than you usually like?" I remember nothing about Victor's height, but most men are shorter than Janet so I take the gamble—I want to make peace.

"We're the same height," Janet says. She's defiant. "And he doesn't care one bit if I wear heels—*he likes it.* He's past any superficial hang-ups. He's *mature.*"

Seth makes a face that Janet doesn't catch and I try not to laugh. I'll get the whole sordid story from him later.

None of us wear a watch, but it must be past nine, maybe later and our conversation has devolved into small talk. I don't dare bring up Victor again and after we're all tired of walking down memory lane, Janet and Seth talk about work and I lose myself in another martini. I lost track of the number I had some time ago. Why do people want to talk about work when they're out for drinks? I pop the last shrimp of my shrimp cocktail into my mouth. Isn't the whole point of going drinking to forget about work?

By the time they move on to real estate prices and Williams-Sonoma kitchenware I'm drunk and exhausted—but I don't want to leave. I look around: the room is filled with new, anonymous faces—more shaggy bobs, less chignons. People dance and a live band plays trippy lounge classics. Janet has switched to water and keeps checking her phone as she describes a butter chicken recipe she calls "otherworldly." She's waiting for a message from old, gross Victor, I suppose. She goes on about the recipe and then Seth takes out a pen and starts writing it down. At first I think he's joking, but when he starts asking questions about the best brand of garam masala, I know he's not. Food is for eating, not making, and this is supposed to be a fun night out, our special reunion, not a recipe swap.

I almost cheer when Seth starts making up fantastical stories about the people in the bar, imagining transsexual mobsters and hermaphrodite spies. It's something he's done as long as I've known him.

Seth goes on and I notice that the maître d' looks my way now and then, sneering. I smirk. I must be a terrible reflection of his abilities as Enforcer of the Dress Code. Janet keeps her eyes trained on her phone. She looks worried and is off in her head. I tell her she can go, that I'm fine here with Seth and his stories, but with Janet etiquette trumps lust and she stays.

"Maybe we should take this back across the street," Seth says, cutting his socialite-cum-secret-freak story-time short.

"What?"

"To your suite—it's getting boring here. Janet?"

"Huh?"

"We should take this back to Mason's suite," Seth says.

"I shouldn't, really. I have an early morning," Janet says. Seth and I exchange glances. I am dying to make a quip about Victor, but hold my tongue. Surprisingly, Seth does, too. "I have to work on the show." She's holding a fashion show at her studio on Thursday to showcase her latest collection.

"I guess it's just you and me, Mason."

"We should get the check," Janet says.

Check? Shit. I have no credit card and this is an emergency, precisely the things I have been racking up a tab to forget. "Um, I don't suppose one of you could cover me? It's just—I saw the lawyer today and he canceled the card I had and I can't get my mother's money and there's taxes and everything's frozen. Ron said he would…but I can't and—"

"No worries," Janet says and puts her hand over mine. My heart is speeding and my breath is short. My eyes well up and for the first time since my mother's death, I cry.

NORTH BEACH

Maybe I shouldn't be surprised that the key the estate lawyer gave me works, but I am. It would be just like my mother to have bequeathed her apartment to me only to have changed the locks as some kind of "lesson" for me to learn. But the key works and Seth and I trip through the door—still drunk—laden with bags.

It's dark and the curtains are drawn and the rooms smell of garbage and dust and Shalimar. I step over my largest suitcase and fumble for the light switch.

"Holy shit," Seth says.

I am speechless. Everything—the furniture, the walls, the art, everything—is white. The last time I stepped foot in this flat eight years ago, it was still kitted out like some retro Asian bordello, with red and velvet and rich dark wood. Now it's streamlined, sleek, spare and calm—so unlike my mother.

I head immediately for what was once my bedroom expecting to find a workout room with all-white equipment or a weird meditation room or a library where all of the books have white spines and blank pages.

"Holy shit," Seth says. His vocabulary is limited by booze, though his words do accurately sum things up. Everything in the room—all of it—is exactly how I remember: my bed, my desk, my books, the three-hundred-dollar-a-roll Italian wallpaper with the black bats. I open the closet and it's full of my clothes circa nineteen-ninety-something, when I was twenty and walked out with nothing. I've only been here once since—maybe for an hour or two—after my mother lured me here under some false pretense I can't remember. That was eight years ago. I left for good after that. I never imagined I'd be back.

Even through the numbing layers of martinis I feel a twinge of—something—as I look around. It stabs me again when I pick up a framed photograph off the bureau: me, Seth, Janet, that guy I was dating at the time who turned out to be a total prick snob. I think his name was Davis. I squint my left eye and Davis's face blurs. That's better. It's one of the only photographs of myself that I like.

Seth dives onto my king-size bed. "Ow!"

"What?" I place the picture back on the bureau and turn to Seth, who sits up and pulls a book out from under him.

"Ooh, the Secret Diaries of Mason McDonald," he says as he flips through the pages.

I recognize the book's cover immediately—it's a journal collaged with Bryan Ferry pictures I snipped from a stash of old British music magazines I found at a rummage sale. I would have been fifteen or sixteen. "Give me that!" I lunge at Seth, but he darts and I fall face-first into my goose down comforter. It's red and Egyptian cotton and hand silk-screened with black-and-grey geometric shapes.

"My mother (aka Satan) is acting like more of an evil bitch than

usual. She had a dinner party tonight and of course everyone got drunk on wine and one of her retarded friends (the one who wears too much perfume and has bad breath) starts talking about her twelve-year-old daughter and puberty and blah, blah, and it's totally disgusting and I swear I just about puked. But then my mother starts going, 'Oh, that's nothing. I remember when Mason started to develop, blah, blah.' And she's being awful and telling these stories and all of her retarded friends are laughing like, 'heh, heh, heh,' and the guys (who are completely gross) are looking at me in this dirty way, so I tell her to shut up and fuck off (seriously), and she just laughs and says something about 'teenagers' so I go to my room and smoke a joint with Seth (at least he was here). I even left the door open and didn't smoke out the window. I don't care if she knows. She's such a bitch.

"Wow—that's fucking awesome, Mason. You should publish this—it's hilarious!" Seth leans over and kisses my cheek. "And thanks for the shout-out." Seth lays the journal in his lap and I grab it. "Aw, come on, Mason—it's funny. Let's read some more!"

"Fuck off."

"Pleeeease…"

"No." I'm so pissed off I'm shaking. Not so much at Seth, but at my mother. She's been—what?—sitting on my bed and reading my teenage journals. I decide that this is an all-new low and pull Seth up off the bed and charge out of my room, dragging him behind me.

"Where are we goooing? Your bed is commmfy." Seth can be such a whiny drunk.

"I think we should read *her* journals," I say as we traipse through the living room and march into her den.

I'm not sure my mother ever kept a journal, but if she did and it's here, I'm determined to find it—or at least something personal and embarrassing that she wouldn't want me to see.

It's not like she knew she was going to die and had time to destroy or hide anything, which is what I vow to do first thing tomorrow. I'll burn my journals and any other incriminating evidence of embarrassing youth.

"What do they looook like?" Seth really needs to stop using the whiny voice.

"I don't know."

"This is boring."

"Go find some wine and bring it back here," I say.

Seth claps his hands, suddenly chipper, and heads for the door.

I'm sitting on the floor and my back hurts, a sure sign that I'm getting old and decrepit. There are papers all over the floor: stacks of yellow legal pads filled with nearly illegible column notes, receipts for lunches and charity donations, pre-release galley copies of self-help books she'd get at the paper, but no diaries.

An unexpected blast of music jolts me out of my head. I look up and see a white speaker discreetly embedded in the white wall, Whitney Houston or Celine Dion blasting out of it. "Seth!" I crawl to the doorway and shout down the hall. "What the fuck!" The music cuts out and I lay back on the floor, but quickly sit up—not so much because the room starts spinning, but because whenever I am flat on my back it's yet another reminder of my age as I feel my squishy breasts sink into my armpits.

The music starts up again, but this time there's no top-40 power ballads. Seth has obviously been rooting through my mother's extensive collection of kitschy midcentury lounge music and I can tell from the full sound and occasional static blips that it's the original vinyl. I don't want to smile, but I do. My mother's records—the Xavier Cugats and the Esquivels, *not* the Celine Dions and Whitney Houstons—are pretty much the only things of hers I could ever possibly want.

Seth appears in the doorway with a glass in each hand, a box of crackers under his chin and a bottle under each arm. "Red or white?" he asks.

I stand up and grab the box of crackers. I should have white. It's lighter and the hangover isn't as bad. But I've had all of those martinis, which means I probably shouldn't have anything but water. I take a bite of salty goodness. Fuck it. "Red," I say.

Seth pours us each a glass and we toast. I almost say, "To my mother," because that's what a good daughter would do, but Seth beats me to it.

"To Britt," he says, so I don't have to.

"It could have been worse," Seth says. He's moved out of his drunk-whiny stage into his drunk-wise-man stage. I don't know which is more annoying.

"What?" I ask, and I drink two gulps of wine.

"Your mom," he says. "I know you think she was this raging bitch, but seriously, Mason, it could have been way worse. It's not like she hit you or let her boyfriends fuck you."

"Jesus, Seth!"

"See? She doesn't seem so bad when you think about it that way."

I can't believe Seth is defending her. No, actually, I can. He liked her. Janet liked her; she kept it to herself, but I could always tell. Men loved her. People—some of them, anyway—must have liked her because they read her column and wrote her letters saying so. She'd show them to me, and later, after I moved to Canada, she'd send copies in the post or scan them and e-mail them to me.

I never did understand those people who wrote the letters: were they losers with no lives of their own? Did they think she was amusing or insightful? Who would want to read every little thing about someone else's life unless they were someone famous or smart or interesting? Did they wonder about the effect those columns had on the people in them? Did they ever stop to think about me?

ART

It takes me a moment to figure out who this Aaron person is and why he might be calling me. Then I remember it's Aaron-Aaron, my ex-stepbrother Aaron, and flashes of that night at The Cecil swirl around in my head: the dancing, falling and the gross, sticky floor, the pearls scattered everywhere and the laughter of the Irony Girls. My shoulders bunch up as I cringe at my thoughts.

"So, I was hoping you'd come with me to an art opening tonight. I know it's last minute and you probably already have plans, but it was really great to see you again and I think it would be fun because the artist is a friend of mine who does these really great—"

"Sure, I'll go," I say, cutting off Aaron's rambling. I don't have anything better to do and there is always free food and booze at art openings.

I arrange to meet Aaron at the gallery. He said he'd pick me up, and while I would like a ride, I tell him I'll meet up with him instead. I hate walking, but the prospect of having to rush around and clean up after the mess Seth and I made the other night is worse.

It's been years since I've been in a gallery, or at least in a gallery that sells work other than bronze cowboy sculptures and oil paintings of mountain landscapes. Wearing black is always a safe, if predictable, choice. My entire wardrobe is black, and I'd love to wear my favorite black pants and my big cowl-neck sweater, but the pants are a bit too tight and both pieces are in my closet in Canmore.

For a gallery, I need something sophisticated or angular and Japanese. I try on a long black skirt with tights and my lace-up Doc Martens ankle boots and decide it works. But I need a top.

After rejecting everything in my suitcase and my teenage wardrobe, I head to my mother's bedroom. She was really into color, but there has to be something black I can wear. I go through her sweaters and shirts. I am *not* wearing anything that could be called a blouse. I find a black V-neck cashmere sweater and try it on. It's tighter on me than it must have been on my mother, but it looks okay, though a little boring. I pull my arms back out of the sleeves and twist the sweater around until the V is in the back. You always see pictures of celebrities in low-back dresses and tops and I think I read somewhere— maybe in a magazine on the plane—that the back is the new erogenous zone. I line and fill my lips with MAC Russian Red lipstick and touch up the kohl around my eyes. I tug the front of the neck down, so it sits flat where the label is. That's better.

It's not Aaron who first greets me at the gallery: it's Edgar. I'm surprised to see him there. Art didn't really strike me as his thing. "Clients," he says, nodding in the direction of two middle-aged men in suits contemplating a triptych of blank white canvases with one tiny black dot on each. "They wanted to experience the *bohemian* side of San Francisco, so I took them to the Haight this afternoon and they bought their kids hoodies at the Gap."

"That's so boho," I say with a laugh.

"They're from Ohio."

"Ah."

"There you are!" It's Aaron. He gives me a kiss on the cheek and holds out two plastic glasses filled with wine. "I didn't know if you preferred red or white."

"Both," I say and grab them from his hands. I down the white like a shot but when I take a sip of the red I nearly gag. It's awful.

"Are you okay?" Aaron asks. "I'll get you some water."

"I'd stick with the white—at least until you're sufficiently drunk enough to not be able to taste the red," says Edgar.

"Good plan," I say.

Aaron returns with a glass of water and another glass of white wine. I drink them quickly in succession. I look around the gallery. All of the walls are covered with giant white canvases, each having one small black dot painted somewhere on them. You have to get really close up to find some of them. The artist's name is j.— lower-case, no last name.

"The restraint he shows is remarkable," says Aaron. "It's quite amazing."

"It's bullshit," says Edgar. I smile at him and he winks.

"Then why did you just buy one?" Aaron asks.

"What Candice wants, Candice gets," he says.

"Edgar's wife," Aaron says to me.

"This guy's the latest greatest thing, so she has to have one. In six months, it'll be up for auction and I'll be staring at some new overpriced painting by the next best thing," Edgar says, then turns to Aaron. "Do you think they have any scotch?"

Edgar goes off in search of scotch and to entertain his clients. I'm not exactly sure what he does, but it must be lucrative for him to afford those smart suits and to be able to drop ten thousand dollars on a painting he doesn't even like.

Aaron and I circle the gallery and he tries to convince me how important and revolutionary j.'s work is. We run into a few of Aaron's artist friends and they, too, are full of praise for j. and his revolutionary dots. I scan the room to see if I recognize anyone, but I don't. I suppose I shouldn't expect to—the city has changed so much in the years I've been gone. I tell Aaron I'm going to get another drink.

I walk the long way around to the drinks-and-snacks table, past the businessmen and gallery reps, the real artists and the wannabes. The patrons are obvious—they're dressed in high-end office attire and the women wear heels and hose. The artists are just as cliché in their paint-splattered jeans and expensive glasses with asymmetrical European frames in any color but black. The wannabes are in layers of scrubby clothes and the girls wear tights with clunky boots. They're dressed like they think artists dress, not like actual artists. I look down at my big black Doc Martens boots. It's not the same at all—I'm not trying to pretend I'm an artist.

"You go to SFAI?" I turn around to find a young woman with dreadlocks facing me.

"Excuse me?"

"CCA? AAC?" she asks.

"Oh," I laugh. She wants to know what art school I go to. "No."

"That's cool. I like your skirt."

"Thanks," I say. Hers is almost identical but about three sizes smaller to fit her tiny frame.

"You know him?"

"Who?"

"j."

"Not really. Well, not at all actually. My—" What is Aaron? "My friend knows him."

"You're with Aaron Neilson, huh?"

"Not with-with him, but I'm here with him—yes."

"His work is pretty good—better than j.'s."

"And he has a last name," I say, but the girl doesn't laugh.

"Art cannot truly be art if it is bought or sold," she says. I think about this. It sort of makes sense. "Come on, a bunch of us are going to smoke a joint out back."

"I shouldn't."

The girl shrugs and turns to go. "Suit yourself."

I look over at Aaron. He's talking with Edgar and two other men in business suits. "Wait," I call after the dreadlocked girl. "I think I will go with you."

"Everyone always says we are living in a patriarchal society, but they've got it all wrong—we're really living in a *matriarchal* society. It's our *mothers* who fucked us all up," says Nathan, the boyfriend of the dreadlocked girl, whose name is Tamara.

"That's so true," I say.

"I mean, look at those suit guys over there—who do you think they're trying to impress?" Nathan points to Edgar and his friends. I don't see Aaron. "*Their mothers*—they're trying to impress their mothers. That is what my work is about—breaking free of the matriarchal repression we're all victims of."

I catch Edgar's eye. He winks and waves. I blush and shrink down the back of the metal folding chair I'm sitting in. After a quick toke with Tamara and Nathan, we're back inside the gallery, stoned and drinking and eating carrot sticks. I would die for a bag of chips.

"You know those guys?" Tamara asks.

"Sort of—one of them. Not really—it's a long story. He's, well, my brother—sort of—he was—kind of. So is Aaron." Nathan rolls his eyes. "You know what they say, you can't choose your family."

"But you can," says Tamara. "We can all pick who we want to be in our true family."

"The traditional family unit is dead," says Nathan.

"Blood is bullshit," says Tamara. She raises her plastic cup of wine and we toast.

"What's bullshit?" It's Aaron. I didn't notice him walk over. I'm stoned and everything is in slow-motion.

"Family, matriarchal repression, art," says Nathan.

"That's quite a list," says Aaron.

"It's true," says Tamara.

"SFAI?" Aaron asks and both Nathan and Tamara nod.

"What's up?" I ask.

"Edgar wants to know if we want to join him for drinks at the St. Regis."

Nathan makes a face.

"I don't know," I say. I wonder if they sell potato chips?

"He's expensing it—those guys are clients of his. They wanted to see some San Francisco culture, but I think they've had enough," Aaron says with a chuckle.

"Oh, sure—okay," I say. If the drinks are free, why not?

Nathan and Tamara roll their eyes. "People are so predictable," says Tamara.

"You can come, too," Aaron says to them.

"Really?" Nathan asks. Aaron nods.

"Let me get my coat," says Tamara.

I can't help thinking what an odd group we make: Aaron and me, Edgar and his Ohio businessmen, Nathan and Tamara. We settle into a table in the lobby bar at the St. Regis and for a moment I'm afraid that this is a huge mistake, that no one will have anything to say, but then the drinks come and the chatter starts and there's laughing all around.

When I lean back in my chair I find Aaron's arm. "Sorry," he says.

"It's okay," I say. It's kind of nice to be out, meeting new people, casually drinking on someone else's expense account and talking about art. Well, talking mostly about TV, but that can be art—like the shows on HBO. And I don't mind having Aaron's arm around the back of my chair. There's a feeling of safety and warmth that comes over me when a man has his arm around me. It's not very feminist to admit this, but it is really comforting.

Aaron asks me tons of questions about my life, my plans. I don't have very good answers, but I try to make myself sound intriguing with a little exaggeration here and a purposely self-deprecating comment there. He seems genuinely interested in what I have to say and he looks straight into my eyes when he speaks. It's almost too much, and every once in a while I have to look away.

"I hope this is okay," Aaron says. He's leaning in and talking close. I can smell the scotch on his breath. After all that wine at the gallery and now the scotch that just keeps coming, I know tomorrow will be painful.

"What's okay?" I ask.

"This," he says and points first to himself and then to me. I don't get it.

"You? Me?"

"Exactly."

"I don't—*oh*." This is a date. I am on a date with Aaron. I had no idea I was on a date. Can it have been so long that I can't even recognize a date when I'm on one? *Am I okay with this?* Aaron is my ex-stepbrother and aren't there rules or laws about that? No, I suppose not since we're not really related. And my mother was married to his dad such a long time ago and for such a short time. I look at Aaron. He *is* attractive in a boyish, sensitive artist kind of way. I have dated so many assholes—I deserve someone nice. I could date Aaron, I think. For now, anyway, until I go back to Canada. It could be something to do; it might be fun.

Another two glasses of scotch in and I'm resting my head on Aaron's shoulder. I'm woozy and drunk. He has an arm around my waist. I notice Tamara giving me strange looks— and Nathan, too. They're sitting across the table from us. "So, what kinds of things do you like to do?" I ask them. Maybe I can get some tips—places Aaron and I could go on dates, things like that.

"What do you mean? Like in bed?" Tamara asks.

"God, no! I mean, good places to go—restaurants, bars, shops, whatever," I say.

"I get you," Tamara says, but she's still acting weird. It could be that people like them simply aren't used to being in places like this. I should make them feel more comfortable.

"What's your favorite, most romantic spot in the city?" I ask.

"Why?" Tamara asks.

"I think Mason's looking for suggestions," Aaron says. "I hope Mason's looking for suggestions." His voice is slurry. I laugh and he leans in closer, kissing me lightly on the lips.

"Ew," says Tamara

"What?" I say.

"I have no idea what kind of fucked-up incest shit you two are into, but I don't want anything to do with it," says Nathan as they collect their things.

"Wait," I say. "It's not like that—he's not my brother, not my *real* brother, well not anymore. It's just that my mother—"

"Really, you don't have to explain," says Tamara, as Nathan pulls her toward the exit.

"But, we're not—"

Aaron laughs. "Forget it, Mason."

"It's not funny."

"It sort of is," he says.

"What's funny?" Edgar asks from the other end of the table. "Where'd your little art friends go?"

"They got freaked out because they saw me kiss Mason and they think we're siblings—it's a misunderstanding."

It was embarrassing. Aaron and Edgar think it's hilarious.

"They certainly weren't very open-minded. And they call themselves artists—*tsk, tsk,*" Edgar says.

"I should go," I say.

"I'll take you home," Aaron says.

"I'll get a cab," I say.

"Use my car service," says Edgar. "There's a town car right out front. I'll call my driver now."

"Oh. Okay. Thanks," I say.

"I'll walk you out," Aaron says.

Edgar stands as he slips his phone back into his jacket pocket. He walks over to me and gives me a hug and a kiss on the cheek. "You're a naughty girl, aren't you?" he whispers. I can't help but laugh, although I have no idea where this came from. He pulls me closer. "You know you are. Just be careful with him." He nods towards Aaron. "He's not like you and me."

SHOWTIME

I've never seen one of Janet's fashion shows. Before I left for Canada she was designing cargo pants and backpacks for a local eco-clothing company that went under after it was revealed they were using sweatshop labor and the press pounced all over them. Janet swore she didn't know a thing about it, and she's a person that's hard not to believe. She really should be on TV.

This is not like a big runway show or anything, just a tea-style presentation in her studio, which is way bigger than I could have imagined. And she has staff—there are stylish young men and women flitting around, chatting people up and handing out something they're calling a "look book." I flip through mine and pretend to be engrossed. I don't know a single person here. Where is Seth?

The "look book" is basically a catalog without prices and with better photography. The only giveaway that it's not some fashion magazine insert is the subtle names and numbers taste-fully printed at the bottom of the page: *Annette blouse, #7395,*

Marion trouser, #2849, and so on. Naming every piece in a collection seems like a weird thing to do, but what do I know about the fashion business? I say: get a look and stick with it. It makes life easier and it worked for Andy Warhol.

There are no assigned seats. One of Janet's smiley staff told me that. She was cheery and wearing a beige linen suit—all the staff members are wearing sharply cut beige suits with black dress shirts, open halfway. I bet the suits aren't beige, but *ecru* or *sand*. Fashion is so pretentious and everyone is so skinny. I feel like a lump. Maybe I should have asked Aaron to come with me—he called earlier to invite me on a trip to Edgar's ranch in Montana for the weekend, leaving tomorrow. My first instinct was to say no—after the other night, and the kiss, and Edgar's weirdness—but I fought the instinct. Is kissing your ex-stepbrother really that wrong? It's not illegal. I looked it up online just to be sure. But it's—I don't know—it's sort of wrong, but not in a bad way. Maybe I am naughty, like Edgar said. A smile creeps onto my face. I kind of like that idea, the idea of me as the mischievous coquette. What does the modern mischievous coquette wear on a ranch in Montana?

I take a seat in the back so I can continue picturing myself as a saucy vixen-on-the-range in peace. I don't want to have to move later because some beige-loving lady can't see over my hair. I watch the crowd and wish this wasn't Janet's show, that instead we were there together in the audience, snickering at the uptight crowd.

"Mason?" I look up and see a blonde woman smiling at me. I can't place the face. "Oh my God," she says and opens her arms. I think I'm supposed to stand up and hug her or something, but I don't. "I can't believe it's you," she continues, taking the seat beside me. "Janet said you were coming, but I couldn't believe it." She takes my hand. "I was so, so sorry to hear about your mother. I wanted to be at the funeral, but we didn't get in from Tokyo until last night. I'm so, so sorry."

"Thanks," I say quietly. Am I supposed to know her?

"Diedre!" Seth comes bouncing up and the blonde woman leaps to embrace him.

Diedre? D.D.? No, it can't be. Shit. Where's the black hair and the heavy eyeliner? What happened to her bad skin and huge tits? It can't possibly be her. She's not stoned, and she would never wear that outfit: a simple pink linen dress and tiny matching cardigan. And she's smiling, which is impossible—D.D. was the grumpiest of all the grumpy goth girls in high school.

"Love the look," Seth says to the woman that can't be D.D.

She twirls around. "Miss Janet's, of course."

"Naturally," says Seth. "You should see some of the winter-white coats she's showing today—gor-geous. Cashmere and silk, like you've stepped out of some forties movie."

Janet could never completely commit to an all-black life-style. She dabbled, sure, but there was always some other color in there, like white or red. And she never dyed her hair. The closest she came is that one time in high school we put purple streaks in her bangs, and even then, the color was only a rinse and was gone in a week. I think she hung out with us because she was so tall and everyone called her a freak. We were all freaks; D.D. was a *huge* freak.

"This is so cool," Seth says. "All of us back together again."

"Sure," I say.

"Is Rob coming? Please tell me Rob is coming," Diedre says. *Is Rob coming? Is Rob coming?* This woman is definitely D.D. She was always in love with Rob Wilson, supergoth, king of the freaks.

"He'll be here. I talked to him last night," Seth says. I had no idea they were still in contact. "Where's Trevor?"

"Where else? At the office," Diedre says, rolling her eyes. I notice a wedding band on her left ring finger.

"Too bad," Seth says.

"There's Rob!" Diedre lights up and starts waving across the room to a man dressed in a blue T-shirt and jeans. He's wearing glasses with chunky black frames and has bangs that flop in his face. Jesus, that's Rob?

"Hey, Mason," he says. "Great to see you. Sorry about your mom."

"Thanks," I say.

"You look great," Rob says, smiling. "Exactly the same."

"I know!" says Diedre. "Doesn't she?"

"So what have you been up to?" Rob asks. What's with all the smiling?

"I don't know," I say. "Just work, hanging out, the usual."

"Janet said you're living in Canada," Diedre says.

I nod. "Yup."

"Great investment opportunities up there," she says.

"Tell me about it," Rob says.

The tasteful background music cuts out abruptly and people rush to find seats. Everyone is quiet—it's weird. A track of classical music starts up and the show begins. The models walk slowly past us, winding their way through and around the seats; everyone gets an up-close look. The clothes are classic and beautifully made. Only three pieces in the entire collection are black.

I recognize Victor Durrell when he hands Janet a giant bouquet of exotic flowers as she comes out to take her bow at the end of the show. He *is* old. He *is* gross. I can't imagine sleeping with him. I can't imagine Janet sleeping with him. She could do so much better.

Amid the applause and congratulations, Seth takes me aside and fills me in on D.D.—*Diedre*—and Rob. Diedre never really got over Rob, but actually married his brother, Trevor, and they're both market analysts. I don't know what market they're analyzing and don't ask. She had breast reduction surgery and has two kids. It's too depressing, but not as bad as Rob's story: he sells internet virus-detection software to big companies and plays keyboards in an all-eighties-hits cover band. It's so sad when people try to cling to their youth like that.

"I'm afraid I have to run," Diedre says, looking at her watch. "But we should have drinks while you're in town."

"Definitely," I say. She hands me her business card. Diedre has an M.B.A. She's married to Trevor Wilson. He was such a geek loser.

"I gotta bail, too," Rob says. "Client dinner." Diedre nods and so does Seth.

"Sure," I say. "It was nice to see you again."

"You, too. Drop me a line when you guys get together for those drinks," Rob says. He scribbles something on the back of *his* business card and hands it to me. "My band is playing at a pub in Redwood City this weekend—you should come." I nod and smile. I'd rather die than trek all the way to suburban Redwood City for anything.

"Would you care for another glass?" Victor Durrell asks me. He's holding a bottle of champagne. Why not?

"Sure," I say. We're making a meal of tasty hors d'oeuvres left over from the show. All the guests except me and Seth—and of course, Victor—have gone. Janet should be celebrating but she's distracted, going over the orders some of her clients

placed immediately following the show. Victor goes to top
up her glass of champagne but she preempts him by placing
her hand over the top. I guess it's just me and Seth and Victor
doing the real drinking tonight. Actually, it's just me and
Seth—Victor doesn't drink at all. It's some kind of A.A. thing.
I don't know how he can sit there and fill up our drinks and
not have one himself.

"I didn't know you kept in touch with Rob and D.D.," I
say to Janet.

"What's that?" She wasn't even listening.

"Never mind," I say and gulp down my drink. Are we
going to do something or just sit around here all night?

"Anybody want to get a movie?" Seth asks.

"I'd be in," says Victor. Of course he'd be in, he's *ancient*.

"Sure, yeah, whatever," says Janet. "But nothing too
heavy."

"I'll get a comedy," Seth says. He's serious. He's seriously
suggesting we rent a movie. It's Thursday night, Janet has just
had a fashion show, the three of us are together again for the
first time in years and we're going to rent a movie? I take the
champagne and pour what's left into my glass. "You want to
go to the store with me, Mason?" Seth asks.

"Not really," I say, but quickly remember that if I stay I'll
be stuck here alone with Janet and Victor. "But I'll go."

"Get something with that Will Ferrell—he's hilarious," says
Victor.

"You're funny," I say to Seth. He's holding a copy of
Anchorman in one hand and *Blades of Glory* in the other. "What
about this?" I pass him the latest installment of the *Twilight*
series. He makes a face.

"*You're* the one who's funny," he says.

"You love vampires."

"You're not joking, are you?"

I point at the Will Ferrell films he's got. "Aren't you?"

Our standoff is silent. Finally, Seth takes the movie from me and marches up to the checkout counter where he pays for all three—and for the bag of salt-and-vinegar potato chips I sneak onto the counter at the last moment.

Janet and Victor both fall asleep partway through my movie. Seth watches with me. I knew he'd like it. When the film ends, I know I should go, but can't muster the energy. Plus, Seth wants me to check out one of the supporting actors in *Anchorman* who is starring in a film Seth is scouting locations for that's shooting here this summer. He says they're going to simulate blowing up the Golden Gate Bridge.

"I don't know," I say. I don't know if I can sit through a Will Ferrell movie. Not that I've ever seen one. But I've seen previews and that's enough.

"Come on, Mason. I sat through that *Twilight* thing." He says this like I owe him.

"Fine," I say and cross my arms over my chest. Janet's place is too far to walk home from and I don't even have enough money for bus fare.

"Just give it a chance, Mason," Seth says. "It's funny."

"What's funny?" Janet asks in a woozy voice.

"*Anchorman,*" Seth says.

Janet sits up straight and nudges Victor in the ribs. "Oh, goody."

LIVINGSTON

It isn't until I pull up in a taxi in front of my mother's apartment in North Beach that I remember I have no cash and no emergency credit card. It's just past ten in the morning—once *Anchorman* started it was my turn to fall asleep. I woke up this morning on Janet's couch with a blanket draped over me.

We dropped Seth off first, at his place. I am beyond tired and am tempted to draw the blinds, turn off the phones and hide from the world, sleep until the legal/taxes thing is sorted and I'm free to go home. And this time I swear I'm never coming back, which obviously won't matter to anyone here because Janet is practically middle-aged and Seth has Diedre and Rob and probably all kinds of other friends I no longer know. Plus, I'm sure he'll be hanging out with Janet and Victor since they're clearly all so close.

But before that, I need to deal with this taxi situation. I rummage around in my bag looking for something I know I'm not going to find. The fare is twelve dollars plus tip. I am fucked.

"Excuse me," I say to the cab driver in my best sweet voice. "I can't find my wallet. Would you mind waiting here for a minute—I can run up and get some cash." My mother had to have kept some cash somewhere.

"You leave your purse," the driver says in heavily accented English.

I'm not sure what to do. If I leave my bag and I can't find the cash then I'm fucked. If I leave my bag he could just drive away with it and then I'm fucked. I could leave my bag and go find the cash and he could give me back my bag and everything could be fine. But what are the chances of that? Since when does anything ever go my way?

I take a moment to think and weigh my options and the inevitably dreadful outcomes. I stare out the window. There's a man sitting on the steps of the building. He's wearing sunglasses and he looks familiar. Shit.

"Just a sec, okay?" I say to the driver. It's not a question. I grab my bag and wedge myself out of the taxi, leaving the backseat passenger-side door open to the street.

"Hey, Mason." Aaron says.

"Hey."

"I've been waiting for you. Are you ready to go?"

"Look, do you happen to have fifteen bucks?" I try to say this like it's not the most humiliating thing in the world to have to ask your ex-stepbrother who you barely know but have kissed to lend you money.

Aaron stands and digs a hand into his pants pocket. He pulls out his wallet and out of the wallet, a twenty. I snap it out of his fingers and dash over to where the taxi is idling. The driver smiles and roots around for change. "Good time to see your boyfriend," he says.

"He's not my boyfriend," I hiss at him and slam the door. He can keep the goddamn change.

I walk slowly back to where Aaron is standing, grinning and looking like an idiot. "Thanks," I say. That's all he's getting from me. There's no way I'm getting all *ooh, you're the best, you saved my life, what would I have done without you?*

"No problem. Glad to help. I tried to call you at the hotel, but they said you checked out."

"Oh."

"Did you know that your mother's address is in the white pages?"

This doesn't surprise me. "She wasn't a very private person."

"I didn't think she'd be listed."

"Oh." The last thing I feel like doing is talking, to Aaron or anyone else. What is he doing here?

"So are you ready to get out of here?"

The words are like magic. All I want is to get out of here. I nod.

"Great. We should get going. You packed?"

I stare at him, puzzled. Packed? Shit— Montana. I honestly, truly forgot. I need a calendar, maybe a PDA.

"Edgar's hired a plane. They're waiting."

"Give me a couple of minutes."

Aaron is sitting beside me on the jet and I'm drinking champagne and eating grapes and trying to look like it's something I do every day. Edgar and his wife, Candice, are here, too, as well as Candice's friend, Amanda, and her husband, Joseph.

When Aaron excuses himself to use the washroom, I stare out the window and try to block out the drone of Candice and Amanda. They're debating the pros and the cons of various private preschools. Both women have one-year-old twins, though no one would guess it judging from their superfit, skinny bodies. Plus, neither of them is thirty. I wonder for a moment where their children are, who they're with, and decide that twentysomething mannequin mommies with deep fake tans are neglectful shrews destined to get some sort of skin cancer nobody yet knows is caused by excessive use of spray-tanning services.

Joseph is reading the *Wall Street Journal* and Edgar is staring at me. I keep catching his eye and it's making me self-conscious so I stare out the window, pretending to be absorbed in thought.

"Nice view, isn't it?" Edgar says, sliding into the seat beside me.

I nod and turn my head slightly, looking at him out of the corner of my right eye. He's still staring at me. Is there something on my face? I casually touch my cheeks and give a quick rub under my nose. There doesn't seem to be any snot hanging from it. "I have to apologize, Mason—I don't mean to stare."

"No, it's fine—I mean, I didn't even notice."

"You're so full of shit," Edgar says this to me in a whisper. I can't help but laugh, but am horrified when it comes out as more of a high-pitched giggle. Candice and Amanda stop yammering for a second while they whip their heads around to see what is so funny. Edgar ignores them and continues talking with me. "It's just so good to see you after all this time. Surreal, isn't it?" I nod again and this time turn to fully face him. He's not wearing a suit today, but jeans and a soft sweater. I notice the black Doc Martens on his feet. He notices me noticing and brushes his leg up against mine until our feet are touching. I'm wearing my clunky Doc ankle boots which I now realize I should have polished or at least wiped down with a cloth. "Great minds think alike," he says, again in a whisper, like we're co-conspirators or in on the same joke. It's a cheesy thing to say, but I let it go and simply grin.

It takes me a moment to realize that Aaron is standing there, hovering, waiting for his brother to move and relinquish his seat. He's clasping the stems of two more champagne glasses between the fingers of one hand and balancing a fruit plate with the other. He must know Edgar has people to do those sorts of things—there are two flight attendants for the six of us.

"Sorry, mate," Edgar says, as he stands.

The men swap places and I snatch a glass of champagne from Aaron before he can even get settled. I raise the glass to Edgar before taking a sip. He winks. "I'm glad you're here, Mason. It's going to be a stellar weekend."

"He can be such a prick sometimes," Aaron says under his breath, obviously irritated. If he dislikes his brother so much, why are we here? He'd better hope he didn't drag me out to Montana to spend the weekend watching some ridiculous male pissing contest. I take a deep breath that when I exhale escapes as laughter. Edgar and Aaron did used to have bona fide pissing contests when we were little, on the long, paved driveway leading up to the Sonoma house—I'd draw a line in chalk and they'd take turns standing behind it and peeing out as far as they could. Then I'd measure the distance and record it in the notebook we kept as a diary of their various and frequent competitions. I can't believe I used to measure their piss.

"What's so funny?" Aaron asks.

"It's just—never mind." I decide to keep that particular memory to myself.

Still, I can't erase the image right away—especially that look Aaron would get on his face when Edgar inevitably beat him. Edgar was older and he always won the pissing contest, but that never kept Aaron from trying and he never once cried when he lost.

★ ★ ★

After dropping our bags at Edgar's place, Aaron and I borrow one of his vehicles and head into town. We visit a few art galleries that are surprisingly good. We chat with gallery owners who seem to be from anywhere but here and when Aaron gives them his card they know who he is. We lunch at a busy place on Callender Street that could easily be mistaken for one of the many fusion tapas places you find in Los Angeles. I scan the room. Aaron says the restaurant is owned by the brother of a famous writer I've heard of but whose work I don't know. Patrons are outfitted in casually chic clothing: jeans, sweaters, leather jackets. It's that subtly expensive look; no big logos or blaring designer names, but it's the details— the cut, the perfect topstitching and pure cashmere sweaters that don't pill—that give the price tags away. Who are these people?

"A lot of writers and producers from L.A. have places here— and novelists. Edgar told me that guy—what's his name? The guy who writes those satirical novels? He lives near here."

I nod. "Oh, that guy, yeah." I have no idea who he's talking about.

"Yeah, yeah. And that other guy—Edgar says he writes really 'male' books, but he's really famous—he lives around here, too."

Again, I nod. "People love his stuff." Just because I work in a bookstore doesn't mean I read the books or have any clue which writers Aaron is referring to. But he has answered my question about the restaurant's clientele without me having to ask. We must be in one of those weird hybrid towns I've heard about—the ones where a bunch of L.A. people buy up half the property and live there on weekends, the kind of place you'd find in a "Stars Without Makeup" issue of one of those trashy supermarket tabloids I sometimes secretly buy.

LADIES

I'm grateful for the two drinks we had before coming back to Edgar's ranch. Candice and Amanda are insufferable and tedious and I've been abandoned by Aaron: he's outside somewhere with Edgar and Joseph, at the stables, petting horses, being one of the guys. I'm stuck with The Ladies in the kitchen with its faux weather-beaten woodwork, gathered around the island that sits in the middle of the room, vintage-style pots with copper bottoms dangling above us. The only thing keeping me from reaching up and grabbing one of the pots with which to knock myself unconscious is the bottle of vodka between us—and that's rapidly disappearing. I thought this weekend was supposed to be fun. I want to be numb.

The Ladies have finally exhausted their discussion of Bay Area private preschools and have moved on to hair and fashion talk. I have, so far, learned that "Grace" and "Gail" were telling Candice about the most fabulous shoe shop in Hayes Valley. I learn that it's a little *bohemian*, but they are the *exclusive* source in Northern California for some French brands I can't remember, or pronounce. *Really?* one asks. *Really,* the other responds. Their voices are quiet—hushed. I want to laugh. This is the way these people talk. I roll my eyes and the reflection of the sun hitting the pans burns my pupils. When I look away, everywhere I turn I see big black spots. I hope Aaron gets back soon.

I eat my way around the platter of hors d'oeuvres in a spiral pattern and do my best to drown out the endless talk of shoes and handbags and hair, but the more I try, the louder The Ladies' voices seem to get. Their *Really? Really* tones are no longer hushed. Instead of being numb and deaf—and potentially blind if I keep staring at the sun's reflection in the copper pots—I have developed some kind of hyperhearing abilities and every word that comes out of The Ladies' mouths sounds like a scream.

Their screaming goes on for what seems like forever, but is eventually silenced with one word: Janet.

They're talking about clothes, expensive clothes I can't afford and probably wouldn't want even if I could. This designer and that one, the pros and cons of navy blue, how high a dress hemline can climb before becoming *vulgar.* They are such ridiculous, stupid women. And then: Janet—*my* Janet.

"You *have* to see the dress she whipped up for me for the Grossman benefit," Candice says.

Janet does not *whip things up.*

"Lally is always using her—gorgeous clothes," Amanda says. What kind of a name is *Lally?* I bite my tongue and suck back more vodka. And by the way, Ladies, this Lally person doesn't *use* Janet. She's not a slave or a dish towel.

"I couldn't make it to her show last night, but I have an appointment next week at her studio—you should come. I'm sure she won't mind," says Candice.

Janet may very well mind. These people have no respect for anyone.

Amanda nods. "That would be fabulous—it's always so much better to meet directly with the designer than buying off the rack."

"Absolutely—it's worth every extra penny," says Candice.

"Isn't she involved with Victor Durrell?"

"Oh, yes—for a while now. I hear it's rather serious."

"It is," I say. Both women stare at me.

"*Really?*" asks Candice.

"Really," I say.

"*Really?* Hmm," says Amanda.

It's the *really* game all over again and this time they've got me as an unwitting player. "She's my best friend." There's a pause and more looks. I feel another *really* coming on.

"*Really?*" Candice beats Amanda to it.

"Since we were seven," I say. "You seem surprised."

More looks and awkward silence before Candice finally speaks. "You just seem very *different* from Janet."

"*Really?*" It's my turn to choose the game.

"Candice doesn't mean that in a *negative* way, Mason."

"*Really?*"

"No, no, of course not," Candice says. I think I've shaken The Ladies.

"I'll have to tell Janet we've met," I say. The Ladies look at each other and this time it's an easy read: panic.

"Oh, indeed, be sure to give her my best," Candice says. Her voice is shallow and fast.

"I certainly will," I say. "And I'll be sure to let her know how much you appreciate her *whipping things up* for you."

The Ladies laugh nervously. "Oh, you don't have to do that," says Amanda.

"Oh, but I will." They both shudder but neither correct

me. "I'm sure she'll enjoy the feedback." How Janet can deal with these people every day is beyond me. They may have money and be her clients, but my God, is it worth it?

"Oh, look!" Amanda says as she tilts her head toward the giant kitchen window with the view of rolling hills and the appearance of three men and their horses riding toward the stable.

"The boys are back!" Candice claps her hands.

"They're probably starved," Amanda says.

"I'll call Kate," Candice says, pulling a glittery pink phone from the pocket of her slim khaki pants. "We should get some snacks going." Candice looks at her gold watch and shakes her head. "She should have been here by now to start with the dinner prep."

Kate cooks and cleans and is a general slave to Candice. It's hard to watch, especially because Kate is all smiles and so genuine and friendly as she serves us home-baked multigrain crackers with goat cheese and orange-fig jelly. I want to take her into a corner and tell her it doesn't have to be like this, that it isn't right and she doesn't have to put up with abuse from anyone, no matter how rich. She could get another job. I'd maybe even be willing to help her escape.

My thoughts of freeing the slave are interrupted by Joseph of Amanda-and-Joseph. He's standing over me, reaching his hand out. I'm unsure whether to shake it or hold it or if he's asking me to dance to the terrible pop-country music Candice asked Kate to put on. I tentatively reach up. He places his other hand atop mine and I'm sandwiched in a mysterious handhold. Jesus, these people had better not be swingers. There is no way I am fucking this guy.

"I just wanted to express my condolences—your mother will be missed by many."

Oh. "Thanks, *Joe*."

He smiles, almost laughs. At least he has a sense of humor. "Indeed, I always enjoyed her column."

"Really?"

"Indeed, Amanda and I often remarked at how amusing and witty she was—such an outrageous character."

Amanda used to read my mother's column? I'll bet she filled Candice in on all the gruesome details if she didn't have them already. I suppose they must know all about me: Britt Castleman's disappointment of a daughter. No wonder they've been so awful. They think I'm some sort of loser, a joke. I'm a thirty-four-year-old woman who once racked up a three-thousand-dollar bill on the emergency credit card paid by her mother, having a torrid month-long relationship on a virtual reality website with a character called "Rage," who turned out to be two teenage girls having a laugh.

"Thanks." I force myself to smile at Joseph and he releases my hand. Then I stand up and walk out of the room without a word.

I meander through the house, ending up in the games room, leaning against a billiards table and helping myself to scotch at the built-in bar. It isn't long before Aaron catches up with me.

"Mason, what is it? Are you okay?"

"What do you think?"

"You're obviously upset—I want to understand why. Is it your mother? Did I do something?"

Yes and yes. "You left me here alone—with those women. They hate me."

"They don't hate you—you just have to give them a chance to get to know you."

"They'd still hate me."

"If you didn't want to stay at the house, you should have come along—you were invited."

"That's not the point."

"Then what *is* the point, Mason?" Aaron shakes his head, his seemingly unflappable, easygoing manner shaken. I suppose I can't blame him—I know better than anyone the kind of stress being around your family can cause.

"Everything okay in here?" I turn and see Edgar's head poking around the corner.

"It's fine," Aaron says and forces a smile.

"It's fine, all right," I say under my breath. Aaron shoots me a dirty look. I sigh. About a million truths could come spilling out, but at the last moment I purse my lips. Now it's my turn to shake my head—all the way out the front door, past Edgar and out of this stupid house.

EDGAR

There's nowhere to go. I'm standing about fifty feet from the front door of the main house, smoking. I smoke my cigarette down to the filter and drop it on the ground, stamping it out with my foot. I can't help but steal a glance over my shoulder, back at the house. The huge windows are like bright yellow shapes; every light in the house must be on. These people have no regard for the environment. I start another cigarette and exhale the smoke straight up and into the black sky.

There are so many stars. The city is so congested with light or fog, you can rarely see stars. This sky reminds me of home—Canmore—and I'm stabbed with sadness. It's not so much that I'm homesick, I'm just not sure anymore if it is my home. My job is boring and I don't have any close friends. Sure, there are always people to drink with and small-talkers abound, but it's a transient place. People come, they work, they ski and snowboard, and drink and fuck and then they leave. Everyone else has a family—or money. There's nothing keeping me there. The call I got from Megan a couple of days ago is the only call I've gotten from anyone since I've been away, and that's because she's my boss at the bookstore and she wants to know when I'll be back to work. I still haven't returned her call.

My self-pity party is abruptly interrupted by the sound of the front door opening then clicking shut. Aaron, I'm sure, but I don't turn around. He's going to have to do some serious groveling before I'm going back in there. I hope he brought me a drink—and a sweater. It's getting chilly and I can feel the goose bumps popping up on my arms.

"You have an extra one of those?"

I jump at the sound of Edgar's voice. Where is Aaron? I was ready for Aaron. I turn around and find Edgar holding a bottle of bourbon and pointing at my cigarette. I hand him the package. It's a bit squished—I guess I'd been holding it tighter than I thought. Edgar slides a cigarette out—it's bent, but still smokable. He holds it up to examine; he probably wants a perfect one. "Thanks," he says and hands me the bourbon while he shakes the mini-lighter out of my pack and sparks the bent cigarette. I unscrew the top of the bourbon bottle and take a big swig. It softens all my limbs as it burns though my body. I'm no longer cold.

"Dinner is on the table," Edgar says in what I think is a slightly bitter tone, but I can't be sure—the bourbon may have softened my perception, as well.

"I'm not hungry," I say.

"C'mon, Mason. It won't be any fun without you."

"Yeah, right." I gulp back more bourbon and hand him the bottle. He does the same.

"I'm serious—you have to help me," Edgar says. He's using the whispery voice again. Goose bumps run up my arms again, but this time it's not from the cold. His breath is hot and thick with liquor and so close to my face.

"I somehow don't think you need anyone's help," I say, dropping my finished cigarette.

"You have no idea," he says.

I shake my head and take a step back, almost tripping and falling. Edgar grabs my arms and hangs on until I regain my balance.

"You're having a terrible time, aren't you?"

I shrug. "It could be worse," I say. This is true. I could be dying of cancer or being tortured or raped.

Edgar laughs. "I'm sorry it's such a drag. Aaron *did* warn you, right?"

"He didn't tell me anything," I say, my anger bubbling up to the surface.

Edgar sighs. "Well, that's Aaron. He's gets so caught up in his own thing sometimes—he should have told you what a bore we all are."

I can't bring myself to say *no, no, you're all simply fascinating,* so instead I say nothing and take the bourbon from him and sit on the ground. Edgar sits beside me and we drink and smoke. He tells me about the town and all of the weirdos and freaks and alcoholic comedy writers who live there. He makes me laugh and when Kate the house slave opens the door to tell Edgar that Candice is waiting and dinner is served, he says, "Tell everyone to start without us," and I blush and feel like the prettiest, most popular girl.

The moment the door shuts Edgar leaps up and pulls me up off the ground. "C'mon—we don't have much time!"

He runs toward the driveway, dragging me behind him. "Where are we—"

"No questions." We stop when we come to an old Land Rover. "Here," Edgar says, handing me the bourbon. He digs around in the pockets of his jeans until he finds his keys. "Get around the other side."

I do as I'm told. My heart is beating fast and I'm out of breath. It could be from the running, but maybe not.

"Edgar!" I hear Candice calling out from the front of the house. "Edgar, dinner is getting cold!" Her voice is shrill and there's no question she's displeased. Edgar starts the engine and unlocks the passenger door. I hop in and before I can close the door, we're peeling out. I get the door shut and just as I do I look out and see Candice standing on the front doorstep, hands on her hips. "Edgar!" She keeps yelling but it's only seconds before I can no longer hear her and the house is a tiny speck of light disappearing fast into the night.

We can't stop laughing as we enter the diner. Edgar has driven us into town and to an old-fashioned diner. It's Friday night and the place is packed with locals, enjoying all-day breakfast with beer, or burgers or clubhouse sandwiches with sides of onion rings or fries. We seat ourselves at a small table with a smooth Arborite top. We're in a time warp, caught in a cinematic dream. I pass Edgar the bottle of bourbon underneath the table and we take turns drinking from it until the waitress comes by and asks if we'd like a drink. This sets us off again, and we're laughing so hard I drop the bottle and it rolls out from under the table. The waitress stops it with her shoe, which is white and the kind nurses used to wear. She picks it up and tucks it under her arm. "Anything to drink?" she asks again.

Edgar clears his throat in an attempt to gain control of his laughter. "Beer, I think," he says. His voice is very low and deliberate and he sounds like a robot in a B movie. This gets us laughing again and we can barely keep it together for long enough to tell the waitress we'd like two orders of chicken fried steak.

The chicken fried steak is why we're here. When we were

talking as we drove into town and Edgar was telling the stories of the weirdos and freaks and comedy writers, he said something about somebody eating chicken fried steak. It wasn't a story or even an anecdote about chicken fried steak, but when he mentioned it, I said I'd never had chicken fried steak and he said it was completely insane and disgusting and that you could practically feel your arteries hardening with every bite. He said I had to try it, that I hadn't lived a truly American life if I hadn't, and so we're here. He never did finish the rest of his story.

I am drunk and I don't think my eyes are focusing properly. I lean across the table and speak very quietly. "Is that guy eating—"

"Yup," Edgar says. At the table beside us there is a family, or at least I think they're a family: mom, dad, and a boy and a girl who have to be in their twenties and look like they have fetal alcohol syndrome—they have that face that's kind of slack and their eyes are too close together.

I close one eye so I can be sure I'm seeing this right, not all blurry and double. The family is definitely a family and there's definitely something wrong with the kids. They're all enjoying breakfast—pancakes and sausages, rolling each sausage up in a pancake and eating them like hot dogs, but dipping it in syrup instead of ketchup. I'm mesmerized; I can't tear my one open eye away. But then the dad looks up from his food and catches me staring. He looks mean and he probably has a gun so I turn my head, pretending to be looking at the kitsch cowboy art on the walls.

"You think that would be a good look for me?" Edgar asks.

"Huh?"

"The pancake dad?"

I swing my attention back to our table. Again, I close one

eye and shift my gaze in the direction of the mean-looking pancake dad. "Holy fuck," I say, probably a little too loud because the couple behind us glares and huffs. I lower my voice. "That is awesome." Pancake dad is wearing a puffy blue ski vest with no shirt underneath, his hairy torso exposed. I was so caught up in the sausage/pancake eating I completely missed this. I must be very, very drunk.

"Hold on a sec," Edgar says. He stands up and steps a few paces over until he's shaking hands with the pancake dad. It's a good thing he's so tall and big—pancake dad still looks mean to me. The chatter in the diner is loud and I can't quite make out what Edgar is saying. I see him reach into his back pocket and pull out his wallet, and just as he does this our chicken fried steak arrives and then suddenly everything starts to shake. I scream and fall to my knees, curling my body up under the small table. I can hear the plates and the salt and pepper shakers vibrate.

"Mason—what the hell? Get up." I see Edgar's hand reach down and I grab it. The rattling and shaking has stopped.

I stand up and the room is silent except for a smattering of laughs. I think people are pointing but I keep both eyes open so everything is blurry. "The earthquake—"

"The *train*," Edgar says, cutting me off. "The diner is right beside the train tracks. It happens every time a train comes through."

I am an idiot. I don't want chicken fried steak. I want to die.

"She's from San Francisco," Edgar says to the room and there is a collective *ah* before everyone goes back to minding their own business. A stranger even sends me over a shot of whisky.

I settle back into my chair and as I reach for a paper napkin

I notice what Edgar is wearing: the blue ski vest and no shirt. "You were right—it is a good look for me."

"I can't believe you did that." I turn to see pancake dad wearing Edgar's sweater. A fifty-dollar bill is tucked under his plate.

"You're a girl who needs to have some fun," he says.

I smile and can't stop. "I think you're right."

CHEAT

Edgar is the bad guy and I got off scot-free—unless you count how much Candice hates me. According to her, it's all my fault. She should really blame herself. If she wasn't such an uptight bitch then maybe her husband wouldn't be taking off in the middle of her precious dinner party. He wouldn't be smoking and getting drunk with me and eating chicken fried steak and then passing out in a small-town hotel room, wearing a ski vest that once we were sober we realized stank of its previous owner.

It was the chicken fried steak that did us in. The rich, fatty gravy replaced our energy with grogginess and upset our stomachs. We stumbled out of the diner and down the street into one of Livingston's many taverns. Edgar made it through two pints of beer while I could barely handle one. I felt massive, on the verge of explosion, a giant balloon that's too heavy to float. It wasn't long before Edgar was looking as green as I felt and we shuffled back up the main street to the Murray Hotel—just for a little lie-down, we said. We passed out shortly after checking in and collapsing on the bed and didn't wake until after midnight when the hotel manager banged on our door, accompanied by Aaron, who was livid and worried—livid with Edgar, worried about me. It was sweet, I suppose. I didn't mention the sloppy kiss Edgar and I shared before blacking out. I was so out of it at the time it could have been a dream.

We sat through an unbearable brunch the next day at Edgar's before flying home that afternoon—a day early. Candice suddenly remembered a meeting she had to prepare for on Monday which was an unlikely story considering she doesn't even have a job. Amanda and Joseph had big fake plans, too. I felt sick and pushed the eggs around on my plate in silence. Aaron rubbed my back and refused to speak to Edgar, who winked at me twice and when no one was looking slipped me his card with his private cell phone number and personal e-mail address scrawled on the back.

I went to bed as soon as Aaron dropped me off on Saturday. He wanted to come in, but all I wanted was sleep. He's called a couple of times since, but I haven't talked to him. I'm enjoying my comfy pajamas and snacks. I've spent the past two days watching bad TV and replaying the kiss that I can't quite remember in my head.

I take Edgar's business card out of my pajama pocket and look at it. I think about calling, but don't. Instead, I dial Seth and stick some frozen chicken wings in the microwave. Whenever I have had man issues, Seth is right there, ready to listen to every gory detail and dole out advice I may or may not heed. He answers on the first ring.

"Hey, Seth. You are *not* going to believe the weekend I had. It was so fucked up—*more* than fucked up."

"Uh-huh. That's great, Mason. Look, I'm kind of in the middle of something right now. Can I call you back?"

"Ooh, are you entertaining a special gentleman friend? Do tell." I hop up onto the counter. It's just like it used to be, complete with chicken wings.

"No. Look, Mason. I'm at work. I'll call you tonight."

"Oh. Okay. Call me later then."

Since when is Seth so concerned about work? He's the one who would always convince me to skip school to see a movie at the Castro or to watch him cruise guys in Dolores Park.

Forget Seth—a little girl-talk is probably more what I need. I dial Janet's number. She has her own business, she sets her own hours, she has always had time to talk. "Hello? Janet?" All I can hear is garbled voices and the hiss of static. I hang up and try again. This time I get through.

"Mason? I'm so sorry—I was in an elevator. The reception in this building is awful. So, what can I do for you?"

I don't know, hang out, come have a glass of wine with me, stay up late and gossip about the people we know like we used to do. "I just wanted to see what you're up to."

"It's Tuesday afternoon," Janet says.

That's not an answer. "So?"

Janet laughs. "Mason, I'm working."

"Play hooky. C'mon. Come over. I have microwave chicken wings." Like me, Janet is a sucker for trashy processed food.

"Yuck. You shouldn't eat that stuff, Mason. It's all chemicals. You know, it's not hard at all to make your own marinade for chicken wings. And there's this great place that sells organic chicken at the farmer's market. I'll e-mail you the address and the recipe."

Since when does Janet not eat frozen chicken wings? I gnaw a piece off the bone of the one I'm eating. "Why don't you come over? You can teach me how to make them."

"I really wish I could, Mason, but I have to work. I have a client coming for a fitting at two and I have a bride at six. Maybe on the weekend? We could get together then."

"Yeah, okay," I say.

"Great. It's a plan. And I'll e-mail you that recipe right now, before I forget."

"Sure. Thanks."

I finish off the chicken wings in the living room. Thank God my mother's apartment has a freezer full of food I can eat. Janet insisted on giving me a bit of money to tide me over until the estate is settled. I told her it was a loan, but she wouldn't listen. And Seth keeps me in booze and smokes, both of which I'm almost out of. I hope he comes over tonight.

I flick through the channels, stopping here and there, but not paying much attention. I could get up, go out, do something, but I'd rather stay here, gorging on chemical foods and displaying my apathy for daytime television.

At some point, my apathy turned to boredom and I fell asleep on the sofa. When my cell rings, it gives me a start. I see the name flashing on the face of my phone and nearly fall to the floor. It's Edgar.

"Hello?" I try to sound cool, surprised—like I didn't program his number into my phone as soon as I got back on Saturday.

"Mason?" He's using his whispery voice. Maybe evil Candice is in the next room. The goose bumps spread up my arms.

"Yeah."

"It's Edgar."

"Oh? Hi."

"Are you busy?"

"Now?"

"Now." It sounds serious. Maybe he's in crisis, maybe everything is falling apart, maybe it's all my fault.

"Okay."

"I'll be over."

"The address is—"

"I've got it."

"Okay."

"See you in about ten," he says and hangs up.

I stare at my phone in disbelief. What is going on? I slide the phone shut and think. I look down at the pair of black-and-red pajamas I'm wearing. I think they're cute and the stripes are vertical, which Janet always says is slimming; maybe I won't look as big as I feel.

"I like the pj's—cute," is the first thing out of Edgar's mouth. Why is he here? And how is it possible to have goose bumps under flannel?

"Thanks."

"Can I come in?"

"Oh, yes, sure, of course." I lead Edgar into the living room.

"Nice place," he says, running a hand along the back of the white couch. He's in jeans again, with another tapered sweater.

"Can I get you a drink?"

"No, I'm good. Thanks, though."

"Water? Juice?" I have no idea what to say. I still have no idea why he's here.

"Sure—water is good."

I excuse myself to go to the kitchen. I get some glasses and a chilled bottle of sparkling water. I don't hear Edgar sneak up behind me, but I jump and drop a glass the moment I feel his breath on my neck. He's wearing cologne but I can smell the faintest trace of bourbon and beer. He takes the bottle and the other glass from my hands and sets them on the counter. "I don't want any water."

"Okay, then. Maybe juice?"

Edgar laughs and moves closer to me, backing me against the wall. "No juice." He reaches down between my legs and rubs me through my pajamas. I think my legs will give out—I haven't been touched in so long. I spread my legs a little and in an instant, his hand is down the front of my pajamas and into my panties. He alternates rubbing my clit and shoving his fingers inside me. I am so fucking wet. He takes his fingers away as I'm about to come and pushes them into my mouth. I've never understood why guys do this and I've never liked it, but with him somehow I do. I want him to touch me again—finish what he started. When he slides his fingers out of my mouth I try to push his hand down again but he doesn't budge. He has other plans.

Edgar pulls my pants and underwear down to my ankles and then I'm exposed, in my mother's kitchen and he's licking my clit. I buck against his face—I can't help it—and I'm panting and grabbing his hair. I want to come, I want to come, but again he stops when I'm right on the brink. He stands and kisses me on the mouth. I taste myself again on his tongue and am so glad I had a shower today.

I reach for his buckle but can't get his belt undone. He swats my hand out of the way and does it himself, and then pushes his jeans and underwear down until his cock is out. I look down—he's so hard and I can see drops of pre-cum shining on the head. Now it's my turn to drop to my knees. I grab his cock and guide it into my mouth. I get it dripping with saliva and use my hands, alternating hand-mouth-hand-mouth, just like Seth says men like it. Edgar seems to like it because he's moaning and pushing his hips at me hard. I give up one hand and reach down between my legs: I need to come, I need to come. But Edgar stops me, and pulls me up from my crouched position on the floor. My face is wet and I can only imagine the state of the red lipstick I applied minutes before Edgar arrived. He kisses me anyway and now my mouth tastes like both of us.

The kissing doesn't last long, though. Edgar turns me around. I'm up against the wall. He pulls my hips back and spreads my legs as far as they will go, my pajama bottoms and panties stretched to their max around my ankles. He places his hands on my hips and guides his cock to my pussy. He rubs the tip against my clit and I almost scream. I need to come, I need him to fuck me.

"Oh, fuck me, just fuck me," I say.

"So you want me to fuck you," he says.

"Please, just fuck me."

"Like this?" he says as he pushes his cock all the way into me in one stroke.

"Fuck me." I can't say anything else. I'm in a trance. I need to come.

Edgar fucks me hard. And then when he reaches around and teases my clit with his finger I come and come, all over his cock, and he finally lets himself go and as he pulls out semen runs down my legs, which are shaky and spent.

"Holy fuck," I say as I pull up my pants and underwear. Edgar's business card falls out of the pants pocket. I kick it under the dishwasher before he has the chance to notice.

"I wanted to do that Friday night," Edgar says and kisses me again on the mouth.

"Really?"

"Really."

DINNER

After Edgar leaves, I defrost a six-pack of bagels I find in the freezer. The tub of cream cheese in the fridge smells okay; it isn't past its best-before date, but I can't help thinking it tastes funny. Whether it's off or not is soon irrelevant. I scarf down two bagels, then toast a third. I cut dry, hard corners off a poorly wrapped block of cheddar and melt cheese on a fourth. I'm stuffed but I can't stop eating. I replay the events of the afternoon in my head and am jolted out of my bagel-induced food coma only when the buzzer rings.

I stumble to the door and press the "talk" button. "Who is it?"

"Mason?"

"Aaron?" Shit. I straighten my pajama top and suck in my stomach but to no avail.

"Can I come up?"

"Sure—yeah, I guess." I press the button that releases the lock downstairs. I have about a minute before he makes it to the third floor, maybe less—Aaron looks like he's in pretty good shape. I turn the dead bolt and rush to my bedroom. What the hell is he doing here? Why didn't he call first? Doesn't he know the rules? I reach into the front pocket of my pajamas and find my phone. The ringer is off and there are four missed calls, all from Aaron's number.

In my bedroom, I strip off my pj's and grab the first thing I lay hands on: my mother's leopard-print kimono. I used it after a shower the other day. I pick it up and force my arms through the boxy sleeves. I tie the fabric belt to cover my food-baby bagel belly—anything that helps to disguise that is fine with me, even leopard-print silk.

"Did I wake you? I called but kept getting your voice mail," Aaron says as soon as I step into the living room.

"No, I was—" I was what? Fucking your brother? Stuffing myself with bagels? No. That cannot be what I was doing. "Well, yeah, to tell you the truth I *was* sleeping. Sorry about that." Whenever someone threatens to tell you the truth chances are whatever they say is anything but. Seth once dated a shrink who told me that.

"Don't worry about it, Mason. I just wanted to make sure you were all right—and see if you were up for a late dinner. But I can go."

I should want him to go, but I don't. I want to know more about Edgar and Candice. "Just let me change."

"No need to get all dolled up or anything—I was thinking casual, French, that bistro on Fillmore."

"Sounds good," I say.

I tell Aaron to help himself to a drink—there are a couple splashes of vodka left in a bottle in the freezer, but he holds up a bottle of expensive-looking red wine. He says he'll open it and pour us each a glass. Now if only I could find something to wear.

every little thing

★ ★ ★

Every piece of clothing I brought with me needs washing. I take a hopeful second whiff under the arm of my favorite black shirt; it's long and drapey and stretchy but not tight. I like that when it bunches across my tummy it looks like it's the style, not my gut, and the three-quarter-length sleeves conceal my fleshy arms. But it stinks, so it's out. And apart from a fleece pullover I bought when I was going through my hiking phase that got no further than me buying a pair of boots and this ugly fleece thing, I have nothing to wear. What I thought I'd do with it here in San Francisco, I don't know.

I *could* wear it, I suppose. I laugh under my breath at the thought. *No need to get all dolled up or anything,* he said. He's thinking *casual, French, that bistro on Fillmore.* I'm sure I don't know this bistro on Fillmore, but I am positive that fleece would be frowned upon. I hate it when restaurant people get all snotty about what you're wearing or if you're chewing gum or whatever. I drop the leopard robe and grab a T-shirt from my dresser that I know will be too tight, but who cares; no one will see it—it'll be under the fleece.

The hostess doesn't look twice at me or my fleece. Obviously, she's new in town or has become so immune to tourists wearing worse that my schlubby look doesn't register on her fashion radar. In any case, this can't be a very reputable French bistro if the sight of me doesn't evoke at least one dirty look or tsk.

I don't think I could—well, I *shouldn't*—eat a thing, but there's *cassoulet* on the menu and *foie gras* appetizers there's no way I can resist. It doesn't help that there are all of these people sitting at tables all around us, *eating.*

Aaron orders the wine in French, which is pompous. First

he doesn't even flinch at the fleece and now he's bilingual. It's a bit much—he's easy to hate.

Aaron talks about me and my mother and his brother and his dad and the year we lived together in Sonoma on the vineyard. He tells me things I don't remember but may well be true. We were all so small. As much as I want to hate Aaron for being a tony, pretentious, bilingual twat, he makes me laugh hard when he describes how he'd spy on me and Edgar when we'd play and hatch plans to get our attention, no matter what the cost.

"Remember when your mom was into that whole animal rights thing?" he asks.

"I remember her spraying some lady at one of your dad's parties with a tiny bottle of red food coloring because she was wearing fur." The memory flashes in my mind, clear and real, like it was a scene in a movie I saw a long time ago. I can't believe this has been buried in my brain all these years. What else is in there?

"That was classic. She was so ballsy—nothing fazed her."

I open my mouth, but for once nothing comes out. Aaron's right—nothing fazed Britt: not wrecking some lady's fur, not sleeping with other women's husbands and certainly not me, no matter what I did.

The wine comes and the waiter pours a splash in each of our glasses. I watch Aaron sip and nod, then he watches me as I bring the glass to my lips. I sip. I scowl. "I don't know…" I say. "It tastes funny."

The waiter looks puzzled. "How unusual," he says. "It's a—"

Aaron raises his finger to the waiter, stopping him mid-sentence. He takes another sip and shakes his head. "It *does* taste funny. I'm afraid we're going to have to send it back," he says.

"Very well," says the waiter. He's curt. "Would you like to try another of the same or something different?"

"Definitely different," I say. I grin, but don't let the laugh that's bubbling up my throat escape.

"Champagne?" Aaron asks. He, too, looks like he's holding back.

"Sounds great," I say, then look up at the waiter. "Whichever one you'd recommend."

"Very well," he says again and skulks back to the bar, our barely splashed glasses and bottle of red in hand.

"You're so bad, Mason," Aaron says.

"What?"

"There was nothing wrong with that wine." He's whispering now.

"I know."

PINK

I've left seven messages for Edgar in the past week but he never calls back. He's shown up twice, though, unannounced, since that afternoon in the kitchen. We don't talk much—there's never time. And we've never had sex in my bed, only in the kitchen and on the living room floor. Last time, I tried to lead him to the bedroom, but he wouldn't budge. He said he couldn't wait. Just thinking about him makes me wet.

I have told Seth everything and sworn him to secrecy. It's like it used to be—late nights and wine, analyzing the smallest details of what he said, what he did, what I said, what I did, and listening to Seth's advice but not necessarily taking it. At first he was all about how slutty I was, what a bad girl, but the last few days he's changed. He keeps saying that maybe I should back off, really think about what I'm doing. He says he doesn't want to see me get hurt. It's not like that, I told him. It's very modern: I know he's married, he knows he's married. I'm not asking him to leave his wife or to be with me every second—it's strictly sexual, there are no expectations. There are no strings.

"There are always strings when someone goes out of their way to say there are no strings," Seth says.

"Oh, that's so deep," I say. Seth of all people should know about no strings. "You always say you have all kinds of 'no strings' sex. *You've* fucked married men."

"Of course I've had 'no strings' sex, and who hasn't fucked married men? But that's not the point—I'm not *you*."

"What is that supposed to mean?"

"Oh, don't get all defensive on me. It's just that you tend to get attached."

"I do not get attached," I say. "And it's not like I even see him much—we've only fucked three times."

"But how many times have you called him?"

"Not that many." I hate Seth. He's probably jealous. He said himself that Edgar was hot.

Seth shrugs and wags a finger at me. "Don't say I didn't warn you."

Later that afternoon, Aaron and I are standing outside my building. We've been for a walk, one of those kinds where you don't have a particular destination in mind, but just wander up and down random streets. I'm usually not one for listless walks, or walks of any kind, but I needed to get out. I've been sequestered for days, watching TV and jumping every time the phone rings. And I've searched my mother's place top to bottom, but have given up hope that she kept some secret, special diaries. Everything in her life was out there, in public, in her columns. When I get really bored, I start reading them—the really old ones she wrote before I was born. It's hard to believe that the woman who wrote those things about her life, who wrote about *everything* in her life, was my mother. It's hard to believe she's gone.

"Are you okay, Mason?" Aaron asks.

"I'm, I'm—" *Am I okay?* The words won't come. I start to shake and my breath gets fast and short. "I'm—" Goddammit. Why can't I say *fine? I'm fine.* That's what people say—whether it's true or not.

"Shit. Mason, let's get you inside," Aaron says. He puts an arm around my shoulder and I lean into him as we walk up the stairs. I fumble for the keys. He doesn't let go. "Here," he says and takes them from me once I find them. He ushers me inside quickly and we start up the stairs. As lovely as my mother's building is, it's old and there's no elevator, just flights of wide marble steps.

Aaron makes me tea. He finds some biscuits in the cupboard and arranges them on a plate he puts in front of me. They're stale, but I eat them anyway—I'm hungry. I'm on the sofa, half lying, half sitting.

"Do you need more pillows?" Aaron asks. He's sitting across from me in a perfectly white easy chair. He pulls a cushion from behind his back and offers it to me.

I don't need it but I take it. "Thanks."

"Can I get you anything else? I could order some food. You seem hungry."

I'm starved. "Sure. I could eat," I say quietly.

"Chinese? Thai? Pizza?"

"Not pizza." Seth brought pizza over last night.

"How about Thai? There's a great place not far from here. I could call and see if they deliver—or go pick it up?"

"Sounds good." In fact, it sounds great. "And could you see if they have any big bottles of Coke?"

"No problem," Aaron says as he takes out his phone.

★ ★ ★

I am stuffed full of spicy Thai goodness. I'm also hepped up on sugar and caffeine thanks to the Coke.

Aaron and I talk and laugh. He almost makes me forget about his brother. Aaron reminds me of guys I knew during and after high school, the ones who are nice to me and like it when I swear and do outrageous things they only wish they had the balls to, like sending back expensive wine at elegant bistros. They like that I can drink them under the table and revel in introducing me to their dullard friends. *I'm the ultimate novelty girl.* This familiar feeling pumps me up but quickly deflates. I'm the ultimate novelty girl—that's all, nothing more, and it doesn't seem that Edgar even wants that.

"Mason, what's wrong?" Aaron asks.

I shake my head. "Nothing. Forget it."

"Are you sure?"

I nod and put on my best happy face, but look at my feet. Aaron moves closer until our thighs are touching, and our upper arms. I can feel him breathe. "Hey, look at me," he says.

I cock my head slightly toward his but keep my eyes on the ground.

"You seem so sad, Mason. And I know you just lost your mother and you should be, but please let me help. I could do a dance. Sing? No, you don't want that, trust me. Or I could stay here with you for a while?"

I nod. Tears well up in my eyes. I hate crying. I hate it.

"It's okay," Aaron says and leans in to hug me, which makes me cry more. He strokes my hair, then the back of my neck. He doesn't let go of me, but pulls his head back until we're facing each other, noses nearly touching. I graze the side of his face with the back of my fingers and he brings his lips down on mine. It's nice; he's nice. I stop crying, but then I start thinking and the moment is gone. How would Edgar like that—me kissing his brother? Probably not so much. I sit up and lean over, reaching under the coffee table for my handbag. I find my phone. There are no missed calls. *Fuck you, Edgar,* I think and drop it back into my bag.

"Are you expecting a call?" Aaron asks.

I turn to him and smile. "No, not at all," I say and kiss him again.

I'm not lying when, a couple of days later, I tell Aaron I'm not feeling well. It's not a headache, but more of a general ache, with my breasts at the epicenter of the pain. Plus, I feel nauseous and generally disgusting. Aaron offers to bring me ginger ale and soda crackers, but all I want to do is sleep. If only I could find a comfortable position—if I lie on my side and my breasts squish against each other, it's bad, if I lie on my stomach it's worse. All I can do is lie on my back and stare at the ceiling.

Edgar still hasn't called or made one of his impromptu visits in over a week. I shouldn't care. I don't, really. It's just a bit rude. And the last few times, I wasn't calling him to say hi or to see if he wanted to come over. I had a question. I just can't remember what it was right now.

I haven't had much to drink this week, so that can't be what's causing me to feel this way. The past two nights Aaron has brought over a bottle of wine and we've sat on the sofa sipping it slowly and watching PBS. He kisses me good-night and we sleep in my bed together, fully clothed. It's very grown-up and can be boring as hell. It must be what marriage is like.

I feel sorry for Edgar, being married to a bitch like Candice. I kind of feel sorry for her, too—she must not be able to give him what he wants, otherwise, why would he be seeing me? Well, not *seeing* me—*fucking* me.

I touch my breasts lightly. They're hard and swollen and so incredibly sore. Sometimes, it gets a bit like this before my period, but this is extreme. I think I read something about this but can't recall where. It could have been in one of those old issues of *Cosmo* I found stashed in my mother's office. Perhaps I didn't read it at all—maybe I saw it on *The View*. Seth makes me watch it sometimes when he comes over for breakfast and we watch TV in the mornings. I wish those women would just shut the fuck up and keep their opinions to themselves. My mother would have loved to be on a show like that.

Then I remember: it was in one of my mother's old columns. Yes, that's it. I lift myself up to a sitting position, which somehow is more comfortable than lying down. I slide the file box marked COLUMNS #1 toward me and start digging. It doesn't take me long to find it. It's in the column where my mother announces to the world that she's pregnant. The aches, the sore breasts: it's all there, described in every painfully excruciating detail.

I laugh out loud. There is *no way*. There is a way, of course, but there is *no way*. *There is no way. There is no way.* This loops in my head as I put on my boots and pick up my purse and walk out the door. *There is no way.* I head straight for the pharmacy around the corner and up the street. I shouldn't bother—it's silly. *There is no way.*

At the cash register with the box in my hand, I start shaking. I pay for the test with a twenty-dollar bill. Aaron knows I'm broke and always makes sure I have five twenties in my wallet. He sneaks them in when I'm not looking. We don't talk about it, and I try not to spend too much of it. I tell the clerk I don't need a bag and shove the pregnancy test in my handbag. *There is no way.* I tell myself that all the way home. I say it out loud when I'm in the bathroom peeing on the stick, but mostly on my hand. I repeat it like a chant as I wash my hands and stare at my face in the mirror while the time on my cell phone turns over one minute, then two, then three. I shift my eyes to the stick on the top of the toilet. There are distinctly pink lines. I grab the instructions and double-check. There is no way. Double pink means pregnant. I am double pink. *There is no way.*

CLOSET

I am pregnant. I bought four more tests—all with Aaron's money, but I'm trying not to think about that, and to smile and let him kiss me when he comes over. I went to a clinic and peed some more and they took my blood. It's now official, but nothing I didn't already know. I thought you weren't supposed to be able to tell you were pregnant for three months or something like that and that you wouldn't feel sore and sick only two or three weeks after conception. I feel like death. Those teenage girls on those cable shows who say they had no clue they were pregnant until—presto!—they have a baby in the high school bathroom before ditching the kid in a Dumpster and heading back to class—those girls are liars. There is no possible way a person wouldn't know if they were pregnant.

I haven't called Edgar since I found out and he hasn't called me, which pisses me off since this is half his fault. I have a pamphlet in my handbag called, *Motherhood: It's the Most Natural Thing in the World*. I want to find whoever wrote it and explain that, no, getting knocked up by your boyfriend's older brother—both of whom are your ex-stepbrothers—when you're in town for a brief time, broke and waiting for your mother's estate money is not natural at all. It's probably some pro-life propaganda anyhow. I'll toss it out later, but Seth is here right now—he came over for dinner last night and fell asleep in my mother's bed, where he still is now—and the last thing I need is for him to find out. I have an appointment at the clinic on Monday, and it will all be taken care of. But I do need cash to pay for it, and someone to take me home afterward, and the list of candidates I can borrow from is short.

Edgar should go with me, Edgar should pay for it, but he's acting like a prick and doesn't even deserve to know. If he doesn't call me soon I will never speak to him again.

I'm exhausted. I swear I could sleep all day *and* through the night. But there's no rest for me. I've been invited to a special memorial some women writers' group is holding for my mother. It's nearly two—it starts in ninety minutes and I have to wake Seth. So far, nothing—not me banging around with saucepans in the kitchen, not knocking politely on the bedroom door, not the smell of coffee nor the blare of Whitney and/or Celine—has worked.

I shower and pull on my mother's leopard-print silk robe. I need to find something to wear. Every piece of clothing in my suitcases is dirty, smelly or horribly wrinkled. I haven't washed a thing since I've been here. I hate everything I own.

There must be something in my old closet I could wear. It's all black, that I know. And yes, it's all old, but layers of black-on-black-on-black should make me look like a big black blob and no one will notice the age of whatever I'm wearing. And anything that's ten years old seems to be considered "vintage" nowadays and most of the stuff in there is older than that so there's a chance—however slight—that I might be right in style.

I pull on a pair of black leggings and choose to ignore the fact that even the stretchiest of fabrics cuts into my stomach, pinching my waist. A fold of skin flops over the waistband of the leggings. I grab for a shirt, a long, blousy one made of T-shirt fabric in a swingy trapeze shape. It doesn't put pressure on my breasts, which are already bigger. All the things I didn't think would happen until much later are happening now: enormous breasts, nausea, incessant peeing. I've been making sure I have a glass of water in my hand at all times and keep dumping it out in the sink or in one of my mother's potted plants when Seth or Janet or Aaron are around. It makes my frequent bathroom runs less suspicious.

I look in the mirror, hoping I'll see someone new, but it's just the same old me in the same old clothes, and those don't even fit anymore. I used to wear this top as a minidress with tights. Now it's a shirt, and thankfully it covers my floppy stomach and the top half of my ass. I'll need a skirt. At the back of the closet I find one that's short and stretchy. I wore it so much that the elastic gave out, which, as it happens, means it fits me perfectly now. Socks and boots and it could be nineteen-ninety-something all over again.

For a moment I reconsider my swingy, comfy look and think about forcing myself into the black Versace suit again—the one my mother tried to fancy me up with—but it's wrinkled and besides, I hate it. I hate it so much that I find the suit, bundle the skirt up in the jacket and march it to the kitchen. I open the cupboard under the sink and am hit with the smell of potato peels—Seth made mashed potatoes and meat loaf for dinner last night. My morning eggs rumble up from my stomach and I vomit into the deep, stainless steel basin. The weirdest smells have been setting me off. It's like I've developed some superhuman smell-power and most normal smells are now gross. I add that to my growing mental list of things I don't know about pregnancy as I wipe my mouth and open the kitchen window wide. I hold my breath and pull the garbage bag out of the bin and quickly twist tie the top. I grab the bag, the suit and the keys and rush out of the apartment, down the stairs and out the door to toss the bag into the Dumpster.

"Mason? My goodness, dear, is that you?"

I spin around and find Pearl Lee, my mother's next door neighbor, standing in front of me. God, she looks old. "Hey."

Pearl steps closer, wrinkles her nose and takes me into a tentative hug. "I'm so sorry about your mother—she was a lovely woman."

Pearl is lying. She fought against my mother's initial application to buy into this building and was forever filing "anonymous" complaints with the co-op board. There were too many parties, too much noise, too many men, the smell of marijuana. Each time she complained, my mother sent her a gift basket of fruit and cheese or a bouquet of flowers, not as an apology but as a gesture to say, *I know it was you, you bitter old cow.* It was a ridiculous, but hilarious game. My mother was prone to such mischief and wrote about it with abandon and glee. In her column, annoying neighbor Pearl became annoying neighbor *Patricia.* I loved it when she wrote about *Patricia,* the pathetic rich old biddy next door—it was funny when she wrote about Pearl/*Patricia,* and it meant she wasn't writing about me.

Pearl pats my shoulder and steps back, her nose still wrinkled and her face sour. "If there's anything you need, Mason, please don't hesitate to ask. You'll be requiring a good Realtor, I'm sure—I know a wonderful young man—I'll slip his card under your mother's door."

I'm confused. A Realtor? She thinks I want to sell. I

do—well, I think I do. I'm not up on local real estate prices but this place was worth a fortune when my mother bought it; it must be worth more than a fortune now. Oh, Pearl would love that. She'd probably be the one to buy it—then she'd have the whole floor to herself. She bought old Mr. Tenny's place years ago and doubled her already sizable apartment. With my mother's she could triple it. How much space could a childless widow possibly need? "Actually, *Patricia*—oops!—I mean *Pearl*, I won't need that card. I'm not planning to sell."

"I see," she says. Her voice is terse. "You do know that any tenants must be approved by the board. I'm the president now—I can get you the forms. But I'll warn you, it's a bit of a process."

"Oh, that won't be necessary. I think I might stay—live here myself." I won't, but I could. She couldn't stop me.

"Well then, I suppose we'll be seeing you," Pearl says as she turns to go.

"Yes, I suppose you will."

I'm not really staying—not after I get this whole pregnancy business and the estate-taxes-legal thing straightened out. But Pearl doesn't need to know about any of that. I could take the double-the-fortune I'd make on this place and buy a great old house in Canmore. I wouldn't have to work or do anything. I could start sewing again or get a personal trainer. I could read all of the books I've bought since I've worked at the bookstore but haven't yet read. I could do anything—or nothing. This prospect is at once daunting and depressing. What do people do when they don't have to do anything?

I contemplate this as I trudge back up the stairs. It's not like I have a ton of friends, but I wouldn't make a good hermit, and I could never pass as a lady who lunches. This, along with the fact that climbing three flights of stairs has me winded, sends me into a panic. I try to remember all the things I wanted to do when I was little, the things I wanted to be when I grew up, but all I can recall is that I did not want to be my mother.

FAT

Janet is late meeting me at the memorial—probably stuck in traffic again coming back into the city from Oakland. I still can't believe she's having sex with Victor Durrell. He could be the most talented, smartest, funniest man—everything that Janet says he is—but that doesn't change the fact that he's only months from sixty and completely gross.

This particular memorial for my mother has been organized by some women's writers' group she was president of a few years back and is being held in the posh café at the Hotel Majestic, a boutique inn on the edge of Pacific Heights. There are little salmon snacks and a waiter dressed in white circling the room with bottles of good Napa wine. When I grab a glass of white off his tray, he looks startled. I raise it up and gag it down. I'm momentarily afraid I'll puke, but once the first one is finished and I put the empty glass down on an unoccupied table, my body relaxes and I'm ready for sleep.

I know no one here. It's all women, most of whom are around my age, in their thirties, definitely younger than my mother. That photograph of her—the one that's over twenty years old, of her in the magenta lipstick—is propped up on a table that's littered with flowers, flickering candles and cards. The music is quiet and French and the hum of conversation is like white noise punctuated with the occasional burst of laughter, which is of course totally inappropriate.

I move around the room. Women smile and nod. I know none of them. I catch a glimpse of myself in a mirror on the other side of the room. I knew this shirt was oversize, but I look positively huge. I smooth down the front of the top and wish I had a belt. I thought wearing something big would camouflage all of my trouble spots, namely my stomach and my ass. But all it's done is make me look enormous, fat—like I'm pregnant. Christ. No wonder everyone is acting so weird with the friendly smiles.

The clean-cut waiter darts in and out of range. I catch him looking at me sideways and he scurries ten feet away each time I move one in his direction. I charge toward him when he's at the bar switching out empty glasses for ones that are full. He's in a corner and can't get away. I snatch two glasses from his tray and pour the wine myself. He stares at me like I'm some sort of Satan-lady, but I couldn't give a fuck.

I continue to walk through the room, a glass in each hand. The women's smiles disappear and are replaced with the same Satan-lady glare the waiter gave me. They can all go to hell. I wander, stopping every now and again at the makeshift shrine to my mother. I eavesdrop on conversations that make me glad I know no one here—these women are so catty and the ones that aren't are boring and depressing, talking of nothing but work and cutbacks.

"Could you imagine sleeping with him?" I'm hovering near a red-haired woman and her bleached blonde friend who's wearing too much lipstick. They're too engrossed in their chat to notice me.

"God, no. But could you imagine sleeping with her?"

The redhead shudders. "Disgusting—they deserved each other, I guess."

"Do you remember the Christmas party last year?"

"The making out? I thought I was going to throw up."

The bleached blonde looks at her watch. "How long do you think this is going to take?"

The redhead shrugs. "Hopefully not long. I have a dentist appointment."

The bleached blonde laughs and lowers her voice to a near whisper. "I'd rather have a root canal than be here."

"Tell me about it."

"Did Monique find someone to speak?"

"I think she bribed Cassie."

"With what?"

"How do you think she got the *Countdown* assignment?" The redhead looks smug. *Countdown* is the big action movie being shot here this summer that Seth was talking about. The one that guy from *Anchorman* is going to be in.

"Seriously?" The bleached blonde's eyes are wide. "Cassie is such a star fucker."

"Yup. And in a way it's kind of fitting—she is, after all, the heiress apparent to Britt Castleman."

"I can't believe she changed her byline every time she got married."

"I can't believe they paid her to write that awful column for that long."

"Cassie's is a bit better, I guess."

"Give it twenty years and she'll be writing about her husband's mustache and her plastic surgery and her moron daughter. I mean, *who gives a shit?*"

The women wave to an older woman across the room I recognize as my mother's editor, Monique. I stand, red in the face and perfectly still, paralyzed by the things the women said about my mother. I want to hit them, wrestle them to the floor one-by-one and tell them that they don't understand a thing. I want to defend my mother, brush the talk off as jealous lies, but I can't because everything they've said is true. I feel queasy but it's not the wine.

I drink more and listen in on conversations around the room and find they're all a version of the same. A memo issued by Monique is the source of much derision. All of the female reporters from the newspaper, save for a handful of metro writers and editors who were off the hook thanks to juicy crime stories and pressing deadlines, were expected to attend today's service. She asked for volunteers to speak, but only this Cassie person stepped up and that was only after she was given a movie-star story. My mother was a bitch and a joke. She was out of touch with reality. She couldn't write. She fucked bosses and coworkers. She didn't earn her big office and she made too much money. She made out with Ron at the Christmas party last year and the women in this room with the exception of Monique and maybe this Cassie person are either indifferent to or pleased about her death. It's tough times in the newspaper business, but there's column space in a major daily newspaper and a big fat office up for grabs.

Janet has yet to arrive; I've had three glasses of wine and am quite sure the waiter is still avoiding me. I put my empty glass down on the table with my mother's picture and the candles and the flowers and the cards expressing disingenuous sympathy. At least the newspaper is paying for this farce; my inheritance isn't feeding the vultures.

I spot Monique across the room talking to the redhead and

the bleached blonde. I knock back a glass of ice water and pop a stick of gum in my mouth, then make my way over. I'm casual and smart, my black top swings when I walk. My mother may have painted me as a moron but it's time these women learned I'm not.

"Hi, Monique." I lean in for double-cheek air kisses and she gives me that look, the one people get when they know they should know you but have no idea who you are. This infuses me with energy. This is going to be fun.

"Hello, you," Monique says. "It's been a while."

"It has." I look at the redhead, then the bleached blonde and then at Monique. I'm waiting for an introduction.

"God, I can't remember when I saw you last. Wasn't it..."

I'm not going to bite, fill in her blanks. I say nothing and smile.

"I'm Teresa." The redhead sticks out her hand for me to shake.

The bleached blonde follows suit. "I'm Angela."

"Good to meet you both," I say but don't offer my name. There's only silence and all three women shift their weight, look at Monique, the floor, anywhere but at me. "So, you all work at the paper."

They nod.

"Please tell me they've painted over that mural in the conference room—that thing was hideous," I say, hoping this will further confuse them. From the looks on their faces it does that and more. I go on. "God, I remember when they first banned smoking and those two editors—what were their names? Tom, I think, and James?—when they would sneak cigarettes in the women's washroom so no one would suspect them and they ended up triggering the smoke alarms and the sprinkler system. That was hilarious." I have hundreds of stories like this—probably thousands—that my mother would column. She wrote about me incessantly, documented my every move and mood, for better or worse—whether it was embarrassing for me or not was hardly her concern.

"The estate sounds lovely," Janet says. "Is it still in the family?"

Edgar shakes his head. "My Dad sold it years ago and we moved back to the city. I wish we could have stayed—I loved it out there, all that space to run around. Right, Mason?"

"Yeah, sure," I say. I think I remember the summer in Sonoma, the heat, the three of us running through the vine-yard when the sprinklers were on.

"Edgar's place in Montana is a bit like that," Aaron says.

"Well, there's lots of space," Edgar says. "But we have to buy our wine in the shop like everyone else, I'm afraid."

"I thought you lived here," I say, confused.

"I do. Montana's just for weekends. We should go some time, take you out there." Edgar throws back another vodka in one shot. The bottle is nearly empty. "You'd love it."

"Everyone loves it," Aaron adds.

"I'm sure," I say as I toss back the vodka the way I watched Edgar do. But instead of nonchalant and smooth, the burn gets stuck in my throat and I start to cough, sputtering wet goo onto my sleeve. Janet rubs my back again and Edgar hands me a cloth handkerchief he pulls from his jacket pocket. Aaron fetches me a glass of water as Seth gazes off into space.

"Are there real cowboys in Montana?" he asks.

THE CECIL

Several full glasses of vodka have propelled us across town to The Cecil, which is the same as always: dirty, divey, selling cans of Pabst Blue Ribbon for a dollar. There was a show tonight at the Warfield, the concert hall on a sketchy stretch of nearby Market Street. Some nineties British band I think I know but could very well be confusing with Oasis performed, and now everyone is here, crammed into the tiny bar, drinking gross cheap beer and slouching. In the corner, two girls dance to Michael Jackson's "Thriller." They're laughing. They think they invented irony. They're maybe just legal and their skin is perfect. I dance alongside them in my faded black dress and pearls.

I smile at the Irony Girls, letting them know I'm in on the joke. They stare back at me with big eyes and then look at each other. I shuffle around until my back is to them, moving in a slow groove, a nearly finished can of beer in one hand. I down what's left and look for a place to set the can, but there's nowhere. I could drop it on the floor, step on it, crush it with the heel of my sensible black pumps and belch the way Seth taught me to do when we were twelve. But I do none of these things and dance the song out with the empty can in my hand.

"Thriller" segues into New Order's "Blue Monday" and the Irony Girls disappear into the crush around the bar. Now it's me, dancing alone, wishing I had worn a more supportive bra. I'm careful not to move too fast or sway my upper body too much for fear that any sudden movement may cause my breasts to swing and bounce in ways that give away my age.

Aaron and Edgar are the only ones in the bar not drinking beer. They're standing together, drinking highballs and looking out of place in their designer suits. Edgar taps a toe of his polished black loafer in time with the music. I cringe for him and spin around. I wave to Seth and Janet and beckon them with my finger. *Come dance.* Janet shakes her head—she doesn't dance except if she's at a wedding or a fancy party and it's a waltz or a fox-trot and her date is taller than her even when she's in heels. Seth will dance and as he pushes his way through to me, I catch the Irony Girls staring, pointing, whispering to their friends. They must recognize me; not only did my mother write about me obsessively, she liked to run pictures with her column.

Seth hands me a fresh beer and now I'm dancing double-fisted. I throw the Irony Girls a look that's more of a smirk than a smile. It's my *yes-it's-me* look. I had perfected it by the time I was ten and now it's second nature, though I haven't had to use it in a while. Living in Canmore, the smile/smirk is rarely called for. The locals—the wannabe hippies and summer students and Aussie snowboarders—don't know about my mother or her column and neither do the rich weekenders from the city.

I pour the second beer into my mouth, swallowing as it

fills, and drink until it's gone. I spot the corner of a low table jutting out between the stalks of hipster legs outfitted in three-hundred-dollar jeans they bought purposefully filthy. I duck and lean, still keeping my rhythm, and reach my left arm out as far as I can. I set one can on the edge of the table and then stretch my arm again, hoping to drop the second empty beside the first. But my balance fails and gravity pulls and I'm on the floor, sticky and tired, close to tears with an aching hip. I bite my lower lip till it bleeds and Seth helps me up. I don't want to—I shouldn't, I know—but I look at the Irony Girls. They are sneering. They're horrified. They start to laugh and I know it's at me.

My lips are bleeding and chapped, my blond roots are show-ing and I hate, I hate, I hate these ridiculous black pumps and these stupid, stupid pearls. Seth holds me up and I walk the best I can, lopsided and gimped. As we make our way to Janet, who is talking to Aaron and Edgar, I step out of my shoes. The concrete is wet with liquor and littered with garbage. Scraps stick to my feet and I cringe, but anything is better than those awful pumps I'll gladly leave behind.

And the pearls—the pearls have to go. I tug at the strand around my neck. They really aren't that great anyway—the quality isn't so high. There's no knotting between the indi-vidual pearls and if you look closely under the right light you'll see they aren't all the same size or color. I give the necklace another tug and this time Janet notices and so does Seth and he tries to stop me, to grab my hand away, but he doesn't think and I don't let go and the pearls fly and scatter. One lands in Aaron's drink. I notice one of the Irony Girls crouch down, pretending to tie her shoe, but it has no laces and I see her pocket a pearl. Let her have it.

"What the hell, Mason?" Seth says. He and Janet are crawl-ing around, scooping up as many of the pearls as they can find.

Even Aaron and Edgar fall to their knees, scrambling for stray pearls.

"Please stand up," I say. Everyone is looking. I just want to be normal, to blend in, to have friends who respect my right to drink and fall down and abandon my sensible pumps and shoddy pearls. "It's not worth it—please." Finally, Seth stands and brushes himself off. Edgar pulls Janet to her feet. I kick Aaron lightly in the thigh and he stands, too. They try to hand me the few pearls they've found but I refuse. "I don't want them."

Janet collects the ones the men have found and slips them into my handbag. "You might in the morning."

My laugh comes up as a snort. Someone taps my shoulder. I turn and it's Aaron, holding out another pearl. He tries to press it into my hand, but I shake my head and shirk away, avoiding his touch. "Keep it," I say. "Or give it away."

"Come on, Mason, just take it."

"No. Really. But thank you." I turn away from him, but he doesn't budge.

I move back and step on a pearl in my bare feet. "Ow! Fuck!" I bend over and scrape the pearl off my foot, letting it roll into the crowd.

"Are you okay?" He touches my shoulder but I slap his hand away. I narrow my eyes; I think I growl. I want to slink away, but the only way out is to walk through the bar, and everyone's looking; my hair is too big to ignore. My mother called it *the rat's nest*. My mother. The pearls. She's dead in fur and big earrings, lying on Ron's bed. Janet squeezes my hand. Fuck the pearls, the earrings, my mother, Ron—I'll just get through the rest of this week and then I'll be back in Canmore, where everyone thinks I'm a witch. I have no boyfriend and no prospects and my job at the bookstore is boring and going nowhere, but anything is better than this.

Aaron hands me a drink I begrudgingly accept. He looks amused.

"What?" I ask.

"Nothing. It's just…you are exactly how I remember you."

"Clumsy? Stupid? Drunk?" I am offended, incredulous, humiliated, a bitch.

"No—funny." Aaron knows nothing. "And the way you'd get Edgar into trouble—I loved you for that." Aaron says this and I fight a smile, the sudden flood of memory. There was the time Edgar and I tried to run away from home after being yelled at for something we almost certainly did, though I can't recall what it was. We packed our bags but didn't make it as far as the gates—which were at least a mile from the main house—before being rounded up by Edward in his Jeep. There was also the time I mixed wine with apple juice and fed it to Edgar when he was sick. I told him it was medicine. He drank glasses of it and was drunk by noon and threw up on my mother. And then there were all the times we ruined my mother's expensive makeup and dressed Aaron as a girl.

I take a big sip of beer, trying to calm myself. I keep my lips tight and try not to laugh but the picture in my mind of three-year-old Aaron in bright lipstick, blue eye shadow and cheeks rouged like a clown is too much and the beer I was holding in my mouth sprays out and onto Aaron. This makes me laugh more and soon I can't stop. My stomach hurts and my head feels like it may explode. I double over and collapse on the disgusting, sticky floor. Everyone is staring. Aaron lifts me up by my underarms. I'm shaking with laughter, my body limp and heavy. I look at his face and see the makeup and hair I curled and feathered. He's wearing one of my mother's sequined tops as a dress. She's angry and I blame it all on Edgar. That was one of the few times she didn't write about me in her column; I haven't thought about that in years.

LAW & TAXES

Now I know why people hate lawyers—and the government—and mustachioed past-middle-age men who keep trying to hug them when they don't want to be touched.

I'm standing with Ron on the sidewalk outside of the estate lawyer's office, smoking, and trying to reflect the sun with the Medusa-head gold buttons of the ridiculous Versace suit my mother bought me years ago, during one of her attempts to fancy me up. If I could just get the perfect angle I'm sure I could blind one of these lunchtime busybodies who keep elbowing past and glaring at me for what could be any number of reasons: my smoking, my hair, my suit, my boots, all of the above. Or it could be the fact that I'm standing in the middle of the sidewalk and everyone has to walk around me.

I have no intention of moving. Instead, I move my legs as wide apart as the suit skirt will permit, and take up even more room. It's not very ladylike and my mother certainly would not approve. But I don't care about anything—other than getting Ron to stop touching me and shutting him up.

He keeps telling me it's going to be okay, that everything will work out, that he's there if I need him, that if I'm short on cash, he's glad to help out. I'd rather turn tricks, but that may not be very lucrative considering the state of my body, with its jiggle and bruises and lumps. At best, I'd be a street whore, queen of the five-dollar blow job. I couldn't pass for a high-end escort and I would rather die than strip.

I could get a webcam and talk dirty, looking sexy and stoned, for businessmen and suburban dads who haven't yet made the leap to the hardcore stuff, the ones who pretend if it's not actually sex then they're not actually cheating. I could get them off then listen to them talk—or type—about their guilt, their shitty marriages, how it was never supposed to be this way, about how they're old and can't believe they're bald. I'd charge by the minute and rates would escalate the more they whine.

None of this is very realistic. I will not be a whore. I will get in the taxi and go to the hotel. I will pack up my things and check out. Room service, dry cleaning, concierge, everything—it's gone—just like my emergency credit card, the one my mother gave me, the one I used to pay for my flight down here, the one I was using to pay for my suite at the Fairmont Hotel. The estate lawyer said it will be canceled this afternoon. I explained I was broke and therefore was experiencing a genuine emergency. He smiled and leaned forward, resting his arms on his big desk. "I know this is a difficult time," he said. "But there is a set way of doing things." And by things he meant that there are taxes and expenses to be paid before the estate can be settled. It could take months, or at best, weeks, and until then my mother's accounts are frozen. I have nothing and am stuck in San Francisco with nowhere to stay.

"You're more than welcome to stay with me," Ron says as

we stand on the sidewalk. The taxi is taking forever to arrive and I wish I had a snack in my bag. Unfortunately, San Francisco is not the kind of city where you can easily flag down a cab on the street. You have to call and order and wait. "I know it could be—" Ron pauses and looks down. "I know it could be *uncomfortable* for you, being at your mother's apartment."

I'm not really homeless, out on my ass giving cheap blow jobs to junkies and fuckups in the Tenderloin. And I don't have to stay with Ron or ask Seth or Janet to stay with them. In my bag I have the keys to my mother's apartment in North Beach. She bought it in the mid-seventies, shortly before I was born, when she fancied herself bohemian. We lived there between her marriages and she always wrote there regardless of what man she was involved with. She called it her refuge and couldn't have been more delighted when the neighborhood gentrified, going from alt-ethnic enclave to Yuppie haven, as her seventies' pseudo-bohemian persona morphed into a eighties' money-hungry conservative in royal blue and shoulder pads, with a bag of blow in her jewel-encrusted clutch. She is—*was*—such a cliché.

"I mean, I know that you and your mother didn't always see eye to eye and that this must be very hard on you, Mason, not having seen her or talked to her in some time…it's understandable that you might not be comfortable staying at the apartment." Ron is blathering. He needs to shut up. And why does he keep saying *you'll be uncomfortable, you'll be uncomfortable?* I wouldn't be uncomfortable—it's where I grew up, sort of, sometimes. I have a bedroom there. At least I think I still do. My mother would say that: "There's always a bed waiting for you. You can always come home."

"Britt—your mother—she called it her refuge, you know," Ron says. He's getting weepy, red-faced on the verge of blubber.

"I know she did." I say this through clenched teeth, angry, not sad. Ron's mustache is disgusting. It makes me think of the column my mother once wrote about mustache versus non-mustache oral sex. I get a flash of my mother laid out on Ron's tacky bed, wearing magenta lipstick, Ron's mustache *tickling her monkey,* as she wrote in her column. I feel sick. I try to conjure other images in my head, of puppies, fast food, Seth and cowboys—anything. But I can't erase it. *Tickling my monkey.* Oh God. *"I did* know my own mother," I snap at Ron. Where is that fucking taxi?

"Mason, I'm sorry. I didn't mean to imply that you didn't. Of course you knew your mother. You don't have to be close or keep in touch to know someone. I'm just saying—"

"You've said enough." I'm not falling for his passive-aggressive bullshit. *You don't have to be close; you don't have to keep in touch.* He's probably pissed that he only gets a fraction of what I do of my mother's estate if there's anything left after the lawyer's fees and taxes.

I turn my body as far from Ron as I possibly can once we get in the taxi that has finally arrived. I open the window and let the dense spring air blow onto my face. We drive past familiar spaces that are now something new. We drive up Kearny through downtown and I notice that the Hello Kitty store is gone. I'm sad about this but couldn't say why. Seth and I used to load up on Hello Kitty notepads and pencils we'd buy at shops in Japantown when we were teenagers, and use them in school. People were always so surprised: the pair of us who dressed head-to-toe in black, using cutesy pink paper and pens with kitties and hearts.

Then Hello Kitty got huge, went superglobal. There was the video cartoon series and this pissed us off. The original, authentic Hello Kitty had no mouth—not until the videos. It was better when she couldn't speak. When the big Sanrio store on Kearney opened it was immediately packed with tourists and little girls. Seth and I burned our Hello Kitty things in the fireplace in the home of my mother's fourth husband.

Anything plastic—the key rings, the soft, miniature binders—smoked and smelled. The alarm triggered and the fire trucks came. We were ushered onto the street as we tried to explain. Neighbors gawked and my mother's fourth husband, Gregory, had a fit. He was rich, old money—very private, he liked to say. That was crap, of course. If he was really so private, he shouldn't have married a newspaper columnist with a well-known habit for writing about every embarrassing detail of her life and the lives of those around her. As if everyone didn't know he was "Griffin," her rich, society husband. As if he didn't secretly love it. They all did until they started to hate the things they thought they loved about my mother in the first place.

The Hello Kitty false alarm was some sort of final straw between Gregory and my mother. Their arguments escalated and became more frequent, and soon we were back in North Beach spending my mother's substantial alimony checks on an extravagant red-and-black lacquer early-nineties makeover for the apartment. I demanded baroque wallpaper in red and gold with flocked, flying black bats. It was specially ordered from Italy and cost three hundred dollars a roll.

The Hello Kitty store is gone, no longer poised for Seth and me to walk by and roll our eyes, aghast at the branding of toasters and vibrators and cars with her image. We can't just happen by on our way to Nordstrom—if we were, for some strange reason, going to Nordstrom—and remember the Hello Kitty false alarm and how we used to scour the shops in Japantown. The store's not there to act as a prompt for us to complain about how Hello Kitty is such a sellout and how things aren't at all like they used to be.

"Will I see you again before you leave?" Ron asks as a bellhop opens the taxi door to let me out in front of the hotel. I don't offer to pay or chip in. I'm broke. He can pay and get all passive-aggressive about it later. I'll mail him a check for my part of the fare when I get my inheritance. I'll owe him nothing and we'll never have to speak again. "We could have lunch?"

Lunch? What is he on about? And I wish he'd stop using that horrible, patronizing tone. He doesn't have to talk to me like I'm retarded or some horrible daughter who wasn't close to her mother and didn't keep in touch.

"Mason?"

I sigh and look over my shoulder. "Fine. Yes. We can have lunch," I say just to get him to shut up. There will be no lunch. I barely know the man.

THE MARK

Before checking out of the Fairmont and meeting Seth and Janet across the street for drinks, I changed out of the Versace suit in favor of a black wrap skirt and a men's sports jacket I wear over a T-shirt featuring a silk-screened bunny with X's for eyes. The maître d' and Enforcer of the Dress Code at The Top of the Mark does nothing to hide his disdain after giving me a quick once-over. *What?* I glare at him and shrug.

The Top of the Mark is one of San Francisco's Great Rooms, with its polished wood, Art Deco vibe and a view of the city so breathtaking I question how I could have left this place for a lazy Canadian mountain town where everyone thinks I'm a witch. Then I remember: my mother made me do it. Suddenly, I miss Canmore and my boring job at the bookstore, but mostly I miss the quiet. There is no silence for me here.

Seth is chatting up two ladies with matching chignons. I don't see Janet, so I plant myself at a table in the corner, and read the extensive list of extravagant cocktails I can no longer afford. I read it two, three times. Seth is still chatting with the chignons. I read the menu once more, wave the waitress over and order myself a drink and the Mediterranean appetizer platter on Seth's tab.

"Mason, hi, I'm so sorry I'm late. I was in Oakland and got held up and it took forever to get across the Bay Bridge." Janet is breathless and harried; her forehead is damp. She dots her face with a pad of fine pressed powder. She takes a white elastic from her bag and twists her long hair back and up, securing it in a high, messy bun that is more high-end fashion model than rat's nest. Everything is so easy for her—it's like her life is effortless, with only momentary blips like getting stuck in traffic trying to make it back from Oakland during rush hour. She collapses into the seat beside me.

"Wait a minute." Now I'm confused. I narrow my eyes and push my face closer to hers.

"What?"

"Since when do you go to Oakland?" I wrinkle my nose and sniff at her shoulder.

Janet ignores this and takes the glass from my hand and finishes what was left of my martini. She laughs and raises her hand to smooth her hair, but it's already up and just-so. "Oakland's changed, Mason. All the artists who were driven out of the city during the dot-com boom have all set up there. It's great—like Brooklyn, but ten years ago."

"So you go to Oakland a lot?" I move closer again and sniff at her, and again she fusses nervously with her hair.

"A bit, yeah. There are some great little places—I have some clients. A couple of shops are carrying my line. It does really well there."

"Really?"

"Yes, really. Why are you acting so weird? Can we please get a drink?"

tell at the dinner table. She dragged me to the newsroom once in a while, and though I was very young, certain things stand out in my mind, like that terrible mural and how dreary and gray the walls and the people looked after political correctness swallowed any character the place once had. When I was little, there was laughter and cursing and people tossing things at each other. There was good-natured teasing, men with whiskey breath and pinups of topless women tacked up in front in their cubicles. It seemed like a fun place to work.

"When was the last time you were by the newsroom?" Monique continues to fish.

"It's been years," I say.

"Did you work there?" Teresa the redhead asks.

"Not exactly," I say. "I was more of a source." Their expressions are priceless. I wish I had a camera.

The waiters must have changed shifts because the one who walks by stops and presents fresh glasses of wine or refills with a smile. He's younger than the other one who was avoiding me. Monique and Angela each have their glasses refreshed, but Teresa refrains. "I have to see the dentist later," she explains.

The waiter moves quickly after serving the other ladies, without offering me anything. He's worse than the guy before him.

Monique excuses herself with double air kisses and says how great it was to see me again and that we should have lunch together sometime soon. I'm left with Teresa and Angela, but fucking with them is getting dull. I notice that Teresa keeps looking at her watch. "Looking forward to the dentist? Or just looking forward to getting the hell out of here?"

"Tell me about it. It's fucking painful."

"I take it you weren't the biggest Britt Castleman fan, either?" I ask.

"That's an understatement," Angela says, chiming in.

"She was such a ridiculous woman," I say. Teresa and Angela clink glasses. I raise an invisible cocktail.

"Oh, my God, I am so sorry—we should get you something," Teresa says, putting her hand on my shoulder. "What would you like? Water? Juice? Soda?"

"White wine would be nice," I say.

Teresa looks at Angela and they laugh nervously. "I'll bet you can't wait to have a drink. I seriously don't know if I could do it," Teresa says.

"Do what?"

She laughs again and Angela does, too. "You types always make it seem so easy. And I really admire you for keeping your own—" Teresa looks me up and down "—*sense of style.*"

"Thanks?" I'm not sure if that was a compliment or not.

"So, when are you due?" Angela asks.

"What?" Oh, come on. They think I'm pregnant, too? But I am pregnant. I just don't look *that* pregnant. Or at least I'm not supposed to.

"The baby." She points at my midsection. "When are you due?"

I look down at my outfit and want to tear the stupid trapeze shirt off and set it on fire with the flames from the candles on my dead mother's pretend shrine. I need to get out of here. Where the fuck is Janet? I put on my best sweet smile and talk through gritted teeth. "Oh, any time now. Could be today. Actually, I'm overdue."

"Wow," Teresa says. "You're so *small.*"

"Just lucky, I guess. Well, it was just lovely to meet you both, but I should pay my respects and be off," I say, my voice dripping sugar.

"Of course, one must pay *respect* to dear old Britt," Teresa says.

"You're not staying for Cassie's speech? *That* should be something to behold," Angela says.

"Nah, I really should go. There's only so much Britt talk I can take in one day," I say.

"I know *exactly* what you mean," says Teresa.

Angela nods in agreement. "How did you know her, anyhow?"

I pause and stare hard, first at Angela, then at Teresa. "She was my mother," I say, pushing the words out and hoping my voice won't waver.

SMOKE

"You want one?"

"Excuse me?" I turn to find a petite Asian girl with black-rimmed glasses and a pale pink pixie haircut holding out a pack of Marlboro reds. We're standing outside the hotel where the girls-only memorial is being held.

"I like your hair," she says.

"Thanks," I say, and help myself to one of her cigarettes. "And thanks."

She flicks her metal lighter and I lean in, taking a long drag. God, this feels good. I haven't smoked much in the past few days—not because I'm pregnant, but because the smell was making me feel sick. "You looked like you could use one," she says. "You here for the Britt Castleman thing?"

I nod, too drained to lie. "She was my mother."

"I'm so sorry. Dead moms are no fun—mine died last year."

"I'm sorry," I say.

"Thanks. I'm Kelly, by the way." She offers me her hand and I shake it.

"Mason—McDonald," I say, making it clear I didn't change my last name every time my mother got married. "Are you a writer?" I ask.

"Editor, mostly."

"I guess you've got some horror stories about my mother, huh?"

Kelly shakes her head. "No, not really. I didn't know her that well. I was talking to her recently about maybe writing something for me, but, well—"

"She died?" I finish Kelly's sentence.

"Bingo."

"You don't work for the paper?"

Kelly laughs. "Used to—for about five minutes about a million years ago. Nah—I'm better suited to doing my own thing. I don't always play well with others."

This makes me laugh. It's like something I wish I had said. Maybe I can use it sometime. "So what do you do?"

"This." She hands me a business card. What is with everyone and their goddamn business cards? *Kelly Lo* it reads, and below: *editor and publisher,* Barbarella *magazine.* "It's my baby."

Baby—it's her baby. I have a baby—my baby. I'm pregnant. Oh God. What am I going to do? I touch my stomach. I'm bloated, sure, but there's no baby in there, not really. It's just cells and chromosomes or whatever. There's no baby. I have no baby. Out of nowhere, a Madonna song pops into my head: "Papa Don't Preach." I remember the video: she's pregnant and she's keeping her baby. I close my eyes and try to think of Morrissey or Smiths lyrics, but Madonna is too strong and the song plays louder. What the fuck? I don't even like Madonna.

"Hey, are you feeling all right?"

I nod out of habit, but say nothing.

"Why don't we lose this downer scene and grab a real drink?" Kelly suggests.

"Sure," I say. It's not like I have other plans and any distraction that gets my mind off the baby I'm not going to have is welcome.

We settle into a booth at an upscale lounge. I order a beer, but Kelly nixes this idea and orders a round of shots. The Madonna song is still lodged in my skull.

"Agh!" I don't mean to say this out loud and Kelly looks startled.

"What's up?"

"I have a Madonna song stuck in my head."

Kelly laughs. "That's the worst. Which one?"

I don't want to tell her, give myself away. She seems to be the only person today who *doesn't* assume I'm pregnant. My bloat is hidden beneath the table in the booth and the waitress didn't flinch when I ordered a drink. I'm keeping my handbag on my lap, though, covering any would-be evidence. I'm not taking any chances. I try to think of other Madonna songs. Some of her early work is almost tolerable. "'Borderline,'" I say and immediately regret it. Somehow, it reminds me of Edgar and Edgar reminds me that I'm pregnant. I should have chosen "Holiday."

"That's not so bad," Kelly says. "I like her early stuff. Well, not 'Like a Virgin.'" Kelly laughs. So do I. "So, do you write—like your mother?" Kelly asks.

I am nothing like my mother. "No," I say. I brace myself for the follow-up: *What do you do? Do you have a card?*

Kelly nods but doesn't ask me anything. It's weird. I like it. I take a closer look at her. She's older than I first thought, but Asian girls are tricky that way; they don't seem to age as fast, but I can see the lines around her eyes. She's maybe thirty-two, thirty-three, maybe my age. "Great—thanks a lot, Mason," Kelly says.

"What?" Can she hear what I'm thinking?

"Now *I've* got that stupid Madonna song in my head."

"'Like a Virgin'?"

"Don't even say it—it will just make it worse. You owe me for this."

"Sorry."

"It's all right—I'll get you back."

"Yeah?"

"When you least expect it."

We do more shots and the soundtrack in my mind changes from "Like a Virgin" to "Open Your Heart" after we tell the waitress about our Madonna troubles and she puts on the song. We sing along and I don't care that Kelly knows I know the words. After all, she does, too.

"You're funny," Kelly says after we recover from our latest bout of hysterical laughter. "How old are you?"

Isn't that one of those questions you're not supposed to ask people? Screw it—who cares? "Thirty-four," I say.

"Good."

"Why? How old are you?" I may as well ask.

"Forty-one, but that's not the point. I think you might—"

"Seriously? You're forty-one?" I cut Kelly off. She looks about twelve. I wish I were Asian and small and looked so young.

"Seriously—I'm forty-one. I'm too old."

"For what?"

"The Window."

"Huh?" I don't follow.

"The Window—it's this bullshit culty life course thing that everyone is into. Basically, their whole thing is that women have between twenty-five and thirty-five to get their shit together and get a career and have babies," Kelly explains. The word *babies* winds me like a sucker punch. "You haven't heard of this? It's huge."

I shake my head. "Open Your Heart" plays over a backdrop of fuzzy images of children and pets.

"Anyway, I have clearly missed *The Window* and can't get into one of their indoctrination seminars. They actually make you bring your birth certificate and government-issued picture ID. But I'm dying to have someone go and write about it, but not in the usual journalist-reporter way. I want the reaction of a *real* woman, someone who owns her life and isn't about to let some ridiculous program dictate how she lives."

"Sounds fun." It does.

"So you're interested?"

"What?"

"Would you be interested in going and checking it out and writing something for me on it?"

"I don't know. I'm not really a writer."

"I'm not looking for a writer, I'm looking for something *real,* someone to tell the truth, who isn't afraid to say something is bullshit."

"I can do that." I'm good at that.

"Great. When can you go? There's a seminar on Saturday— the magazine will pay for it, of course."

I run through the calendar in my mind. I have my appointment at the women's clinic on Monday and I still haven't come up with a plan to get the money. Every time I think of asking Janet or Seth I am dejected by what I imagine they'll say and the look on their faces. "And would it, I don't know, pay?"

"Give me a thousand words, I'll give you five hundred

bucks." If I add in a few of the twenties Aaron sneaks into my wallet, I'll be covered. "Just send me an invoice with your story and I'll pay it out within thirty days."

My relief is short-lived. "Thirty days?" I can barely croak out the words.

"I'm guessing you could use it sooner?"

I nod. "Sort of."

"Estate bullshit?"

No, abortion. But I nod.

"Tell me about it. It took forever when my mom died—almost six months."

My nausea rises and I fear I may puke. My body is over-heating and I'm starting to spin. I excuse myself to go to the bathroom and splash cold water on my face, but all this does is make my makeup look uneven and blotchy. My hand shakes as I apply a fresh coat of red lipstick. It can't take six months. I need this abortion and my money and I need to get out of here. I can't stay. I don't care what I have to do. I'll sell the apartment. Let Pearl Lee have it. It was never much of a home.

When I return to the table, Kelly is on the phone. She's booking a place for me at The Window seminar on Saturday. Her voice is syrupy sweet. "Thanks again!" she says, signing off. "Toodles!" She snaps her phone shut and places it on the table. "Fuck me, those people are perky. You'll have so much fun—I'm jealous. And look, if you need the cash, I can spot you. Just get the story to me and I'll pay you right away."

"Really?"

"Sure—I know what you're going through," Kelly says.

I doubt that, but I'll take what I can get.

CRASH

I should have known something was wrong. Janet is rarely late and she's never once stood me up. I should have called her again. I should have worried when I kept getting her voice mail. Seth and I are waiting in line at the coffee place around the corner from my mother's apartment. I'm still tipsy from the shots I did with Kelly. It's unlikely that a cup of coffee will be enough to completely sober me up, but I figured showing up at the hospital drunk was worse than taking the extra minutes to stop for coffee. At least they'll know I made an effort.

Janet's mother, Margaret, called the apartment while I was out. There was an accident getting back into the city. Janet's okay. She has a concussion and the doctors want to make sure it gets no worse so they're keeping her overnight. Margaret told Seth that Janet insisted she call me to apologize on her behalf for not making it to the memorial this afternoon.

I feel sick in the same way I did when Ron called to tell me my mother had died. In the taxi, Seth works the phone, calling people—friends of his and Janet's. Other than Diedre and Rob, they're all names I do not know.

We should have brought coffee for Margaret—and even for Victor, who's in with Janet. His back is to us, but I can see into the room: Janet is propped up and has a bandage on her forehead; Victor is holding her hand.

Margaret hugs Seth and then me. She tells me I look great and seems so happy to see me. Margaret is my dream mother, always smiling and helpful. She can cook and would always listen when I'd show up on their doorstep late at night, in tears over something my mother wrote or a boy who didn't call. She'd make tea and later when we were older, Irish Coffee, and talk me down off the ledge. Margaret is kind and calm, and tall and gorgeous like Janet. She married only once and always seemed so happy with Nick, Janet's equally tall and attractive dad who died five years ago, suddenly, from a heart attack. Janet was devastated. I called her almost every night for a month and sent a card, but I should have come down for the funeral.

"They've assured us she's going to be fine," Margaret says, but her sunny smile doesn't mask the tight lines of worry on her forehead. She's a widow. Janet is an only child. She must be terrified. I wish I knew what to say.

"I'm sure she'll be great. I mean, they've probably done all kinds of tests, right? To see if her head is bleeding or whatever inside. There was that actress, remember? Who hit her head and was fine and laughing and talking and then she died the next day because her brain was bleeding? But I'm sure they have to check for that."

Margaret's smile disappears. Seth glares at me. Jesus. I am such an asshole. "I'm not saying that could happen to Janet—

she's totally fine. You shouldn't worry. I'm sorry—I don't know why I said that. Just forget I'm even here—please."

"Mason?" Victor Durrell pokes his head out the hospital room door. He is completely gross and about a million years old. He's tanned and leathery; his hair is silver and slicked back.

"Hey." It's best I keep my talking to a minimum.

"Janet wants to see you," he says. "And you, too, Seth."

"Of course she does." Seth steps forward and gives Victor a man-hug, the slappy-back-of-the-shoulders kind, pelvises miles apart. I had no idea Seth and Victor were like this together, that they're *friends*. Seth and Janet have this whole other life that I know nothing about. I wonder whether Janet would have told me about Victor at all if I hadn't accidentally tricked her into confessing about their relationship. And since when can Seth keep a secret? There was a time when he would have told me the minute I got off the plane, or would have called to tell me when it first started, which is who-knows-when. Maybe Janet's been with Victor for years and has been keeping it from me. Maybe I don't know her—or Seth—at all anymore.

I try to defuse my angry thoughts with a smile, the way Janet and Margaret do so well. I think I need more practice—my face feels lopsided. "Hey, there," I say as I walk into the hospital room. I move close to the bed so I can squeeze Janet's hand. I should hug her but I don't. I can smell the booze on my skin, and I know from experience that if I can smell it on me, then it smells ten times worse to the people around me.

"I am so sorry I didn't make it this afternoon," Janet says. "I wanted to call but the police and the ambulance came. I don't know why I have to stay here. I'm fine. I wish I could have been there, Mason. And you have to know that I would have called if I could."

"Don't worry about me," I say. "Just get some rest and get better." I've heard people say things like this on TV medical dramas.

"How was it?"

I shrug. It was awful, the women were awful, the waiters were awful, everyone thought I was a pregnant lush so I split and got drunk with a stranger. "It was fine," I say. "Uneventful—I didn't stay long. You didn't miss much."

"Are you okay?" Janet reaches out and squeezes my hand. My eyes sting with tears that I immediately squint out and brush off my face with the back of my sleeve. I'm wearing another one of my old black shirts that I know is unflattering and makes me look fat—but at least it doesn't make me look pregnant.

"I'm fine—just tired."

"And drunk," Seth says.

"Not anymore," I say and give Seth a dirty look. I want to clarify that I'm not a total degenerate.

Seth starts to tell Janet about all the good wishes their friends sent, the ones he was talking to on the phone on the way over. I take a deep breath and slip out of the room. I need some air.

Dying suddenly would be best, I decide after looking up and down the hall, seeing people in those papery gowns on gurneys and shuffling past with IV stands, needles shoved into their veins. My mother was lucky in a way. She was lucky she didn't have to be hospitalized—we're all lucky for that. I can't begin to picture what a saga that would have been, all weepy goodbyes and keeping vigil and watching her waste to nothing while she chronicled every detail in her column before finally slipping away. No, it would be better to go without warning.

"I was so sorry to hear about your mother, Mason. I meant

to offer my condolences the night of Janet's show." It's Victor Durrell. "She always put a smile on my face—such energy!"

"Thanks." Oh God, was my mother sleeping with him? It's entirely possible. *She always put a smile on my face.* Ew.

"How are you holding up? Janet feels terrible that she couldn't be with you this afternoon. And when I got the call about the accident, I meant to call you right away, but I didn't have a number for you and Seth's phone was off." Janet gets in an accident and it's *Victor fucking Durrell* who gets the call? This situation is more serious than I had thought if he's her call-in-case-of-emergency person.

"Don't worry about it—I just want her to get some rest and get better," I say. I am a robot, an automaton.

"We all do," Victor says. "Look, Mason, I understand that this might be strange for you—me and Janet—and knowing you through David and your mother, but I hope you can see how much Janet means to me."

I nod. Again, it's best I don't speak unless necessary. And it's not hard to see what a girl like Janet would mean to an old, gross guy like Victor. I just don't get what he means to her. Perhaps this bump on the head will knock some sense into her.

A squeal comes from Janet's room and interrupts my little heart-to-heart with Victor Durrell. We both rush into the room, as does Margaret. Seth is holding Janet's hand and jumping up and down. She has a big smile plastered on her face. I stare at her face then I look at her hand to make sure I saw what I think I saw. Yep, there it is. It's big and so shiny I can't believe I didn't notice it before. Janet hasn't had any sense knocked into her: she's getting married.

DRESS UP

From what I can tell, the company Edgar works for buys other, smaller companies, fires people and then resells the companies for more money. There are tons of articles about them, mostly saying that if your employer is bought out, it's a good time to start looking for a new job. Kelly gave me the access code for this periodical database she subscribes to so I could do research on The Window, but I got sidetracked. I was only taking a short break when I entered Edgar's name into the database's search engine and then all this stuff started coming up, way more than when I looked him up on Google. There are pictures, too, mostly of Edgar speaking at this conference or that, but a few from social events where he's standing next to a beaming Candice.

She has the same fake smile in all of the photos, the kind pop stars and actors always have when they pose at red carpet events. You push your tongue against the back of your teeth as you grin, that way the smile is never too wide and your gums don't show. But unless you have perfect veneers, you can always see bits of fleshy tongue poking through. I enlarge Candice's mouth on one particularly unflattering photo: sure enough, there's her tongue.

Then I come across a picture of her pregnant. Her face is softer, not as angular and harsh. And she's got perfect makeup: big, dramatic eyes and pale pink lips, sort of a sixties look. I could do that. I could look like her. I print the picture out and take it with me into the en suite bathroom of my mother's bedroom. I tack it up on the mirror and get to work.

My mother had so much makeup. Much of it she'd get for free at the paper, or have to pay a nominal fee for when the lifestyle editor held a sale in the newsroom, clearing out all the free stuff she and her staff didn't personally want or couldn't use. The money would go to charity, a fact my mother used to justify her excess. In one of her makeup drawers I find a bottle of dark foundation that wouldn't have come close to matching her skin tone. But it's a big, expensive brand I know is only available at high-end department stores.

I open the bottle and pour a tiny bit onto my index finger. I just want to see what it feels like, if it is really any different than the cheap drugstore stuff I use. I dab it onto my cheek and smooth it into my skin. It dries instantly but looks moist. It's shimmery and light. It would look great on me if it were the right color. My skin is even paler than my mother's, so the makeup looks a bit like sparkling mud, but it feels fantastic.

I finish coating my face and neck and now it looks like I have a really deep tan. I've never had a tan and am surprised how much it makes my blue eyes pop. I move on to the shadows and liner, making my eyes dark and smoky, like Candice's in that picture. I find a peach blush-bronzer and run it on a big puffy brush along my cheekbones. Finally, I paint on a sheer frosted lipstick and take a step back. I don't look real. I'm an alien. I try the movie star smile, pushing my tongue against the back of my teeth. I could be Candice or any one of her doppelganger friends.

Makeup on, I pull the pins out of my rat's nest hair and comb it straight so it falls past my shoulders. It's a big black frizzy helmet. I spray it with detangler and comb it through. That's better. I pick it up from the bottom and twist it into a makeshift chignon, securing it at the top with a clip. I can't see the back, so it doesn't matter.

I think about what it would be like to attend one of those events, the kind Edgar takes Candice to. I could pull it off, I decide, checking myself out in the mirrors of my mother's wardrobe. There have got to be at least eight of them, and they hit every angle; so much for not being able to see the back of my hair.

A sequined evening gown catches my eye. It's fuchsia and hard to miss. I pull it off its hanger. I shed my pj's and wriggle into the dress the best I can—I can't get it to zip fully up the back.

I look ridiculous. Who wears this kind of thing? I wonder. It's so eighties, and not in a good way. *My mother wore this kind of thing.* I see myself in the mirrors; I'm everywhere. *She's* everywhere. I have to get out of here. I pick up the hem of the long dress and make my way to the living room taking short, tiny steps—it's all the tight gown will allow. I ease myself onto the sofa, careful not the split the seams open.

I pour myself what's left of a bottle of expensive French bubbly water Seth brought over into a glass I'm not sure is mine. There's a Milky Way bar on the coffee table. I lean over and pick it up. I don't even like Milky Way bars that much, but it's there, so I shove it into my mouth and pick up the candy wrapper along with an ashtray that needs emptying.

I jump when the door buzzer goes. It's probably Seth. He said he'd be scouting locations around here today and might drop by. He'll love this dress. With the chocolate bar sticking out of my mouth, I scamper to the foyer, press the "door" button and unlock the dead bolt. I'm almost to the kitchen when Aaron's voice stops me dead.

"Nice look."

I spin around and the chocolate bar wrapper falls to the floor. I bite down and pull the Milky Way out of my mouth.

"So this is what you're up to when I'm not around," Aaron says, moving toward me. I step backward. I can't speak—my mouth is full of chewy, chocolatey goo—so I have no choice but to stand silent, chewing and staring, wishing more than anything that I'd taken the time to remove the heavy makeup and change out of the tacky eighties gown that won't zip up the back.

Aaron tries to touch me, but I push him away. "Aw, c'mon, Mason, you look cute. I don't know what the hell you're up to, but it's cute." I put my hands on my hips. I glare and chew faster. Aaron flops onto the sofa. I pick up the chocolate bar wrapper and retreat to the kitchen to toss it out and empty the ashtray.

There's nothing but dish detergent to remove the makeup. It's for dirty plates, not for skin, but whatever damage it does is worth it—I don't want Aaron to see me in this orangey foundation and frosty lipstick any longer. I swallow the last bit of Milky Way. "I'll be right there," I call out in a singsong voice I swear isn't mine.

I squeeze a dollop of green dish detergent gel onto my palm, then lather it up, rubbing both hands together until they're foaming. I close my eyes and wash my face over the sink. I scrub around my eyes, and clean from my neck all the way up to the top of my forehead. Once I'm convinced there's no way any makeup could possibly be left, I turn the tap on and splash my face with lukewarm water. I touch my cheek. My skin feels remarkably clean. Maybe I'm on to something here. Maybe dish detergent is the key to clean skin. I could get some of those little jars and make some labels and sell it as miracle facial cleanser. I could make a fortune. Back in Canmore there's a woman who sells so-called homemade soaps and creams and cleansers. She thinks she's hot shit because some boutique in L.A. carries her stuff and movie stars supposedly use it. It's probably dish detergent.

I reach for a dishcloth and pat my face dry. It's smelly but it will have to do. Feeling refreshed and almost certain of my future as a beauty mogul, I walk back into the living room and to Aaron. I'll chat for a moment, let him see how lovely my skin looks, then I'll make a dash for the bedroom and a proper outfit—that is, if I can find one.

I sit down beside Aaron on the couch. I turn toward him and his smile disappears. "Mason—your face."

"I know," I say. It's so clean, I knew he'd notice.

"Is there anything you can do? Can I get some cream? Do you need a doctor?"

What is he on about? I bring my hand to my face. The skin burns when I touch it. It's no longer smooth but covered in tiny bumps. My dream of being a beauty mogul fades fast as I leap off the couch and sprint to the bathroom.

I bring my knees to my chest. I'm a big flannel in my pajamas. A dense cream is slathered all over my face. Madonna's "Vogue" plays in my head and it won't go away. Aaron runs a finger lightly over the bumps on my cheek. I flinch.

"It's not so bad," he says. "I'm sure it will clear up in no time."

"Yeah, right," I say.

"Come on, Mason—talk to me."

Where does he want me to start? What does he want from me? "My friend was in an accident yesterday."

"Oh my God. Is your friend okay?" Aaron touches my arm. I don't push him away.

"We think she'll be fine, but it's a head injury so you never know. There was that actress—"

"I know! They thought she was fine and then—boom!—she's dead."

Boom? "I don't know what's going on," I say and this is sort-of true. I should really call Janet, see how she's feeling.

"You are having really shitty luck, aren't you?" Aaron says as he reaches up and pushes my bangs out of my face.

"I guess."

"And you miss her, don't you?"

"Who?"

"Your mother, Mason. You can't fool me, I know you've been feeling down, and you're wearing her clothes and everything. Don't push me away—I want to help you."

I raise my head and turn to face him. I kiss him and he pulls me up and takes me by the hand, leading me through the living room and down the hallway to my bedroom.

I let him undress me and for once don't care about my stomach or my hips or the puckery cellulite on my thighs. Aaron takes his clothes off and kicks them onto the floor. His cock stands straight up. It's shorter than Edgar's, but thicker. My whole body is sore and sick, but I've never been so turned on. I've heard about pregnant women who have an insatiable sex drive but always figured it was bullshit. It's not.

Aaron goes down on me and the moment his tongue flicks across my clit, I come. I'm panting and I want his cock. He lifts both my legs up until they're resting against each of his shoulders. He takes his cock in his hand and rubs it against my clit, teasing me—just like Edgar did. I look up and see his face, his blue eyes—just like Edgar's. My body wants him. I shut my eyes tightly and picture Edgar's face.

WINDOW

At The Window registration table, a woman asks to see my ID: a birth certificate and one piece of legal identification with a picture. Someone would have to go to an awful lot of trouble to attend one of these things if their age didn't fall within The Window. The Window is ages twenty-four to thirty-five, but a quick glance around tells me that the women here are all in their thirties.

The no-nonsense registration woman hands me a receipt, a soft-covered book and a name tag. I slip the name tag into my purse. I pass small groups of women, huddled together and shaking hands. The women in pantsuits talk with the other women in pantsuits, while the ladies in jeans congregate in their own corners. Sloppy, overweight women sit at a table together and others—like me—lean up against walls, watching the time and each other, waiting for permission to enter the gymnasium at the high school where the seminar is being held.

Being inside a high school is disorienting and strange. I'm

uncomfortable, though that may just be my pregnant body screaming at me for sleep. I flip through the book I was handed and discover it's a collection of work sheets with blank spaces to write about my goals and my feelings and number every one of my *priorities*. Is having to sit through a day of this really worth five hundred dollars? I remember the appointment I've booked for Monday at the clinic and decide that it is—it will have to be.

The woman leading the seminar is called Pleiades. But before I have a chance to make a crack in my mind about what a bullshit, made-up, fake name Pleiades is, she beats me to it and tells the audience that it's not the name she was born with, but one she chose for herself. We get to choose everything in our lives, she tells us—we get to decide, we're in control.

That's the first exercise: to come up with a name that's all our own. She tells us to tear off our name tags and throw them on the floor. People do this and I'm surprised with how much gusto. Pleiades tells us we'll find another stick-on name tag in the slot at the back of the workbook and sure enough it's there, but I'm not putting it on.

When I was a kid I always wished I was named Gloria. This wasn't because I knew anyone named Gloria or idolized anyone with that name, I simply liked the way it sounded. I don't have any better ideas and I have to go along with the program, lest someone find out I'm actually working on a story so I'll go with Gloria.

I'm a *reporter,* I think to myself. *I'm undercover.* I picture myself talking into a camera, a correspondent for one of those newsmagazine shows. It would be one of the respectable ones, not one of those overly sensational series where all they do is set traps for pedophiles every week by posing online as twelve-year-old girls and arranging meets in McDonald's parking lots.

I would never work on one of those shows. It's good that they exist—nobody wants pedophiles running around luring their kids to McDonald's parking lots—but setting up deviants isn't my thing.

After changing our names for the day and listening to Pleiades talk passionately about The Window for twenty minutes, we are told to open our workbooks. On the first page, we're to make a list of all the things we'd like to do in our lifetimes, no matter how odd or extravagant. Everyone scribbles away and the room is quiet except for Pleiades' breathing—she hasn't turned off her headset.

I don't know what to write. I sneak a look at the list of the woman sitting to my right: make a million dollars, sing in front of an audience, start my own business, get married, have two kids. It's not much help. If I sell my mother's apartment once it's officially mine, I might have a million dollars. I don't like to sing. Owning a business is too much work. Marriage and kids? I'm not really the marrying or the mothering type, I don't think.

I don't know what to write, so I copy what I see the woman on my left writing, which differs only slightly from the list of the woman on my right. She's got the millions, the marriage, the kids, but doesn't mention anything about singing or starting a business. She's into travel and wants to visit all the continents before she dies and see all the seven natural wonders of the world—or is it eight? Anyhow, I like the travel tangent, so I use that one, but skip the natural wonders. I'm more interested in the man-made ones like the Eiffel Tower and the Great Wall of China. I write down *marriage and kids* because I probably should. That's what everyone in this room seems to want and I'm supposed to blend in, not blow my cover by standing out.

On the next page, Pleiades instructs us to write out all the worst possible scenarios we can imagine, the things we fear could happen if we pursue the goals on the previous page. She tells us to let our anxieties loose, let them run free on the page. Then she tells us to rip the page out and give them to the assistants who are suddenly at the end of each row, standing and smiling, wearing T-shirts that say The Window in big block letters and Look Inside underneath in a soft cursive script.

I double-check to make sure my name isn't on the sheet before passing it down the row, but all it says is "Gloria." I notice that all the women around me are wearing their new-name name tags. The woman to my right who wants her own business is calling herself "Crystal"; the woman on my left is "Alexis." I smile to myself, wondering if there will be a *Dynasty*-style cat fight later as I write "Gloria" on my name tag and slap it onto my chest.

"Ow!" I forgot how sensitive and sore my breasts are for a moment and now everyone is looking at me.

"Is everything okay up there?" Pleiades asks. The lights are bright in her face, so she puts a hand up to block their glare, trying to find me in the crowd. I slink down into my seat but she's not giving up. "Everything okay?"

"I'm fine," I say quietly.

"What was that? Come on, dear, stand up—we want to see you," Pleiades says and the audience starts to clap.

I stand up slowly and wave. A T-shirted assistant rushes over and hands me a cordless microphone. I take it from her and bring it up to my chin. "I'm fine," I say into it. My voice is so loud; it sounds foreign and weird. The women clap again and I try to hand the mic back to the assistant, but she shakes her head.

"What's your name?" Pleiades asks.

"It's Ma— I mean, Gloria."

"Hi, Gloria. Come on, everyone, say hello to Gloria."

"Hello, Gloria." The whole room speaks in unison.

"Hi," I say quickly.

"Since we've all met Gloria, what do you say we get her up here to kick off the next part of the session?"

More applause, a few hoots and whistles and then they're chanting "Glor-ee-ah! Glor-ee-ah!" at the top of their lungs. I edge past the women in my row till I get to the aisle and rush up to the stage to join Pleiades as quickly as possible, anything to stop this inane chanting of my not-name.

Pleiades shakes my hand. I look out into the sea of folding chairs. There have to be at least two hundred women here, maybe more—I'm not good with numbers. Pleiades says we're going to play a little game and I've been chosen to go first. An assistant hands me a piece of paper I immediately recognize as the one we all filled out and tore from our workbook minutes before. Only this one isn't mine. Pleiades instructs me to read it out loud. It's been composed by someone not-named "Dana" and there weren't enough lines for her life wish list, so she's continued the list in the margins. I read the list into the cordless mic. It has all of the usual things: she wants to have kids, remarry, etc., but she also wants to write a bestseller, be featured on the front cover of *Vogue,* star in a film with George Clooney and win *American Idol.* I don't know which woman "Dana" is, but I'm pretty sure that there's an age limit for *American Idol* contestants and I'm pretty sure everyone in this room exceeds it.

Her list of worst-possible-scenarios is worse—fatalistic. Getting the fame she craves could result in a murderous stalker, waiting much longer to have a child could mean birth defects and special needs, being a bestselling author just means she'd have to work all the harder to top herself with each subsequent book. The list is depressing, boring, and reading it out loud makes me squirm with embarrassment.

My reaction, of course, is exactly what Pleiades was looking for. What kind of empowerment seminar is this? One that makes you feel shitty in front of a roomful of strangers?

Pleiades lets out a laugh and the audience members follow suit. Great—now I'm a joke. This is bullshit. I don't need to put up with it. I start to walk off the stage, but Pleiades pulls me back. "Hold on there, Gloria. We're not laughing at you. I just wanted to demonstrate how ridiculous we all sound when we catastrophize. It's paralyzing—no wonder we don't achieve our goals. We're terrified—all of us!" I'll bet the only thing Pleiades is terrified of is turning thirty-five and her Window closing. She's got to be over thirty; the clock is ticking.

"We let our fear stand in the way of our success," Pleiades goes on. The bright lights shine in my eyes. I can't make out individual faces but I see plenty of nodding heads in the crowd. "Now, I have to let you in on a little secret." She crouches down and lowers her voice, like she's trying to get a stray cat to come closer. "The list Gloria so kindly read for us—I created it. I used all of the stories from all of the women—women just like you and me—that I've crisscrossed the country talking to. Everywhere I go, I hear the same stories, get the same lists from young women who are unsatisfied with their lives. We're all the same, every one of us. That's why we're going to destroy our fears right here—today—so we can move on and up."

There is a great round of applause as Pleiades stands and raises her hands like some dime-store messiah. I imagine for a moment that the applause is for me, that I'm winning an award for—*something*. Maybe for investigative reporting.

"Now, I'd like to ask one more favor from our friend Gloria." It takes me a moment to realize Pleiades is talking about me. She walks over and touches my arm. "I'd like to you help Angie distribute the lists." Angie is one of the assistants. She's holding a bankers box filled with the lists we handed in. "I'm going to ask you to form groups—not with the women beside you, but with the women in front of you and behind you. So everyone in the seats closest to the aisle, please stand up and make your way over there." Pleiades points to a corner of the gym. The women get up and do as they're told.

Pleiades goes through this exercise with all of the women until they are in groups scattered all over the room. It's my job to help Angie distribute the lists to the groups—everyone gets one that's not theirs. They're supposed to read it to their group and then line up on the stage to "burn" the list. Being indoors, there's no real fire, just a cheap-looking Plexiglas bin with red flickering lights inside.

As Angie and I weave our way through the various groups handing out papers, I feel important and special, better than all of this. Women smile at me like they know me; many of them call me Gloria. It's so sad. When we're done, I start to head back to where Pleiades is standing, but Angie blocks me. "You should join them now," she says, pointing to one of the groups. She thanks me for my help and hands me a free T-shirt and the last list in the box. It only takes me a quick glance to see that out of all of the papers, I've gotten my own.

There are trays of sandwiches and complimentary pastries for lunch, but I feel like something spicier. There's a hot dog place up the street and though we only have a half-hour break, I'm sure I can make it there and back in time for the next part of the seminar. Plus, I have to get away from these women. After the fear-"burning" exercise, we got further into our workbooks, documenting our past successes and writing out a "recipe" to achieve our future goals using all of the "ingredients" that had worked for us in the past. My recipe was short and easy—and probably not that tasty.

After lunch we're going to be doing all group activities. I should feel like having a drink, but I want a chili-cheese hot dog more. I would have thought that would be the last thing I'd ever want to eat, but the past couple of days I've had insatiable cravings for spicy food. Pickles and ice cream are a myth. I scarf down a chili dog in record time and hurry back to the seminar. I take my seat and hope for the best. People are still calling me Gloria.

We work in groups of four, randomly chosen by Pleiades, who pulls numbers out of a hat that coincide with the seat numbers on the back of our chairs. I am stuck with a prissy-looking woman calling herself "Candy," a plain lady going by "Alexandra" and a woman in a business suit named "Barb." She could choose any name she wanted and the best she could come up with was "Barb."

We're halfway through the "sharing circle" exercise when the pain hits me. It doubles me over; there's no warning. I feel like I'm being stabbed from the inside out. The pain is low and deep and I'm scared. The women gather around me, "Alexandra" rubs my back. My body is overheating. I panic. I'm dizzy. *The baby. My baby.* I force myself to stand. I grab my bag and race to the washroom, hunched over like an ogre.

I lock myself in a stall and sit on the toilet. I check myself for blood, but there's nothing—not yet. But it's coming, I can tell. *The baby. My baby.* This can't be happening. It's not right and I'm scared. "Gloria, are you all right in there?" I recognize the voice as Pleiades'.

No, I'm not all right. I'm losing my baby. I'm at a goddamn self-help seminar and I'm having a miscarriage. I can't lose my baby, I need to save it. *I want my baby.*

I have to go, get to a hospital. Maybe they can help. "I have to go," I say. My voice is weak.

"Just unlock the door and we'll get you some help."

I reach up and slide the bolt over. Pleiades and one of the assistants help me to my feet. "Call an ambulance!" Pleiades shouts to someone I can't see. "It's okay, Gloria, just hang on—help is on the way."

BABY

Thank God I still have my Canadian health care card and the whole hospital fiasco is covered. I want to forget it ever happened, but I can't because everything has changed.

A nurse called Kelly for me from the emergency ward. I couldn't have Seth or Janet finding out and certainly not Aaron, who's been leaving me incessant voice mails since we had sex. Kelly was the only person I could think of. She came down right away, before the doctor told me that I wasn't having a miscarriage at all, simply a really bad reaction to the chili-cheese dog. He said I probably ate too fast and should beware of spicy foods while I'm pregnant. I would do anything to erase the image of his smug face from my mind, but I can't. I'm not sure if I'm still writing the story or getting paid since I didn't complete the seminar. I'm going to need the money to start buying baby things.

"You should write about it," Kelly says. We're sitting in my living room drinking tea.

"But I had to go—I didn't finish."

"No, write about all of it—going to the seminar, the chili-cheese dog, everything."

"It's embarrassing."

"It's *real*. People relate to real."

"I don't know." I want to forget the chili-cheese dog, not tell people about it.

"Think about it, Mason. There are all these people out there going through the same things as you are—and even more people who already have—but everyone is so uppity about pregnancy. It's so boring. Let's shake them up, give them something raw and real."

"I don't know, Kelly. I haven't even told my friends that I'm pregnant. I haven't even told the father."

"Seriously?"

I nod.

"Well, you could do it anonymously—we could think of a pen name."

"I could be Gloria," I say.

"Perfect—Gloria…. Gloria something. We can come up with that later. Just write one piece, see how you like it. Be as in-your-face as you want. Just make it real."

"I was joking—about the Gloria thing," I say. Kelly will not let this go.

"I'm not. I'll pay fifty cents a word. Look, I have to run, but promise me you'll think about it," Kelly says, standing up. I walk her to the front door. Five hundred dollars for one thousand words, the same rate she was going to pay for The Window story. I could use the cash. "Promise me."

"Okay, okay, I'll think about it."

"Good. And Mason?"

"What?"

"Congratulations." Kelly gives me a hug. I feel tears well up in my eyes. "It'll all work out. You'll see."

"Thanks," I say and wipe my eyes with the back of my sleeve.

Writing is harder than I thought it would be. Kelly said she wanted something that was real, so that's what I gave her, but she keeps e-mailing the story back to me with notes and suggestions. I thought that's what editors were for—to fix things. I wrote the story in an afternoon, but have spent at least two or three hours a day working on it for over a week now, executing Kelly's changes. It's exhausting, but it gives me an excuse to avoid Seth and Janet and Aaron—especially Aaron. I'm not ready to tell anyone about my situation; I just want to hide. Maybe I could sequester myself for the entire pregnancy and resurface only after the baby is born in better shape than I was before the baby, just like one of those Hollywood moms. But hiding out is not a very realistic option, and it's already getting dull since I've banned myself from visiting any more pregnancy websites and am forcing myself to drink a pint of water every hour. Trolling the sites made me feel paranoid and guilty about my drinking and smoking. What if I've done something wrong—something that can't be fixed? I chug back more water and try not to think about it.

I think about Janet; she keeps calling. She wants to come over and show me the sketches of the dress she wants me to wear for her wedding. I'm her maid of honor. They've set a date: New Year's Eve, four days before my due date. I can't bear telling her she's going to have to redesign whatever she's come up with and rent me a tarp to wear. I was surprised when I got her message about the wedding—aren't people supposed to wait a year or something after they get engaged? How well does she even know Victor? That could be the rush: he's old; he could be dying.

I told Seth I'm *on deadline*. I didn't offer any details and he didn't ask, which stung a bit. People get so caught up in their own lives; he could have asked what I was doing—not that I'm supposed to tell anyone. Kelly made me swear I wouldn't tell people that I'm "Gloria Babymaker," the fictional author of the story I've rewritten too many times to count at this point. I wrote about The Window, the chili-cheese dog, all of it—except the part about getting knocked up by my married ex-stepbrother and then sleeping with my other ex-stepbrother who is *his* brother. I didn't tell Kelly about that, either, and she hasn't asked. People are so self-involved.

I've lied and told Aaron I'm sick and even after I explained that I was supercontagious and basically under quarantine, he still wanted to come over and bring me movies and soup. I don't think I can put him off for much longer.

It shouldn't be a shock when Aaron shows up at my mother's apartment unannounced, but it sends me into a panic. I don't want to have to tell him, but I don't see that I have a choice. And I'm not wearing my signature black eyeliner and red lipstick; he's never seen me without makeup except that time when I scrubbed my face with dish detergent, but I don't want to think about that.

"I brought you soup," Aaron says.

"Thanks," I say, accepting the thermos he hands me. Soup sounds delicious. It's weird how the mere mention of a word will send my cravings into overdrive.

"I know you're not Candice's biggest fan, but her mother's chicken soup recipe is amazing."

"Candice made this?" My appetite is suddenly gone.

"No—I did. It's just her recipe."

My appetite returns. Aaron makes soup. Aaron is kind. Aaron likes me and doesn't run in horror at the sight of my makeup-free face. Aaron would make a good dad.

We watch the movie Aaron brought over. Will Ferrell is in it, but I keep my opinions to myself. I try to tell myself that the film is funny and laugh in the right places. It actually is kind of funny, but I'm pregnant and in addition to crying more than I usually do, maybe I think things that aren't funny are. It's like having some sort of alien implant. I rest my hand on my abdomen. I know it's only bloat and that people can't tell yet, but I really can feel my baby in there. It's not just me anymore—it's me and my baby, and maybe Aaron. He'd make such a good dad.

I do my best to concentrate on the movie—not because I think there's some great insight I'm missing, but mostly to keep myself from chanting *Aaron would make a good dad* over and over in my head. It's true—he would—but I can't. I shouldn't. I guess I could—

I have to stop thinking like this, but the chant goes on. *Aaron would make a good dad.* First the Madonna songs and now this. *Aaron would make a good dad.* I'd give anything to hear "Like a Virgin" again. *Aaron would make a good dad.*

Aaron would probably be happy. Aaron probably wants kids. And it wouldn't be like the baby wouldn't be related to him—they'd share tons of genetic material. They might even look alike. I know it wouldn't be an ideal situation, but it could be—would be—better than the alternative: my baby growing up not knowing her asshole father, Aaron getting hurt, me being humiliated. When I really think about it, it makes total sense. And there's not a thing Edgar could do about it even if he did suspect. It would serve him right. *Aaron would make a good dad.* Everybody wins.

★ ★ ★

It's taken me three days to summon the courage to see Aaron again and we're going to the modern art museum. It's all very civilized and nice and I catch myself thinking that this is what it will be like, our life together—bringing our child to art shows, having long, smart discussions. But the photography exhibition Aaron is so keen on inspires me only to want to fling myself off the Bay Bridge at rush hour. There are only so many grainy black-and-white pictures of Eastern European Goth teen junkies a person can look at. Aaron, however, is loving it. He's full of energy, excitedly pointing out details to me that no one could possibly miss. He's like the high school art teacher who wants to motivate his class but ends up doing everything but. And I am the grumpy girl sitting in the back of the class whom he's chosen to pet.

"This one—" He pulls on my arm, yanking me away from a thorough examination of my chipped black nail polish. "This is the one I really wanted to see."

The photograph is huge, at least six feet high. It's a close-up portrait of a woman's face. She has black messy hair and dark lips. Her eyes are dull and she's older than she looks at first sight. Cigarette smoke escapes from her mouth. I noticed the picture when we first walked into the gallery—its size makes it impossible to miss. From a distance, she looked like a teenager, and even pretty in a way, but now that my face is a foot from hers I see all the lines and the flaws, her age and her sadness.

"She kinda looks like you," Aaron says. "Don't you think?"

He is not helping. I don't answer him and instead glare at his profile. He can't take his eyes off the photo. He reaches for the small black Moleskine notebook he carries everywhere and starts scribbling something. I head off to find a bathroom. He probably won't even notice I'm gone.

I reline my lips in red and fill them in with matching lipstick. The lighting in the washroom is doing nothing for my pale, chalky skin, so I hurry to finish my lips. I don't want to look at my face any more than I want to look at the one of the woman in the photo. She was probably high, another junkie. How could Aaron say I look like her? It's a good excuse to be mad. I still haven't told him that I'm pregnant. I snap the metal clasp on my black patent vintage handbag shut and stomp out of the room. I take a seat on a bench just outside the gallery and wish I could smoke.

"Hey you," Aaron says. "You okay?"

"Fine."

"Sorry I took so long, but you know, that was just what I needed. For the first time in months, I can't wait to get to my studio. Pretty amazing stuff, don't you think?"

"I guess."

"You didn't like it," Aaron says. His voice is flat and it occurs to me that what I think might actually matter to him.

"I did," I say. "I mean, the photos were good, but maybe a bit depressing."

Aaron nods slowly. He's thinking. "But they're beautiful."

They're ugly and make me want to hurl myself into the Bay. "In a way. They're hard to look at."

"But that's the beauty. Difficult images often yield the most beauty," Aaron says. It's a statement, a conviction. I'm not going to argue. I want to tell him, get it over with. I want to shake off the gnawing feeling that what he said wasn't so much about the photographs as it was about me.

There are so many things I'd buy if I could but I'm broke so I can't. I'm grazing in the toy section at the museum gift store. It's one of my favorite shops in the city, with its wall-to-wall art books and fascinating design thingies. But the toys are what always get me: the modernist plastic dollhouses and William Wegman DVDs where the dogs are dressed as people. I could spend thousands. I seriously need to call that estate lawyer after we're finished here.

Aaron wants to buy a copy of the book that accompanies the Goth-junkie exhibit. There's a display table on the way in—the photo of the woman who isn't me is on the cover. I head straight for the toys.

"Mason, c'mere," Aaron calls over to me. I see he already has a small stack of books curled under his left arm. I feel a pang of—what? Homesickness? Guilt? I feel unexpectedly queasy and sad and wish I were in my tiny apartment in Canmore, watching the snow melt and rearranging the art section at the bookstore—I've been meaning to do that forever.

Aaron pulls me over to the jewelry counter, where a young smiley woman in glasses with thick black frames stands holding a heavy glass tray with a necklace sitting atop it.

"Turn around. Hold your hair up," Aaron says. He's more eager than bossy so I forgive him even before I get angry and do as I'm told.

"Wow," I say because no other words will come. I stare down at the necklace resting above my cleavage. It's unusual—a braided leather rope with a carved black rose at the neck and three short strands of black beads dangling from it. It's amazing.

"They're pearls—black pearls," Aaron says.

"The flower is onyx," the smiley salesgirl chimes in and holds up a face mirror for me to see.

"It's gorgeous," I say.

"It's perfect," she says.

"We'll take it," says Aaron.

"I'm pregnant." I blurt it out. I can't help it.

The salesgirl looks at me and then at Aaron. I can't meet his eye. I say nothing. He starts to laugh. "Wow—Mason. Wow." He pulls me into a hug and kisses me lightly on the lips. "This is—wow. I don't know what to say."

Say you want it. Say you want me.

The salesgirl smiles at me. "Congratulations—to both of you."

"Thanks," I say. I don't dare look at Aaron.

"We're having a baby," he says, not to the salesgirl, not to me, but to himself, like if he says it out loud it might be real.

PEACE

Aaron insists on staying over every night and I have to admit it's nice to sleep in and have someone make me breakfast when I get up. He usually heads off soon after breakfast, kisses me goodbye and goes to his studio where he's working on something "top secret." I round out the rest of my morning lounging on the sofa and marveling at the stupidity of daytime television I'm too lazy to shut off.

I get dressed only when I have to. I don't have any "maternity" clothes, and my regular, oversized black garb is starting to look too small. I definitely have nothing to wear to this dinner Aaron wants me to go to at Edgar and Candice's house. The last place I want to be is in a room with that asshole and his bitch wife, but I can't very well say no without raising suspicion. I want to look spectacular—glamorous and glowing—but this is proving impossible considering my growing shape.

At noon, I grab a box of Froot Loops off the coffee table and head to my mother's bedroom. I measure doorways and walls and write down the numbers. As soon as I get my inheritance, I'm starting to remodel. I can't very well live in my mother's all-white minimalist apartment. I'll need a place more suited to me.

I measure the inside of her giant walk-in closet, but not without managing to get trapped under two filmy maxidresses from the seventies. God, she really did save *everything*. I have to pull out one of the dresses to detangle myself—it has long beaded fringe. Carefully, I free each strand then hold out the dress in front of me. It's huge—not like something my mother would usually wear. Maybe that's why she relegated it to the very back of the closet. As I reach to hang it up I catch a glance of the label: Mondrian Maternity, it reads.

I look around, as if to make sure no one is watching. I drop my pajamas and step into the dress. Unlike the sequined gown, this one zips up the back. I look into the eight-way mirrors. The dress is pink, as is the beaded fringe. The neck is low and the bodice is fitted, making my breasts look huge. I almost trip over the hem, it's so long. I look like my mother going to a costume party as a pregnant Cher. I can't help but laugh. I hike the hem up to see what it would look like shorter. It's better, but it's still over-the-top and still pink. But maybe there's more. I grab the dress that was hanging next to it and sure enough, the label is the same. This dress is pink, too, but with less adornment. I flip through the other clothes on that rack, and find they're all maternity dresses. Unfortunately, they're all pink.

I call Aaron at his studio and ask him if he can pick up a whole bunch of black fabric dye on his way home. He says he will and that he's also bringing his top secret surprise. I know it's a painting—he's had paint on his clothes every day.

I find my old sewing machine at the bottom of my closet. I take out a pair of shears and start pinning and cutting three of the most decent dresses. Once they're black, they'll be fine. I am relieved and proud of my ingenuity. There will be no Old Navy Maternity for me.

There is a painting of me, naked, on the mantelpiece in the living room. That I'm four—maybe five—in the picture makes no difference; it's still weird and it's creeping me out. I remember the picture from my childhood—Aaron had to have painted it from an image in that series of slides I remember Edward taking when we lived with him in Sonoma.

I can't believe Aaron has made this hideous painting which, when I think about it, is kind of pervy. Who paints pictures of naked four-year-old girls? If he was taking *photographs* of naked four-year-old girls, he'd be arrested for sure, but it's a painting so it's *art* and *okay.*

I can't look at it dead-on, but from the corner of my eye, I steal glimpses of it. I'm cute, I'm happy, I'm blond and skinny. Now I'm none of those things. No one would ever suspect that the painting is of me.

"It's for the nursery," Aaron says, his voice teeming with excitement. "What do you think?"

"It's *me.*"

"I know!" He thinks that's super. I think it's creepy and depressing. But I put on a smile.

"It's lovely," I say.

"You really like it?"

"Sure. Yes. I do." Can we please change the subject? "Oh— did you remember to pick up that dye?"

"Yeah, of course. It's in my bag," Aaron says.

"Great—thanks." I walk over to his messenger bag and pull out several bottles of liquid dye. "I'm going to get to work on this," I say. I'm planning to hand-dye the dresses in the bath-tub. I used to do this all the time when I was a teenager.

"Oh. All right." I can read the disappointment in his voice.

"Why don't you give me a hand?" I say. I'd really rather be left alone, but he looks so sad and when he looks sad I feel guilty and start to think that maybe letting him think the baby is his is not the best idea, that I should tell him the whole truth, about Edgar, about everything.

"It's perfect," Aaron says.

He's right. The now-black dress does look pretty great. I'm wearing a short-sleeved one with a scoop neck and an empire waistline that shows off my small bump. This is the one I'll wear to dinner at Edgar and Candice's. It's quite chic, I think, especially with the pair of black heels I have on. They were my mother's and a bit big, but I don't plan on doing much walking. I don't plan on doing much of anything except making Edgar see what a dick he's been and that Aaron gets to have everything he's missing.

I have to stop thinking that way. I close my eyes and try one of those visualization exercises we had to do at The Window seminar. I picture the evening, how it's going to go. I'll be attractive and relaxed; I'll be civil and polite. Everyone will like my dress. I'll be at peace with the world. It'll bug the hell out of Edgar.

Aaron drives us to the dinner. I suggested we take a taxi: he might want to drink—God knows I do—but he's not drinking while I'm pregnant. He says he knows he can't feel what I'm feeling, but that we have to have a *partnership*. I touch my neck as we get out of the car in front of Edgar's Victorian-style home. I don't know why but I expect to find the pearls my mother gave me, the ones that scattered all over the floor at The Cecil, but obviously they're not there. I'm wearing the black rose necklace Aaron bought me at the art gallery. I can't do the positive visualization exercise without being obvious. I shut my eyes just for a second and try to make myself see something nice: flowers, rainbows, puffy clouds. But all I can think of is ripping the necklace off. I don't deserve it; I shouldn't have it. I need to calm down, but I start to sweat, and the last thing I want is to ruin this dress.

Edgar smiles and shakes my hand like we're old friends. He tells me he likes my hair. Even when I glare at him and barely mutter *hello,* he smiles and offers to make me a *mocktail.* How could I have ever had sex with someone who says *mocktail?* I don't think the use of dated fad words is genetic, but I can't be sure. I'll have to look that up online when I get home.

Candice is perfectly turned out in a slim yellow strapless dress that shows off her deep fake tan. The twins are nowhere to be seen. When I ask where they are, Candice points to the staircase leading to the second story and simply says, "Nanny," while she sips a glass of white wine.

My drink is too sweet. I want a beer in a frosted mug. I want to be able to tune out the conversation and forget that Edgar is my baby's father. Why couldn't it have been Aaron? I always pick the wrong one.

"Appies—yum!" Aaron says as a woman no one introduces or acknowledges sets a platter of appetizers between us. *Appies?* Now I'm really hoping that the use of dated fad words isn't passed through generations; it must run in their family.

I do love mini-food and dig into the tiny quiche and complicated towers of vegetables and cream cheese on crackers. "Oh dear," Candice says. "You might want to rethink that one." She points at the bite-size wrap I'm about to pop in my mouth. "It has salmon." I put it down on a napkin and Candice smiles sweetly. "Here—have some carrot sticks. Vitamin A is essential for a healthy pregnancy."

Reluctantly, I take a carrot. At least they're small. I hate carrots and most raw vegetables in general. I nod and pretend I'm listening as Candice runs down her personal list of pregnancy do's and don'ts. I can't tell if she's sharing this information because she wants to look smart and show off or she's trying to fill time or if she actually cares. I prefer to think of her as a heartless shrew who's bad in bed.

We're well into the appetizer platter when Edgar's phone rings. I see him look at the number and then he quickly excuses himself.

"Always business with that one," says Candice. "You're lucky." I think she's talking to me. "It would be wonderful to have someone around who's not always running off to a meeting or flying off on a business trip." Her tone is lighthearted, but her eyes are sad. I feel sick, flushed, horribly guilty. *I'm carrying her husband's child.*

"I am so sorry, but I have to run," Edgar says when he comes back into the room. He doesn't say where he's going or what he's doing and Candice doesn't ask. I get the feeling she doesn't want to know.

"All work and no play," says Aaron.

Hardly, I think. It would be a safe wager to bet that Edgar's sudden departure has nothing to do with business.

The three of us sit down to an elegant dinner without Edgar, whose place setting has been discreetly removed by the maid or cook or whoever she is. I can barely get anything down and I definitely can't look at Candice. I shouldn't care; it shouldn't matter—she's a heartless shrew who's bad in bed.

"So, how have you been feeling, Mason? I know the first few months can be rough when you're in the family way."

The family way. Who says that? "Okay," I say. "It's getting better." I'm lying. It's getting much, much worse sitting here at this table. *The family way*. I'm starting a family. *This* is going to be my family. *Candice* is going to be my family. And Edgar. We'll have dinner here, at this table, again. There will be birthday parties and family outings. I feel dizzy and hot. I think I may cry.

"Mason, what is it?" Candice asks.

"Hormones," Aaron says, like that's some kind of answer.

"Never say that to a pregnant woman," Candice warns. "It's not that simple."

Aaron puts his hands up in surrender. "You don't have to tell me twice."

"Do you want to lie down? Do you need anything?" Candice asks. She's up out of her chair and is kneeling beside me, holding my hand.

I shake my head. "The bathroom." It's all I can say. I need to get myself together. I need some room to breathe, some cold water on my face. Candice directs me through the kitchen and down the hall.

When we get to the bathroom, she gives me a hug. My body goes stiff. "I know we didn't get off on the best foot in Montana, Mason, but I'd like it if we could be friends. And you can call me anytime if you have any questions or if you just want to talk. Pregnancy can be a very emotional time."

I nod, but can't speak. All I can do is cry.

SICK

Aaron thinks I'm acting *funny,* and not in a hilarious way. He keeps asking me if I'm okay and it's getting on my nerves.

I have to tell him the truth. But I can't, I just can't. I feel sick and I'm quite sure it's not the hormones. I have to steel myself and face him. In a way, it's all his fault. If he hadn't abandoned me with Candice and Amanda when we were in Montana then I never would have taken off with Edgar, he wouldn't have called or come over, I wouldn't have fucked him and I wouldn't be carrying his child.

Aaron was supposed to come over at noon, but I manage to delay him for a few hours by telling him I have an appointment with my mother's estate lawyer, whom I really do have to call. Having a baby is expensive, that is one thing I know and Aaron's habit of sneaking twenties into my wallet surely won't last past today. I need my own money.

I call the estate lawyer's office and the secretary tells me that she was going to call me to set up an appointment. I ask if someone could simply write me a check but she says I have to come in and discuss *my affairs* with the lawyer. This makes me laugh out loud. I somehow don't think that pesky lawyer-man who's holding up my inheritance wants to know anything about *my affairs*. Or maybe he does—he's a lawyer so chances are he's a bit of a perv. She asks me if I can come in tomorrow.

"Is there any way I could see him today?"

"I'm afraid not," the secretary says. "Tomorrow p.m. is the earliest I have."

Oh well. I thought if I could see the lawyer right away then that would mean I hadn't lied to Aaron when I said I had an appointment with him. I hang up and contemplate the ways to kill time. I sit on the sofa and paw at a bowl of half-eaten corn chips leftover from last night as I play various scenarios in my head. Nothing I see in my mind seems real: it's all a soap opera with flimsy sets and soft-focus close-ups.

I picture telling Janet and we cry and she tells me that she, too, is pregnant and our daughters are born the same day and grow up as the best of friends. I tell Seth and he couldn't be more pleased. I tell Aaron the truth and he's devastated, but loves me so much he gets over the whole pregnant-with-my-brother's-baby thing and we still raise our child together. I tell Edgar and he screams and yells and tells me to get an abortion. I am disgusted with him. I will not have an abortion. I am angry now and another wave of nausea washes through me as I stand up and begin to pace back and forth in front of the fireplace, all the time stuffing corn chips into my mouth.

My anger leaves me winded and I sit back down and hold my head in my hands. A new series of scenes flashes in my brain. I tell Janet and she is disgusted: she can't believe I would sleep with a married man. I tell Seth and he couldn't be more pissed off because I didn't listen to him when he warned me to be careful. *I told you so,* he says. I tell Aaron and he calls me a whore. I tell Edgar and he laughs and denies everything. I am alone with my baby and no one cares. And I can't tell my mother because she's not here.

I start to cry and as much as I will myself to stop, I can't. I see my mother at first insulted—she's too young to be a grandmother—but then she's buying pink things I hate for my daughter and reading columns she'd write as bedtime stories. I know I'd want to kill her and everything she'd do would make me crazy, but she wouldn't laugh, or shun me or call me a whore. She might share all kinds of inappropriate details about me with the entire population of San Francisco, but she'd never leave me—or her granddaughter—alone. I wipe my eyes with my shirtsleeve. Why I'm so sure it's a girl, I don't know.

Aaron brings flowers which makes it so much worse. I should just say it so he can call me a whore and storm out. Yelling would be preferable to crying, which until this second I hadn't thought about, but it could happen—Aaron is sensitive, he's an artist.

We sit on the sofa and he tries to kiss me but I pull away. "What is it, Mason? What's wrong? You can't tell me it's nothing—you've been acting funny all week."

I shake my head. "I'm…"

"You're what?" Aaron takes my hand and holds it.

"I can't do this." I shake his hand away and stand up, my hands on my hips. I have to pee.

I sit in the bathroom and think. There is no good way to put it. I'm anxious and unsure of whether I should tell him at all. I could simply disappear, borrow more money from Janet and go back to Canmore, and never see him again or answer his calls. When I'm eighty I could write him a letter and explain it all and tell him that I loved him best. But I don't love him. I wish I could. I might have loved Edgar, but he's just another asshole who didn't call me back. My anger returns along with the nausea and I vomit corn chips into the toilet.

I run cold water and splash my face. I brush my teeth and rinse with mouthwash, but there's no relief for my rage. I march out the bathroom, through the living room and past Aaron, straight into my mother's office and slam the door. I pick up the phone and dial Edgar's home number—I've never called there before, but know it off by heart. Candice answers and I almost hang up, but instead I put on my best, most pleasant voice and ask for Edgar. I'm surprised they don't have servants to take care of such menial tasks as answering the telephone.

"I'm afraid he's at the office—may I pass on a message to him?"

"Would you mind telling him that Mason called?"

"Mason?"

"Candice?"

"Yes. What's going on? Are you okay?" I wish people would stop asking me that.

"I'm fine, Candice, and if you could please tell him I called, I'd really appreciate it. But I'll try to reach him at the office or on his cell." I didn't know my voice could sound so sweet. Candice says nothing. "It's quite urgent that I speak to him," I continue. "I have some exciting news for him."

"News?"

I stop and close my eyes and take a deep breath in. I'm going to tell her—I'm going to do this. She deserves to know what an asshole Edgar is, especially now that we're practically family. But then I hear it—a scream. No, more of a wail: a baby—one of *their babies*. The words won't come; they're stuck deep in my throat.

"Mason, what is going on?" Candice asks. The baby cries louder and I hang up the phone.

I turn the ringer off in case she calls back and rest my head on the desk. Christ, what am I doing? I could rebook my appointment at the clinic. It's not too late.

MIRROR

"It's okay, Mason. Everything is going to be fine." Aaron's voice is soft. I'm back in the bathroom and he's sitting outside the door trying to coax me to come out. I'm sitting on the edge of the bathtub. There's a mirror on the facing wall, and one above the sink, and another—full length—on the wall opposite the toilet. Everywhere I look I see myself: the messy hair, the blond roots, the lumps of chub that plague my upper arms, my stomach, my ass. My skin looks chalky and tired and lately it's seemed thinner, like tissue paper, and almost translucent. I pull a white towel off the top of the pile on the linen shelf and wrap myself in it. It has *guest* embroidered along the bottom.

Aaron taps on the door. "Mason, could you please come out so we can talk? I'm getting really worried."

I'm getting really worried, too, but less now about Aaron screaming and throwing things and calling me names. I'm worried that he'll be nice and understanding and forgive me and still want to be with me. I had sex with his brother. I'm pregnant with his child. I am forgivable only to the weakest of men. I step over to the door, leaning back and banging my head hard against it—twice.

"Mason! Are you all right? What's happening in there? Should I call an ambulance? The police? Please, can I come in?"

I almost laugh. Jesus, Aaron is such a pussy. I slide my back down the door and then I'm sitting on the cold tile floor. I open my mouth, but nothing comes out. Aaron is quiet, too, and I can tell he's stood up—the tension of his weight against the door pressing against mine is gone. He's gone and I'm alone. I hug my knees to my chest and start to cry, burying my tears in the white *guest* towel. I am alone. But, I guess, not really—there's the baby, my girl, my baby girl. The crying ceases and I raise my head and smile. My mother's precious *guest* towel has big black mascara stains. White towels are a terrible idea.

I stand up and run cold water. I splash my face and when I pat it dry with another white *guest* towel, my chalky foundation and what was left of my red lipstick leave stains. I hold the towel up for examination. My face is all there: eyes, nose, cheeks, lips. But if my face is on the towel, who am I looking at in the mirror? I always think about things like that, or at least I used to. I promise myself I'll write that down when I get back to my bedroom; there are a few blank journals on the bookshelves, left over from my teenage years. I should start that up again, jot down all the important, big thoughts, like this one about my face and the towel. I should keep track of my dreams, as well.

I count to ten and place my hand on the doorknob, but the moment I do, it wiggles and shakes. "Mason—if you won't come out, I'm coming in."

He's still here? I stand up and pull the towel tighter around the top of my breasts. "Ouch." I forgot how sore they are.

"Are you okay? Please tell me you're okay, Mason." The doorknob wiggles again. He must be sticking something in the lock to try to release it. And he probably will—it's not that hard. I've done it before, several times, including once when I was a teenager and having a party. Seth had locked himself in here with some jock guy who got gay when he drank. The toilet had overflowed in my mother's washroom and people were threatening to pee in the kitchen sink if I couldn't get Seth and the jock guy out of the bathroom. I did and there was Seth, pants down, the jock guy on his knees.

The doorknob wiggles again. He's getting close. My options are limited and none are appealing. I square my feet and press my back against the door, forcing all of my weight against it, trying to buy more time. But more time doesn't mean better answers, or any answers at all.

"Ah-ha!" Aaron says, as the lock is released. He pushes against the door, but is met with all the wobbly body force I can muster. "Mason, don't be silly—let me in. We need to talk."

No, we don't need to talk.

"Please," he says. He stops pushing on the door but is still twisting the knob back and forth, probably in celebration of his manly prowess. Men are always like that—gloaty, puffed up and proud—whenever they accomplish anything that could be considered *handy*. "Please, Mason. I'll stay out here all night if I have to." I look down at the doorknob, twisting right, then left, then right—it's hypnotizing. "Come on, Mason—it can't be that bad." Aaron's voice cuts through my brief meditative moment and pisses me off.

"I'm pregnant."

The knob-twisting stops. "I know—"

"It's Edgar's."

Aaron is silent.

"I know it's totally fucked up, and I'm sorry, and I didn't

want to hurt you. It was just one of those things that happened. I was so mad that you left me with those awful women when we were in Montana and then Edgar was so nice to me, and then he kept calling me when we got back to the city and he brought over drinks and—I know it was a horrible thing to do, but—"

I hear a faint click—the front door. Aaron is gone. He didn't even give me a chance to explain.

I sit in the bathroom for who knows how long. There is no clock in here and I don't wear a watch. But I'll have to start wearing one since I'll have doctor appointments and birthing classes and other baby things I'll have to deal with at specific times. Or I could get one of those phone-organizer things when that lawyer finally hands over my money tomorrow. But I might not need one of those until the baby comes and I have to take her places, to playdates.

Nausea hits me unexpectedly and I throw up. I miss my feet, but barely. A couple of chunks splash up onto my calves and the bottom edge of the towel. I step away from the mess and out of the towel. I reach for the other towel, the one with the makeup stains and hold it under running water. I wring it out and then clean up the puke. The process only makes me want to puke more, but this time I'm ready and vomit into the toilet.

I find a garbage bag under the sink and stuff the two wet, pukey towels into it, then open the door just enough to be able to toss it into the hall. I'm not washing them—they're trash. I'll take the bag out later, before I write in the first page of my journal how I cleaned up my own vomit with the towel that was my face. Or maybe it wasn't my face, only *one* of my faces. I'll write something down about this for sure. It seems significant; I wonder what it means?

I pull a clean towel from the linen pile and wrap myself

in it. It's bigger and fluffier and has *Hot Stuff* embroidered in hot pink thread. I watch myself in the full-length mirror as I tuck the corner into my makeshift towel-dress to secure it. My stomach drops, but I don't throw up this time.

Aaron knows. Edgar probably knows or will know soon. I'll have to tell Janet and Seth. Everyone will know and I will be *that woman,* the one who fucked the married guy and got herself pregnant. And if certain people found out—like my mother's media friends or whoever—then it will be a scandal. The society bitches will hate me, but that wouldn't really matter because I'm sure they already do because of my mother. Candice and her friends will definitely hate me. I wonder if Candice will divorce Edgar. I wonder if Edgar will try to give me hush money that I would of course refuse. I wonder about everything. What are people going to say?

Whatever they are going to say, I have to be ready for it. This is my decision and my baby and I know they're all going to sit there and wait for me to fuck it up. But what if I don't? What if I'm a really good mother? Thanks to my mother, I have a pretty good idea of what not to do, and that's got to count as some sort of parenting education.

I sidle up to the vanity and start pulling the black bobby pins from my hair. It takes some doing, but I brush it straight. It frizzes out past my shoulders like the corners of a big triangle. A pointed hat and I would look like the witch those people in Canmore think I am. But that's not my home anymore. I won't go back. Not now, not with the baby, my daughter. This is my home. I should really call Megan at the bookstore and tell her I'm staying. I'll do it tomorrow. I could call my landlord and have him box up and ship my stuff, but there's nothing I want and he's always been a bit of a dick to me. Let him wonder, let him think I'm dead.

A strange, rumbling noise startles me—my cell phone. I forgot I had brought it into the bathroom with me. It's sitting on the edge of the bathtub jerking around in a vibrating circle. The call display says it's Edgar. He knows now, he must. I'd like to see him try to charm his way out of this one.

"Hello?" I answer like I don't know it's him.

"What kind of game do you think you're playing at, Mason?"

"No *hello*? No *how are you*? No *are you available for a fuck in your kitchen?* I'm disappointed—where are your manners?"

"You're telling Aaron you're pregnant with my baby? You're calling my house? You're talking to Candice? What the fuck?"

"So?"

"So—you are obviously a sick fucking person who needs to stop fucking with me."

"So now *I'm* fucking with *you?*"

"Fuck you, Mason."

"Oh, you've already done that—several times."

"*Three* times."

"That's enough to do it."

"Come on, Mason, you can't be serious. I don't know what your deal is, but whatever you're thinking you're going to get out of pretending to be pregnant is not going to happen."

"I *am* pregnant. It *is* your baby."

"You need to get some help. Don't call me again—ever." Edgar's voice is cold and hollow. He hangs up. Edgar is a bigger dick than every dick guy I've ever met in my life combined. I stare at the phone in my hand until the backlight goes off and Edgar's name disappears from the screen.

ROOTS

I couldn't give a shit about what that stupid lawyer thinks about my hair, but he didn't need to be so obvious, sitting there behind his big-man desk with that smirk on his face as I signed the papers. I suppose I could have worn a hat, but I'm one of those people who doesn't look good in hats. Janet looks good in hats. I'm meeting her at the salon she goes to after my appointment at the bank later this afternoon. She says they have an excellent color-correction specialist. She said she'd lend me the money—*five-hundred dollars*—to have the whole mess fixed, but there's no need for that. I have my own money now—my mother's money, all $348,800 of it, plus the North Beach apartment, of course. And that place has got to be worth over a million, so technically I think I am a millionaire.

But there will be no bank and no salon until I get through this coffee-snack thing with Ron. He was at the estate lawyer's office, too. This surprised me, but I guess it shouldn't have— he was my married to my mother. He looked so sad signing off on the last of the paperwork. "It's really over now," he said to no one in particular. So when he asked if I would have a quick coffee with him I couldn't say no. I think I'm starting to feel maternal.

"Your hair's different," Ron says.

"That's an understatement." I pull a piece of hair out from my rat's nest up-do and bring it down in front of my eyes. It's orange. Not redhead orange, but carrot orange. When I was snooping in the cupboard under the bathroom vanity, I found my mother's stash of DIY blond hair dye. I followed the instructions to a tee, not once, but four times, until I had used all of the boxes, and still, it's orange. As I smooth a piece behind my ear, the ends break off and then I'm sitting at a table with my depressed sort-of stepfather whom I barely know holding a small clump of wiry orange strands between my fingers.

Ron smiles. I start to laugh. It *is* ridiculous. This color-correction girl of Janet's had better be as good as she says she is. "It's supposed to be blond," I say.

"Your mother said you were a natural blonde—she showed me pictures of you as a girl."

"My mother wasn't blonde," I say and Ron's smile falls. "I'm sorry. I don't know why I said that."

"So, how have you been, Mason?" Ron asks, changing the subject. "The city treating you all right?"

"I guess," I say, shrugging. This is the strangest conversation—it's not uncomfortable, but it's sad and the silence between our words is too long. Making small talk is hard. It's like we're having coffee, the three of us: me, him, my mother—and Ron and I have to think of something to say to each other while we wait for my mother to return from the washroom, except we both know she's not coming back. I blink back the tears that defy my will to stop them. Ron puts his hand over mine and neither of us says anything for what seems like a very long time.

"I'm pregnant," I say quietly, not wanting to break the silence open too wide.

Ron stares at me with soft eyes and squeezes my hand. He really should shave that disgusting mustache. "That's wonderful news, Mason—isn't it?"

"It is," I say.

"And the father?" Ron waves his hand in front of his face. "I'm sorry, Mason. You don't have to answer that—it's none of my business."

"It's okay," I say. I'm going to have to get used to this, so Ron is as good as anyone to practice on. At least I know he's not going to cause a scene and call me a whore at the top of his lungs right here in this SoMa café. At least I don't think he will. "It's sort of complicated."

"Everything is," says Ron and he's right. I'll remember that and write it in my journal when I get home.

I tell Ron everything. Not all the details about the fucking or anything, but enough so he gets a good idea of what's going on. He shakes his head. I grip the edge of the table. This could be the moment, he flips it over and points and yells and calls me a whore in front of everyone. "And he won't believe you? What kind of a man is he? He does know how babies are made, right?"

"Exactly! He's acting like I'm making it all up. He's such an asshole—isn't he?"

Ron nods. "He's an asshole, Mason, no doubt. Do you want me to talk to him, maybe help you get this sorted?"

The tears rise up again, but I manage to blink them away before any fall. Why is Ron being so nice to me? He doesn't even know me. And after all the things my mother wrote about me, I don't know why he would want to. I can't even imagine the stuff she said to him about me in private. I shudder. "No, that's okay—I'll take care of Edgar myself."

"Oh, I'll bet you will," Ron says with a laugh. "You remind

me of your mother—she wasn't one to let anyone off the hook for crossing her. She'd get this look and you'd just know: *watch out, Britt's on the warpath.* I never heard her raise her voice, though, not once. She always had much more creative ways of going about her business."

"She'd just use her column." It's not that creative.

"No, no, I'm talking about the ways she'd deal with all of those busybodies in the newsroom and the snotty social ladies. She knew everything they said about her, what they thought, but when one of them crossed the line, she always set them straight."

"Like how?" I was sure my mother was oblivious to the rumors and snickering. Maybe Ron is going through some sort of idealization phase, thinking she was better or smarter or more creative than she really was.

"All sorts of ways. I could tell stories for days."

"Really?"

"Oh, yes, my dear," Ron says as he pats my hand. "Mason, it's nearly three—what time do you have to be at the bank?"

"Shit. Now."

"We can catch up again later. I'll catch the check."

Mary, the color-correction specialist, circles me slowly, stopping occasionally to touch my hair and sigh. She's making me nervous, and I've had enough nervous for today, especially after my trip to the bank where they made me wait in a tiny office while two ladies in pantsuits reviewed my application in a bigger office down the hall. I have a check for over $300,000 and I still have to pass some kind of test to be in their club? I was set to walk out and take my money elsewhere, but stopped myself. What would be the point? If that bank was like that, so were the other ones. Banks are all the same as far as I can tell. But I didn't have the time or the energy and I was already late for the salon.

"We're going to have to do this in two steps," Mary says, pulling up a rolling stool and sitting down in front of me. I'm in the big chair. Mary looks very serious and she's been taking notes. It's like being at the doctor. "We can do the first step today, and you'll need a cut—we won't be able to save all of this." Mary reaches out and breaks off another clump of wiry orange hair.

"Will it still be orange?"

Mary sighs again. "No, it will be blond—but a darker blond, darker than your natural color. In a month, after your hair has had a chance to recover a bit, we'll take you back up to your true color. And like I said, we're going to have to cut it."

I was hoping I hadn't heard that part right, that somehow she could save the breaking ends. "How short?"

"Chin length, max. A shaggy bob with bangs, maybe?"

I look at Janet. She nods. In fact, she looks excited. *A bob?* Shaggy or not that sounds, well, *pretty,* and I don't do pretty. Mary stands and swings my chair around until I'm facing the mirror. All I can see is a cloud of orange frizz around my face. "Fine—chin-length shaggy bob it is, then."

"I called Seth," Janet says. "Told him we're running a bit behind."

It's his birthday and we are supposed to meet him for drinks at eight. I have been sitting with gunk on and off my hair for four hours. Mary did a preliminary cut—there was no point in coloring the fucked-up ends—and then proceeded to "lift" the orange out of my hair, once, twice, three times.

It's just after eight now. All Mary has to do is finish the cut and blow-dry my hair. I touch the back of my neck. It's bare and feels weird, but I feel so much lighter.

PARTY

I am blond by the time we get to the bar. Well, I'm dirty blond and I have what Mary called "a *chunky,* razor-cut bob." It was a bit rude of her to use the word chunky around me: I am no longer fat. I am pregnant. I wanted to blurt out the news, but kept my mouth shut. Janet was there and I still haven't figured out how to tell her. She doesn't even know about Edgar. And she's an engaged person now, so trying to explain how I got knocked up as a result of an affair with my ex-stepbrother won't be easy.

Normally, if I had something like this to tell Janet, I'd invite her over. We'd bond and drink tons of wine till we were off our heads, and then I'd spring it on her. She might get a bit angry but then she'd be all mushy and forgiving. Plus, she'd have a nasty hangover to deal with in the morning and my misdeeds would be the least of her worries. But the plan won't work, not this time. Janet barely drinks anymore and I'm not supposed to drink, though in between the bouts of nausea, I've found myself craving cold beer, something Belgian or French.

★ ★ ★

Seth wobbles over and shoves a champagne flute into my hand and one into Janet's the moment he sees us. He's being propped up by a man-boy who can't be over twenty, who's very attractive in that fully waxed body, workout-every-day kind of way. He's not my type at all.

Seth proceeds to pour bubbly golden champagne, some of which makes it into our glasses, but most of which ends up on my hands and on one of Janet's shoes. "We need a toast," Seth says. *Toast* comes out of his mouth like *thost*. He is so drunk.

Seth's new friend takes the bottle from his hand, as it's clear he's not up for pouring with any accuracy. I keep my nearly empty glass at my side and wave the bottle away when Seth's friend gets to me. "I'm just going to get some Coke, I think," I say, hoping it's too loud in the bar or Seth's too drunk to hear or care.

"I can get you one," Seth's friend says.

"What?" Seth lurches between us and pulls us into a huddle. "You want Coke, Mason?" Seth asks. I'm sure he thinks his voice is quiet and that he's being subtle in that way that drunk people do. "I'll tell ya a li'l secret—I got us some super special candy for tonight." Seth pulls a tiny vial from his jeans pocket and takes a loud and exaggerated breath up his nose. A couple standing behind us turn and stare.

"Put that away," I hiss at him.

"I thought you said you wanted coke." He's whining now.

"I did—Coca-Cola—the soda."

"What about the champagne? You *looove* champagne."

It's true, I do. "I think I'll just have some water." Coke might be bad for the baby—I'll have to add that to my list of things to check on. "I'm really dehydrated and if I drink it will get worse." This sounds perfectly reasonable. If I don't make a big deal of this maybe Seth won't and he'll go away or pass out or something.

"Come onnnnnn, Mason. Have your soda laaaater." Seth grabs my hand and lifts it so the empty champagne glass is at his chest-level. He swipes the bottle from his new friend and starts to pour. I shake his hand off mine and he ends up pouring what's left of the champagne onto the floor. Now he's pissed.

"What is your fucking problem now, Mason?" he asks.

"I just don't want to drink tonight," I say through gritted teeth.

"Leave her alone, Seth," Janet says, taking the empty bottle from Seth's hand and the empty glass from mine. "If she doesn't want to drink, she doesn't want to drink."

"But Mason *always* wants to drink—you know that. Everybody knows that," Seth says. He shuffles over until his face is just inches from mine. "What the hell is up with you? You gone all A.A. or something?"

"Fuck off, Seth," I say. I've had enough. I'm tired and I'm starting to feel nauseous again.

"Maybe you're pregnant, right?" Seth starts laughing and can't stop.

I open my mouth but nothing comes out. I start to shake. Seth stops laughing. "Holy shit. You're fucking pregnant!"

Janet looks at me in alarm. I nod. I still have no words. Janet hugs me. "Congratulations," she says softly. "Does Aaron know?"

At this, it's my turn to laugh. "Oh, he knows," I say. Seth joins in my laughter. Janet looks puzzled. Seth pulls me away from Janet and twirls me around. I stop laughing. I may throw up. I steady myself by putting a hand on the back of a chair. The man sitting in it turns around and sneers.

"She's fucking pregnant, you dick," Seth says.

I take a couple of deep breaths, making sure I exhale all the carbon dioxide I can. This is supposed to be good for me during stressful situations. I assume it's good for the baby, too, but I should look that up. "I'm okay," I say, unsure of who exactly I'm trying to convince.

"What about Siouxie?" Seth makes another ridiculous suggestion. We're playing name-the-baby in a booth in a semi-quiet corner of the bar. It feels good to sit down.

"No, no, no—it has to be something classic—like Caroline or Kimberley," says Janet.

"Tessa is nice," says Seth's friend. I still don't know his name.

"What do you think of Gloria?" I ask. This is fun, and the best I've felt since I found out I was pregnant. I don't need Aaron or Edgar or anyone. Janet and Seth are my oldest friends—they will be my family.

"Gloria's good," Janet says.

"I like it," says Seth's friend.

Seth makes a face. "Nuh-uh. No good."

"Why not?" I ask.

"You haven't heard about *Gloria Babymaker?*"

Holy shit. Seth has read my piece in *Barbarella*. I shake my head no. "Who's Gloria Babymaker?" I'll play along.

"Just some idiot woman who can't write," Seth says. His words sting.

"She wrote a story in the new issue of *Barbarella*—you know that online magazine—about being pregnant and eating a chili-cheese hot dog and thinking she was having a miscarriage," Janet says. She's read it, too.

"I'll forward it to you," Seth says. "It's *awful,* but in that can't-stop-reading kind of way—all whiny and me-me-me."

"It's a bit like your mom's column, actually," Janet says.

This stings the most. "I am nothing like my mother," I say through gritted teeth. Janet and Seth look confused.

"We didn't say you were, Mason," Janet says.

"We're talking about this so-called *Gloria Babymaker,*" Seth says.

"*I'm* Gloria Babymaker—you're talking about me," I say as I stand up and walk away from the table. Janet leaps up and comes after me. "I'm going to the bathroom," I say. "Just leave me alone."

"We didn't mean it," she says. "Come and talk to us— please, Mason. We didn't know."

"Give me a minute," I say. Janet nods. I watch her slink back into the crowd and then I make a break for the exit.

KELLY

I have no idea how to do this, what to do or what order to do it in. I spent most of last night in my mother's office, on the computer, lurking in online pregnancy forums, trying to forget about what a mess my life is. But it didn't do me much good: now I have even more questions and not one answer. I shouldn't eat tuna, one woman posted. I shouldn't eat fish at all, posted another. No chicken, no sugar, watch out for gestational diabetes and edema. Most miscarriages happen within the first trimester. Everything I've had to drink and eat since I didn't know I was pregnant matters. Damage may have already been done.

I slept for five hours, but not well. Nightmares of blood and sick babies kept me tossing. When I woke to the sound of my cell phone ringing, I was sure it was the doctor calling to tell me something has gone horribly wrong. This is impossible, I know, considering I don't even have a proper doctor yet, but it made my heart leap with anxiety and for once I was relieved, not annoyed, to hear one of those recorded messages telling

me I've just won a trip to Barbados. I hang up the phone then
pick it up immediately to dial Janet, but quickly remember that
I can't. I can't call Seth, either, but I don't want to be alone
and I have to get out of here for a while.

If anyone asks, I'm not pregnant, just fat. I smoke my way
through the last of a pack Seth left behind last time he was
over. I walk up and down the city's famous hills until I find
myself downtown, not far from the newspaper where my
mother worked, panting, sweaty and surrounded by tourists.
I dip into the first pub I see that isn't a chain or a sports bar. I
sit on a stool at the bar. At least ten minutes and half a glass of
Napa white disappear before I realize that this is the bar my
mother and all the other writers went to.

I look around and sure enough there they are, the writers
and editors with their scotch and microbrew beer, wearing
their casual Friday clothes on this Tuesday afternoon. It's a
bit early, I think, but then, it's tough times in their business
and drinking in the newsroom is no longer considered, as my
mother used to put it, *character-building*. I peer at the clock above
the bar—it's later than I thought, already after six. I touch my
belly—I'm running out of time.

I unfold the entertainment section of yesterday's newspaper
that's sitting on the bar. I quickly learn that a former super-
model has been caught driving drunk and that navy blue is
the new black for fall. Having a dirty-blond bob and hacked-
off vintage dresses are one thing, but navy blue is something
else entirely. It's the color of mommies. Nobody wears navy
blue except kids whose parents won't let them wear black and
dowdy mothers. I gulp back a glass of wine and signal the
bartender to pour me another.

There's an article about an actor everyone knows is gay.

I love women—maybe too much, reads the headline. I let out a little snort.

"I know—what a joke, huh?"

I turn my head and am suddenly face-to-face with Kelly. She's leaning against the bar, waiting on her drink. I feel myself turning red. She's left three messages I haven't returned.

"Hi. Hey—I've been meaning to call you. It's just been so hectic with everything, you know."

Kelly looks puzzled. She moves her face closer to mine. "Oh my God—Mason! I didn't recognize you! Your hair is so...*blond.*"

This isn't a compliment. But Kelly Lo has no business making comments about anyone's hair, not with that pink pixie 'do.

The bartender places a fresh glass of wine in front of me and a tall, skinny can of beer in front of Kelly. It has some illegible words on it—Eastern European, I think. Czech, maybe Polish or Hungarian—lots of strange accents and not a lot of vowels. I keep my eyes trained on my wine but this doesn't stop Kelly from dragging a bar stool over and sitting beside me. "I'm so glad I ran into you, Mason. I wanted to talk to you about doing a regular column for me."

"I don't know," I say.

"Think about it. It would be great, really provocative— exposing the truth about pregnancy," Kelly says.

I choke on my wine and start coughing. For a moment, I forgot she knows that I'm pregnant. I'm in a bar. I'm drinking wine. I surely smell of smoke. I have to get out of here. I dig through my purse until I find my wallet. I pull out a twenty and drop it on the bar. I slide off the bar stool and shove the newspaper under my arm. Kelly touches my arm. "Mason, what's wrong? Did I say something to upset you?"

I should walk out the door, walk out and not turn back,

but I don't. I clutch my purse to my stomach hoping to hide any evidence of this baby I clearly shouldn't be having. The cigarettes, the wine, God, I wonder if it's too late to have an abortion.

"I can't—I shouldn't—I—"

"Hey, relax," she says. "Sit down a sec. Catch your breath. Tell me what's going on."

I shake my head.

"You're right—this probably isn't the best place. Come on—I only live a couple blocks from here. We can chill out."

I nod and go with her because the last place I want to be is here or home. I'm in limbo, purgatory, stuck and alone.

I walk with Kelly up the street and around the corner. We stop at a short building that houses a Chinese restaurant, a convenience store and a travel agency. She slips a key in the door between the restaurant and the store and we head up the stairs. It's a bit sad, really. She's over forty and she's living in a shitty flat over a Chinese restaurant?

Kelly unlocks a door at the top of the stairs and we step inside. I can't speak; I'm in awe. The place is huge and open and everything is pink. There's a pair of vintage mannequins from the eighties in the corner, wearing fifties pouffy dresses and posed like they're telling secrets. There's a Victorian-style sofa with faded floral upholstery and a wall of multisized mirrors in ornate, gilt frames. And on the far wall, there's a painted mural of San Francisco landmarks: a parade of Kewpie dolls walk single file across the Golden Gate Bridge, Gloomy Bear rides the antique carousel at Pier 39 and Hello Kitty climbs the Transamerica Tower like a *kawaii* King Kong.

"My ex painted it," Kelly says, having noticed my gawking.

"It's incredible—this place—oh my God—" *This* is what I want. No more white walls, no more black bat wallpaper in my bedroom—I want that perfect mix of kitsch and cool. Sort of *eccentric*. I want *this*. Only not in pink.

"My favorite movie when I was a teenager was *Pretty in Pink*. I wanted a room like Molly Ringwald's character had—with all that great vintage stuff, that eclectic mix," Kelly says.

Eclectic—that's the word, not *eccentric*. "It's amazing," I say.

"It's taken me years. I started collecting this stuff when I was fifteen. Sometimes I think I should just ditch it all and paint everything white, go all minimalist."

"No!" I didn't mean for it to come out so loud. I put my hand over my mouth.

Kelly laughs. "Okay then, if that's how you feel about it. Can I get you a drink? I have some white in the fridge."

"I shouldn't," I say.

"It's okay, you know. My doctor says that a glass or two of wine now and again isn't going to hurt the baby. She's British—very progressive." I know Kelly has a daughter— she's told me this before—and I'm sure she would have said something if she'd been born with some kind of defect.

"All right then—maybe just one."

"Have a seat," Kelly says. "Anywhere you'd like."

There are so many options. I choose a pale pink vinyl chair with metallic gold stars and dots that look like loose glitter. Kelly hands me a glass of wine and puts a bowl of cashews between us. "Nuts are great for protein," she says.

"Isn't there more of a chance your child will be allergic to nuts if you eat them when you're pregnant?" I'm sure I read that last night on one of those sites.

Kelly laughs again. "That's bullshit. Look, do you want me to tell you what you need to know?"

I nod.

"First, throw out any pregnancy books or magazines you have except one, only keep one that is strictly about your body—how it changes and when, that kind of stuff. You can eat whatever you want except I'd avoid tuna. You can eat sushi—that's all bullshit, too, all that crap about no sushi. What do you think Japanese women eat? And Japanese kids are way healthier than Americans. You can drink a bit. And if you want to smoke sometimes, whatever. I mean, all of our mothers smoked when they were pregnant and their mothers and their mothers and *we're* all fine. This whole you can't do anything while you're pregnant idea is pretty new and it's totally American—it's not like that in Europe at all. My daughter was born in Holland. Nobody gets hysterical over there—it's so much more civilized." Kelly lights a cigarette and pushes the pack toward me. I want to smoke but don't.

"What's your daughter's name again?' I know she told me once before, but I can't remember. Short-term memory loss is common during pregnancy—I read that, too.

"Jean—like Jean Seberg. We call her Jeannie."

"How old is she?" There are school notices on the fridge, a pink backpack on the floor, a CD by one of those thirteen-year-old Disney pop stars on the top of a pile of papers on the table between us.

"She's eight—great age."

"Where is she?"

"At my parents'—they look after her on the weekends, give her a taste of the suburbs."

"So you're from the Bay Area?"

"Yeah. I grew up here. I mean right here. My parents owned the restaurant downstairs and eventually bought the building. We lived in this space—well, about half of it—when I was growing up. When they retired I knocked out the walls and took over the whole thing."

I slide a cigarette out of Kelly's pack and she lights it for me.

"So, I have to ask—you don't have to tell me—but what's your *situation?* With the baby? Dad around at all?"

"No, he's—" He's what? My ex-sort-of-boyfriend's married older brother who is also my former stepbrother? "I'm on my own."

"Good for you," Kelly says and clinks her glass against my empty one. "Another?"

"Sure." It's not like I'm drinking hard liquor. I'll just have one more before I go.

HOME

I'm obsessed with my hair. It's been three weeks since I got it cut and colored and still, every time I pass a mirror I can't help but stop and stare and wonder if it's really me looking back. I see Mary next week when she's scheduled to lift my color blonder and put the final touches on my new style.

People treat me differently. They're nice when I walk into a store. They smile. They ask if they can help me. I went to Nordstrom and bought a new handbag and two pairs of shoes—Italian sneakers and fancy flip-flops. It's summer now and the city is hot. As a peace offering, Janet sent over some loose-fitting linen dresses, boat-neck fitted T-shirts and casual drawstring pants that fit like pajamas. Everything is off-white, dusty peachy-pink or a light peachy brown—no black at all.

At first, I refused to wear the clothes out of principle. Then I started wearing the clothes around the apartment for days, but would change into more typical black attire when I'd go out. But it's hot and when you're pregnant you're hotter and after a week I gave in and started wearing them. Besides, the vintage dresses I dyed are getting too small. I should call Janet to thank her. We should make up. I get soft and nostalgic and am full of forgiveness but then I remember that she compared me to my mother and can't do it.

As hard as it is to admit, I am excited. I love looking at baby things and tiny clothes. I joined an online chat group for other first-time pregnant women who are due in January. Everyone swaps stories and talks about sore breasts and fatigue and sickness and swollen feet, but they're all excited, too, I can tell. But they all have husbands and boyfriends so in a way they are nothing like me.

I'm heavier, I know, but I feel light with my hair, the clothes. I've started making lists of things I want to buy for the baby and things I need to do before she comes. I have piles of these lists. One day, I plucked one randomly from the pile on the kitchen table and went out and bought everything on the list—just like that. I love having money. I have so much freedom, I can do anything. Kelly keeps asking me what I want to do and I know she means for work, for the future. I keep saying "get a massage," and she laughed the first couple of times before growing tired of the joke. What *am* I going to do? The money won't last forever. I could sell the apartment, but that doesn't seem right—it's my home. I will have to work.

I rub the back of my neck and swing my head side to side. I love the way my hair moves. I stand up and walk into my mother's bedroom to face the full-length mirrors in her walk-in closet, the ones that attack every angle. The drawstring pants make my ass look huge, but they're comfy and people can tell I'm pregnant now so fuck it. The stretchy white top clings to my belly and my enormous breasts. The black rose necklace Aaron gave me would look great with this top, but I don't dare wear it.

I go to my bedroom and look around—at the black bat wallpaper, the black lacquer furniture, the tubes of empty red lipsticks I found in the drawer of my vanity dresser. I take out the black rose necklace and bring it up to my neck and fasten the back. It does look great with this shirt.

I center the black rose between the two pointy bones that jut out at the bottom of my neck; I forget what they're called—the clavicle, I think. I was never much for science or school at all, really. I adjust the neckline of my top so it sits perfectly, just skimming the top of my breasts. But Kelly was right when I met with her the other day: I really do need to buy some nude-colored bras. All I have are black ones and under these light clothes they show through and look cheap. At first I didn't care, but now, I don't know. I want to take all of these things in this room—all of my clothes, the books, the wall-paper with the black bats, everything—and throw it out or give it away. It doesn't fit. I don't fit. I wish someone would come and clear the place out, tear up the tiles and the carpet, strip down the walls. I could start from scratch.

Imagining this overwhelms me. I sit on the edge of my bed. I want it gone, all of it. Anxiety replaces the calm and warmth and then I'm seething and scared and the loneliness is terrifying. I'm pregnant, blond and wearing ecru-colored linen pants.

I strip off the ecru and the white and smear on bright red lipstick. I shimmy into a pair of black leggings and my black trapeze-style top that used to be a dress when I was much, much smaller. Miraculously, it still covers my belly. I tease the ends of my hair and spray and back comb some more and spray again until I've built a mini-nest atop my head that I secure with pins. I dump everything out of my fancy new bag and shove it all into my old canvas messenger tote with its Clash and Dead Kennedys pins. I find an almost-empty pack of cigarettes. There are four left—good. I pull on my Docs and put on my sunglasses and head out into the city.

I walk and walk, an unlit cigarette in one hand and a lighter in the other. I'm not heading anywhere in particular; I just follow one of the routes I would as a teenager, away from my mother's apartment in North Beach, down to Columbus. I walk up through the Tenderloin, past the junkies and dealers. I walk and walk, all the way to Japantown where I find myself sticky and out of breath. I buy a bottle of water and keep trudging on down Fillmore to Hayes Valley, with its bistros and shops. I'm dizzy and stop at a cake place. I scarf down a thick slice of double decadent chocolate explosion something-or-other, drink more water and am back out on the street. I see a newspaper box while I'm waiting at a corner for the light to change. There's a banner across the top of the front page above the fold promoting Cassie what's-her-name's column, the woman all the newspaper bitches were gossiping about at my mother's girls-only memorial.

I feed quarters into the machine and snap up a paper. There's a photo of a woman with pouty, glossy lips and sleek curls that fall perfectly over half of one eye. Inside: The Girly Girl—Cassie Acevedo on the Art of Being the Other Woman. Oh, this is perfect. I fold the paper and slide it under my arm. I take the cigarette from my hand and put it in my mouth. It's bent and a bit damp from the sweat of my palms. I light it and inhale. The rush of nicotine makes me woozy, but in a good way. I exhale as I'm crossing the street. A woman walking toward me gives an exaggerated cough. I laugh and take another drag, making sure I exhale just as she walks by.

BAD MOMMY

Kelly wants to do a side-by-side thing called "She Said, She Said." I'd write about my pregnancy and another woman would write about hers. But she's this prissy, uptight, no-sushi mom called Brenda who reads all the bullshit books and runs to her doctor every five seconds. She says it will be stimulating and provocative and *real*. It took some convincing, but I've finally said yes. I'm worried a bit about all the writing and rewriting, but Kelly says that I'll be providing a crucial voice for women who *go against the grain*. It's a public service; I'm nothing like my mother.

There's so much to do. My baby is due in five months, and I want to redecorate and there are tons of things I need to buy. Kelly has been taking me around to all the cool baby and maternity shops. I had no idea those kinds of stores existed—at one of them I bought a onesie with a silk-screened skull on it. I have yet to decide on a name.

Today we're having a lunch meeting at a restaurant on Union Street, brainstorming column ideas in between ducking into air-conditioned stores with adorable things. By the time we make it from the car to the restaurant, we're late for our reservation and I'm laden with bags.

"What about something on shopping for cool baby things?" I suggest. Kelly says I need to write the columns from personal experience and that's what I've experienced most lately.

Kelly makes a sour face. "Too blah," she says. "We need to kick off with a bang. Brenda is writing about navigating the maze of nutrition and health choices for pregnant women. We need a counter voice. How about something about the fear mongering that goes on about having an occasional glass of wine—that's something you know about."

Sure, I've had a few drinks in the past few weeks, but I'm not sure I want to publicize it. I'm writing under my own name now—no more Gloria Babymaker. "I don't know."

"Oh, come on, Mason—have some balls. I need edgy, *real*. But if you're not comfortable doing that then—"

"I'll do it," I say, cutting Kelly off. I have balls.

"Good. Now what else can we come up with?"

Drinking and smoking can be two separate columns. There's another one about navy blue being the color of mommies—I came up with that one; Kelly thought it would be funny and light. I'm also going to write about the excessive, conflicting and sometimes false information available online. I'm also supposed to write about the division between women who have children and those who don't. The only woman I know in San Francisco with kids is Candice and that won't happen. But wait—there's D.D., Diedre. I'm sure I have the business card she gave me at Janet's fashion show somewhere. I could talk to her. And I'm sure she has some other friends with kids she could introduce me to. I'll have to call her later. That column will be easy. But first I have to get through this one about drinking.

I have six false starts before giving up for the night. Every time I try to write, it comes out wrong. I have to focus, know what I want to say. I want to say that it's okay to have a few drinks while you're pregnant. I want to point out that generations of women drank during pregnancy—even many of our own mothers—and we turned out fine. I want to say that drinking all the time when you're pregnant is a bad idea, but that a glass or two—maybe three max—of wine or beer is probably fine. But all of those thoughts combined only suck up about one-hundred words, and I'm supposed to write eight.

Maybe some fresh air will help clear my head. I must be missing something, there must be a trick to doing this. I always got my best grades in school in English and my mother made it look effortless, just tap-tap-tap on the keyboard for a couple of hours and the rest of your day was free. It's a pretty good schedule for a mother, I have to admit—not that my mother was the best mother or anything, but she didn't have to work all the time. She may have shared every little thing about my life with the entire city, but I never had a nanny.

I'm glad I wore a sweater. Even at the height of summer, the wind off the Bay at night cools the city off. I walk against the breeze that feels almost wet on my face. It's so humid out that soon the lovely, cool feeling disappears and my skin gets sticky, and walking through the thick air is like moving in extra-slow motion.

I nip into a late-night café-bar to rest and take in the climate-controlled atmosphere before walking back home. I sit at a table in the corner and wish I had something to read. The free weeklies and complimentary magazines are at the entrance, but I don't feel like maneuvering my lumpy-bumpy body between the tightly packed tables. The waiter comes by and I order a glass of sparkling water.

"Wait a minute," I say as he turns his back to go. "Could I get a glass of your house white, as well?"

The waiter stares at me—at my belly then my face. I'm still in that in-between stage—people can't make a definitive call as to whether I'm pregnant or just fat. The look on his face is priceless. I stare at him hard and do nothing to hide my belly. "Okay, if you're sure," he says.

"Why wouldn't I be?" I ask. This should be good.

"No reason," he says and walks quickly away.

A different man brings me my drinks. He's not dressed in a white shirt and black pants like all of the wait staff so I suspect he's a manager of some sort. He places the water on a napkin in front of me. He hesitates with the wine, but sets it down beside the water. "Anything else?" he asks.

"Could I see a wine list?" I ask. This could be fun. At least I'd have something to read.

"Wine list?"

"Yes."

"I'll be right back," he says.

The man does not come right back. Instead, I see him gather a small group of waitresses and confer by the espresso machine. I know they're talking about me; the girls keep looking over. Finally, one of them brings me a wine list. "Thanks," I say, but she doesn't move. Instead, she sits down across from me at the tiny round table that's only slightly bigger than an extra-large pizza.

"Hi there—I'm Amy," she says. This girl can't be any older than twenty-five.

"Hi Amy," I say.

"Look, I don't mean to pry or step into your business, but we're all a bit concerned about you."

"Concerned?" I ask, taking a big swig of wine. It's not very good. I don't even want it anymore.

"Well, about your—you know—*condition*."

"Condition?"

"You know." She points to my belly.

I almost laugh. "Thank you so much for noticing. I've lost nearly ninety pounds on Jenny Craig." I say this like I'm a commercial spokesperson, all perky and smiles.

The girl turns her head, looking at her colleagues in alarm. They go back to pretending to wipe the espresso machine when they notice me staring straight at them. "Oh my God. Excuse me. I thought—I didn't mean—look, the wine is on the house. I'm so, so sorry."

"Whatever for?"

"I have other tables I have to check on. Please—order anything you'd like, on us."

I flip through the wine list, which is bound in a faux-leather folder. *Order anything you'd like,* she said. I see they have a half-decent selection of real champagne. I could order a bottle, or at the very least a glass. I take another sip of my wine. Yuck. All I want is orange juice—or chocolate milk—and that's not very edgy or provocative. Being a bad mommy is harder than I'd thought.

I leave the part about not finishing my one glass of wine and ordering a pint glass filled with orange juice out of my column and concentrate on the behavior of the staff at the café. I make the manager man meaner and Amy-the-waitress more stunned and aghast than she was. It's *color,* I tell myself. Nobody wants to read about how I couldn't write so I went for a walk. Or how I ended up basically telling a bunch of restaurant people that I was formerly a super obese person on the road to a healthy weight and that while I might be pregnant,

I would rather everyone think I was fat than be vilified. In any case, the truth wouldn't have added up to eight-hundred words.

I send Kelly my column a day early and she sends it back almost immediately with notes and edits. She's chopped out my description of the mood and decor of the restaurant, which I thought was good—it set the mood. It might have eaten up two hundred words, but still. Now she wants facts. She says I need to balance the anecdotal with some research and statistics, maybe get a quote from an expert. She's included the name and phone number of the obstetrician she says is *very progressive*. I don't want to have to talk to anyone. She didn't say that there would be any interviews or research required for this job. I thought it was supposed to be about me.

I am shocked to discover that the staff at that café—or any other restaurant—could refuse to serve me and it would be perfectly legal. It's not like a pregnant lady drinking a glass of wine is exactly *illegal,* but those signs you always see at restaurants, the ones that say things like, "we reserve the right to refuse service to anyone"—those signs are directed at pregnant ladies they don't want to serve. They're not doctors, and even if they were, that doesn't give them the right to decide what I get to do with *my* body.

I'm all riled up as I write. My fingers won't move fast enough to keep up with my thoughts. I really should work on my typing skills. I write about the information I found online about the way pregnant women are lorded over and controlled in this country. There are people who want to make us submit to involuntary drug and alcohol testing for the whole nine months. This country is ridiculous, hysterical. I should move to Europe. Kelly says it's really cool and people are way more laid-back about things. I want to have a drink—just because I can—but the truth is the thought of alcohol makes me queasy. All I really want is chocolate milk.

CHILDREN

Children are everywhere. How could I have not noticed this before? On my way to meet D.D. and her friends at a Starbucks in the Marina, the taxi whizzes past countless kids—in strollers, walking, jumping and playing in parks, crying and yelling at their mothers in the street. One steps onto the curb at a corner and falls into the gutter. I see another let go of his mother's hand to pick up a coin in the middle of a busy crosswalk. And at the end of my harrowing journey, when I finally get to the Starbucks, it's jammed with screaming children. I walk in just in time to see one hoist itself out of its stroller and fall onto its face on the floor while the mother talks to her friend. I will never turn my back on my baby—not even for a second. It's the kids of *these* irresponsible mothers that those pregnancy-watch people should be worried about, not the ones whose mothers like an occasional glass of Napa white.

"Mason!" I'm mortified. The woman with the woman whose kid fell on its face is D.D. She steps around her friend's stroller to give me a hug. "You look great—I love the hair!

I'm so glad you called. This is Susan—and her son Maurice. And that's Lisa and her daughter, Helen." What's with the old-people names everyone is giving their kids? "Oh—and those two are mine: Hugh and Norma." D.D. points to a couple of older children sitting at the table with Susan and Maurice. I'm glad I didn't make a comment about the names.

D.D.'s children are five and seven and not excited about being here. When D.D. introduces me to them, they only say hello after being prodded and the girl tells me my hair looks funny. I will teach *my* child manners.

As soon as I've settled in, we have to leave. Susan's son, Maurice, won't stop trying to free himself from being harnessed into his stroller and as I've already witnessed, he has the skills to do it. "Terrible twos," Susan says to me as if this were some acceptable explanation or excuse for her letting her son fall on his head. Shouldn't she take him to a hospital or a doctor's office to make sure he's okay?

We take our coffees to go and head to a nearby park where the children can play. There are plenty of other kids already there and all the kids are off as soon as we get there. We set up at a picnic table in the shade. Susan produces a diaper bag bigger than most pieces of regulation-size carry-on luggage. "You have one of these yet?" she asks me.

"No—not yet." I was just planning to use a cool messenger bag, something streamlined and Euro, maybe one of those Freitag ones from Switzerland made of recycled truck tarps.

"These are the best," Susan says as she opens the bag. It expands like a cardboard accordion file, with slots for every-thing. "This section keeps the soy milk cool, this pocket is insulated for hot food, there's a pouch for your phone, your laptop, there's a changing pad, diapers, everything you can think of. And it locks and has a remote sensor that you can turn on if you can't find your bag or if someone tries to take it you can put it into alarm mode." Susan presses a button on the remote dangling from her key chain and a loud siren sound starts emanating from her diaper bag. Who would want to steal a diaper bag?

The women work efficiently to set up a base camp at the picnic table which is half restaurant, half triage center. There's a vast selection of drink boxes and water, Goldfish crackers, raisins and tiny rounds of Babybel cheese mixed in among the sunscreen, bug spray and Band-Aid packs and Maurice's and Helen's EpiPens. "He's allergic to everything," Susan says about Maurice.

"At least he can have gluten—you wouldn't believe how hard it is to eat out when your child is allergic to wheat," says Lisa. I sense some competition.

"I'm lucky," says D.D. "With my two it's just peanuts—that we know of—but everyone's kids are allergic to peanuts."

Both Susan and Lisa nod in agreement. Jesus. When I was in school there was one kid who was allergic to nuts and one who couldn't have milk and that was it. "Wow," I exclaim. What else can I say?

"So, you're writing. This is exciting! Not as exciting as this, of course." D.D. touches my belly. "So tell us what you'd like to know."

"Um, it's not so much a formal interview thing, I just want to get a sense of what it's like to be a mother, I guess, and maybe hear about how your life has changed," I say. I didn't really prepare questions. I figured I'd wing it.

"More like, how hasn't it changed?" Lisa says. "Look, just take everything you think you know about kids and parenting and banish it from your mind. It's not something you can be prepared for—not really."

"Forget your life as you know it," says Susan. I swear there's a touch of bitterness in her voice.

"Don't let us scare you, Mason. Having kids is great, it's just, well, not ever the same as before," D.D. says.

"What about your friends? Do you have a lot of friends who don't have kids?" I ask. I take my notebook out of my handbag. I'm poised to write. It's an interview now. Kelly will be so pleased.

Lisa laughs. "Does the babysitter count?"

"My sister doesn't have kids," Susan says.

"But she's your sister—you have to see her," says Lisa.

"Lots of the women I do business with are childless—and I see Janet now and again," D.D. says. The mention of Janet's name makes me wince. I haven't seen her or called since Seth's birthday and now it's been so long I don't know if I can or if I should.

I learn a lot from my Saturday afternoon in the park with D.D. and company, but what stands out the most is how different the three women are. Other than kids, they don't really have much in common. It's weird. D.D. is this have-it-all mommy/businesswoman and she met Lisa through a play-group both of their daughters were in. Lisa works as a retail consultant and sells Avon on the side. Susan's a stay-at-home mom who lives on Lisa's street and they met when Lisa sold her some skin cream.

One thing they do have in common other than children is that they can't stop talking about their kids. Helen did this at eighteen months. Maurice did it at twelve. D.D.'s daughter, Norma, did it while she was still in the womb. I don't even know what most of the amazing things their kids are so gifted at are. And why does everything in baby-world have to be measured in months, weeks and days? Why does everyone have to say *twelve months*? Does anyone realize that they can just say *a year* and we'll all know what it means?

After an hour and a half—ninety minutes in babyspeak—at the park, D.D. and I say goodbye to Lisa and Susan and their kids and walk back to D.D.'s house. From the outside, it's lovely—a skinny, two-story Victorian painted yellow with white trim. Inside, it's chaos.

There is stuff everywhere—piles of it, mounds. The kids rush past me to get to the TV, nearly knocking me over while I slide off my designer flip-flops. "Oh, don't bother," she says. "Keep them on—it's probably safer." She's right: three paces in I step on a miniature metal car. "Hot Wheels," she says. "Norma loves them."

D.D. pours us each a glass of iced tea and we sit on the deck. Doesn't she have to watch the kids? "Will they be okay in there alone?" I ask.

D.D. laughs. "Oh, they're fine. Once they're kindergarten age, they're good. But those three-year-olds—yikes. Watch out. You can't take your eyes off them for even a second. Everyone talks about the 'terrible twos'—that's nothing compared to three."

"Susan said that—the 'terrible twos.'"

"That's because Maurice isn't three yet—he's going to be a terror, that one. But you know what they say about boys."

"No." I don't know anything. This is becoming increasingly clear.

D.D. leans forward. "Everyone says that girls are great and easy when they're little and it's the boys who are into everything and aggressive and difficult. Then, it switches—the girls are a nightmare once they hit puberty and the worst with the boys is over. It's true. I can't imagine what Norma's going to be like at puberty. Did you know that the average age girls are getting their period these days is ten? It's terrifying."

"Oh my God." This can't be true. Why do I have to be so sure my baby is a girl?

"Tell me about it."

"I'm having a girl."

"Really? Oh, congratulations, Mason—that's wonderful news!" After what D.D. has just told me I'm not so sure about that. "Have you thought about names?"

"Not really. I don't know yet."

"Oh, you've got lots of time," D.D. says. "So, I took a look at that online magazine you're writing for. I read that 'Gloria Babymaker' story. That was you, right?" I nod, though I'm not sure if I should, if she's going to call me out as an awful writer or say I'm an idiot like Janet and Seth did. "I could tell—it was funny. It reminded me of your mom's column. You must miss her."

I am not like my mother, not at all. "I guess. We hadn't been really close lately."

"But she was your mother. And soon you're going to be that little darling's mother." She points to my belly. "Nothing will ever change that."

"Would you like to stay for dinner?" D.D. asks, looking at her watch. Dinner? It's already that late? I look at the watch I recently bought. It's only four-thirty. "We eat at five," D.D explains. "The kids are in bed by seven-thirty."

"Sure. Yeah, I guess—if it's no trouble," I say, using my best guest voice. "I could help."

"You cook?"

"Well, no—but I can chop things."

"I was never much of a cook, either, but I got into it after the kids started eating real food and I couldn't stand another grilled cheese or macaroni dinner. You'll see."

"I guess."

"Oh, you must be so sick of people saying that, telling you things, giving you advice—it's endless, I know. I apologize—it's so hard not to do. I hate it when I catch myself getting preachy about parenthood."

"It's okay, really. I need all the help I can get." This is not a lie. I like talking to D.D. She's totally different than she was in high school, but she's okay, she's cool—for a mom.

"Are you sick of being treated like public property yet? You know—strangers wanting to touch you, talk to you, telling you what you should and should not be doing?"

"I know—it's weird. I just wrote a column about how everyone gets so freaked out if you have a drink."

"While you're pregnant? A drink-drink?" D.D. shifts uncomfortably in her deck chair.

"Just wine or beer—nothing heavy, not too much. I went to this place the other night and they almost didn't serve me."

"You're kidding, right?"

"It's not a big deal." I'm confused. I thought D.D. was cool.

"It's a very big deal, Mason. How can you do that to your child—take those risks?"

"You have to drink *a lot* to do anything to the baby—I did the research," I say defensively. I did do the research—sort of. I mean, Kelly said it's fine.

"And your doctor told you this?" D.D.'s voice is high and shrill. She looks like she could hit me.

"No, but think about it—all of our mothers drank and smoked while they were pregnant."

"You're *smoking,* too?"

"Not much." This is true—except for that one day, and that time at Kelly's.

"I think you should go," D.D. says as she stands. "And Mason, please—get some help. Talk to a doctor."

I grab my purse and hoist myself out of the chair. "I have

all the help I need, thanks." She is acting like such an alarmist bitch.

"I feel sorry for your baby," D.D. says. "You're worse than your mother."

Her words bite, but I don't turn around as I walk out the back gate onto the street. I refuse to let her see me cry.

ASHES

People hate me—not just D.D., but lots and lots of people. And most of these women actually sign their names when they've finished calling me a "bad example," an "awful person" and an "unfit mother." I even had one e-mail in which this woman called Alison Jenkins from Ft. Worth, Texas, threatened to notify the authorities about my "irresponsible behavior" and said that they'd make me give my baby away when she's born.

So I wrote about having drinks, and about alarmist robot mommies and about missing smoking pot—what's the big deal? It's not like I said I *was* smoking pot or anything. And I didn't even smoke pot that often when I wasn't pregnant. It was just that one day Kelly was over helping me figure out what to do with this place and I said that it was the kind of day you wish you had a joint. San Francisco is always so hot and sticky in September. As soon as I said it, Kelly snapped her fingers and said, "You've *got* to write about that."

Readers went nuts when I wrote about smoking the

occasional cigarette or drinking wine, or going out for all-you-can-eat sushi, so I could imagine what they'd do with the mention of pot. Kelly says I'm writing about all the things these women are secretly thinking, but are too afraid to admit. I'm known on the *Barbarella* forums as *Bad Mommy*.

Kelly's "She Said, She Said" idea has taken off big-time. The column was mentioned in the newspaper and on *The View* after Brenda, the woman Kelly hired to write the prissy, uptight column, quit when Kelly published my piece last week about having my hair colored while pregnant. Apparently, this is another one of the trillion things women are not supposed to do; the chemicals seep into your body or something and can harm the baby. It sounds ridiculous, but Brenda had a fit. She's just pissed that she doesn't have the nerve to get her roots done. I saw her once at Kelly's and her dark roots had to be longer than an inch.

Brenda is gone, so now it's just me. Kelly was going to change the name of the column to "She Said" but since everyone is referring to me as *Bad Mommy* already, she suggested we go with that. The whole situation is hilarious. I've had women get in my face at the grocery store after recognizing me from the photo that runs with my column, and one time when I was at lunch with Kelly. I was eating fish and chips. According to this woman, no fish whatsoever are to be consumed during pregnancy. I smiled and told her to go fuck herself. One of her little kids started crying and I felt sort of bad about that, but who's to say he was crying over that? He could have been crying over the fact that his mother is a dull, judgmental bitch. Plus, she was wearing navy.

I think I'll finally write about navy after the pot column. Kelly says I can be as "out there" as I want. It's so much fun.

"What time are you meeting Cassie Acevedo?" Kelly asks.

"She's coming over at three." We're sitting in the *Barbarella* office, which is a sectioned-off part of her giant pink flat. She has those metal stands connecting velvet ropes, the kind you see outside of nightclubs, but Kelly's velvet ropes are pink, not the standard red. There are no actual walls, but she says that Jeannie respects the ropes and knows not to go into Mommy's work area without permission. Jeannie is adorable, a mini-Kelly. They even have the same mannerisms and way of talking. I wonder if my daughter will be like that.

It's remarkable that Kelly can put out the magazine from this tiny corner. All of the writers are freelance, and most don't live in San Francisco so she communicates with them only online. She does her own design and coding. Kelly is amazing—she doesn't need anyone else.

"Do you know her angle?" Kelly asks. It takes me a moment to remember that she's talking about Cassie, who called up a few days ago saying she wanted to profile me for her column—which used to be my mother's column, but she didn't bring that up.

"I don't know—*Bad Mommy* on the loose in the Bay Area?"

Kelly laughs. "That'd be perfect."

The buzzer rings early, but I have myself done up. Cassie didn't say whether she'd be bringing a photographer or not, but it's best to be prepared. My hair is big and platinum blond. My eyes are rimmed in black kohl liner and my lips are red. I'm wearing black yoga pants and a maternity T-shirt Kelly gave me: it's black and has an arrow pointing to my belly and the text I'm With Stupid. I think it's funny, but I can bet there are countless women who won't. I'll write about it after the pieces about being accosted by the no-fish woman and the one about navy blue.

There's a knock on the door. "It's open, come on in," I say.

"Mason! My goodness, you look—" It's Ron. What is he doing here? I know he's left a ton of messages for me that I haven't returned, but I've been meaning to. He didn't have to come by. "You look—"

"Fat? Huge?"

He gives me a hug. "I was going to say, glowing and lovely."

"Yeah, right."

"I've been trying to get in touch with you."

"I know—it's just been so hectic."

"I've seen your columns—you've been stirring things up quite a bit."

"There are a lot of uptight people out there," I say.

"That's the truth. Look, Mason, I know you said that you didn't want to be involved with any decisions about your mother's ashes, but some time has passed and I thought that you might want to—"

"Want to what?"

"I'm not saying that you have to do anything, but it's been six months since she passed and I was thinking it might be nice to take the ashes out to Sausalito and scatter them onto the Bay. It was one of her favorite places."

"I remember." When she was in between men and had extra time on her hands, we'd ride the ferry across and spend the day people-watching. I forgot about that. "Sausalito would be a good place."

"You don't have to make a decision this second—I don't want to put you on the spot. I thought I'd leave them here for a couple of days and you can think about it." Ron reaches into the canvas shopping bag he's carrying and pulls out a box. I take it from him and flip the lid; inside is a shiny gold urn. I feel dizzy and sick. That's my mother in there. I push my weight against the wall so I don't fall down. Ron doesn't seem to notice. "We could talk Thursday or Friday, plan something for the weekend. I'm okay with whatever you think is best."

"Really, I'm good with Sausalito," I say, and try to hand him back the box. It's heavy.

"No, you keep it here until the weekend," Ron says.

"No, I think you should—"

Ron takes the box from me and walks across the living room. He places it on the white mantel above the white fireplace. "A couple of days, Mason," he says and starts for the door.

"But—"

"I'll call you Thursday," Ron says and then he's gone.

I shuffle to the sofa and lie down. This is fucked up—Sausalito is fine. He didn't have to leave it—her—here. It's not like I'm going to bond with my mother's ashes if they're here for a couple of days. I feel the baby move and I press my hand against her foot or hand—whichever is kicking or punching. My mother has been dead for six months. It doesn't seem like that long. The baby keeps pushing against my side. I push back and she pushes again—over and over. It's like a game. I keep my hands and eyes on my belly and don't look up. I swear I feel as if someone is watching.

"Mason?" The voice gives me a start. I sit up and see a young woman with long, dark hair and perfect lipstick. "I didn't mean to startle you—I passed your stepdad on the way out and he left the door open for me." She steps forward and reaches out her hand for me to shake. "I'm Cassie Acevedo."

I shake Cassie's hand limply. My stepdad: I'd never thought of Ron that way before, but I suppose he is—technically. Although, is he still my stepdad now that my mother is dead and watching my every move from inside the gold urn in the box on the mantel? "Are you ready to get started?" Cassie asks. Her curled hair is just as it is in her picture.

"Sure," I say, pushing myself up to sitting position. "Have a seat."

Cassie asks me about the column and about how I feel being called Bad Mommy. I tell her it amuses me because it does. Then she asks about how it feels to be a single, pregnant woman. She's hinting around the father question, but doesn't ask directly.

"I think that being a single mother can be empowering—there's no one to answer to or have to make compromises for," I say.

"So, this pregnancy was something you planned?"

"No, not at all—it was a big surprise to everyone."

"Including the father? What does he think of your columns and the controversy you've stirred up?"

"I have no idea. Let's just say he wasn't thrilled with my decision to keep the baby."

"He tried to pressure you to get an abortion?"

"I wouldn't necessarily say he *pressured* me, but it was clear that was the direction he would have preferred me to go in. This situation isn't exactly convenient for him."

"Why is that?"

Fuck Edgar. He's an asshole who used me. He deserves whatever he gets. "He's married."

Cassie actually gasps. I have to bite my lip to refrain from laughing out loud. "He's *married?* I can see how that could be inconvenient for him. I had a fling with a married guy. I wrote about it a while ago."

"I saw that story."

"You should have seen the hate mail I got—every married woman in the Bay Area must have written in."

"They should have been spending that time checking up on what their husbands were up to instead," I say.

"Totally," says Cassie. "I mean, it's not *my* problem that *your* husband isn't into you and is sleeping with me. If she could keep him happy, there wouldn't be a problem. These women are such victims—they need to take a good look at themselves before showing up at your work, hysterical and calling you a whore."

"She did that?"

"You bet. And she wrote to my editor demanding that I be fired—she told *everyone,* made a complete fool of herself. And what kills me is that she's mad at *me,* but she's still with *him.* It's bullshit."

"Have you seen him since all of this?"

"Oh, yeah, we're still fucking."

"I thought my situation was fucked up," I say, laughing.

"What exactly *is* your situation, Mason?"

After Cassie leaves, I grab a box of Froot Loops from the kitchen and head to my bedroom and shut the door. I'm tired after all that girl talk and a bit anxious about what she'll write. She promised she won't name Edgar. I said I didn't care if she did. But she says it'll never get by her editor so she'll *write around* his name. In other words: she'll describe everything about him but leave out his name. This was a common trick of my mother's. San Francisco is a small city, its upper social ranks closed to the general public, and they won't like this at all.

Even though I'm in my bedroom with the door shut I can't shake the feeling of being watched and this time I know it's not Cassie creeping up behind me. It's that urn. It may be in the living room, but it's like my mother is here, all around.

Cassie did ask about my mother—I suppose she had to. I played the good daughter and told her how sad her sudden passing was, how I wish she had lived to meet her granddaughter. She asked me about the parallels between our careers. I said that other than the fact we both ended up writing columns, there's not much commonality. She was always writing about me. I'm dealing with bigger issues. It's not the same at all.

I dig out my tattered spiral notebook from a pile beside my bed. I need to get a cleaning service—mounds of things have grown all over the apartment; it's starting to remind me of D.D.'s. But I'll worry about that later; right now I want to lie down and eat Froot Loops out of the box.

I started the notebook when I was fifteen. I flip through the pages, skimming the endless list of my mother's offenses. God, she really did have to write about every little thing, didn't she? She even wrote about my conception—in detail. I remember the first time I read that column. I had to have been about ten. Seth and I were going through my mother's files when she wasn't home, looking for what Seth called "the juicy parts." I didn't quite understand what he meant until he pulled out a copy of the conception column and read it aloud. It was pretty tame in retrospect—it *was* printed in a daily newspaper, after all—but even so, the mention of *lovemaking* and how *his little wiggly guy found my egg* was more than enough trauma.

I skim a few more pages, then shut the book and shove it under my bed. I eat more Froot Loops and listen to some old cassettes, but I can still feel her presence. Now it feels like it's coming from under the bed, from the notebook. She's probably down there trying to erase all the pages. But she can't because I wrote them in pen.

There seems to be a lot of similarity between your work and your mother's—how would you describe the parallels?

Cassie's question gnaws at me. I don't know how she can think what I'm doing is so much like what my mother did. I'm not putting everything out there. I'm not writing about my daughter, I'm writing about *my pregnancy,* and after she's born, I'll write about *the motherhood experience*. It's not about her, and it's not even really about me anymore.

The sense that something is happening under my bed is starting to freak me out. The Froot Loops are gone and the music isn't enough of a distraction. I close my eyes and reach under the bed until I find the notebook. I get myself out of bed and waddle to the living room. It's got to be nearly ninety degrees outside but I start the fireplace anyway—the apartment has air-conditioning.

As soon as the fire is up I start ripping pages from the notebook and tossing them in, watching them burn. I remove my mother's urn from the box on the mantel and when all that's left of the notebooks is the metal coil and soot, I scoop the hot ashes out with a big spoon and dump them into the urn.

I seal the urn up tight and place it back in the box. I feel a million times better as I walk back to my bedroom, alone, with no ghosts.

DEAL

I guess I shouldn't be surprised, but I am—and a little insulted. Edgar obviously doesn't have the balls to contact me himself, so he's had his lawyer do it. Even Aaron sent an e-mail. It wasn't very nice, but at least he did it himself. He called me a hypocrite and said I was ten times worse than my mother and that he *shudders to think of the issues your child will have growing up with you as a mother.* He topped his temper tantrum off with the line: *Is nothing sacred to you?* My God, he's melodramatic. I can't believe I slept with him and that there was a moment when I wished he was my baby's father.

As far as I'm concerned, my baby doesn't have a father and I would have thought Edgar would be happy to agree. But he doesn't seem happy about anything since Cassie Acevedo's column was published and all of San Francisco society figured out he was the unnamed married father she had written about. The column was written like a mock-scandal story, like the kind you'd find in one of those weekly supermarket tabloids I secretly enjoy so much. The part about Edgar was called

Who's the Daddy? and read like a gossip column blind item. Edgar really should get a sense of humor.

It's not like he's asking to ever even see the baby or have anything to do with her, but he wants me to undergo some sort of psychiatric evaluation before he'll fork over any monthly child support. That's a laugh. I don't want his money. And I'm not seeing some shrink just because his lawyer says so. There's no court order, no nothing. Amongst the jargon in the documents, I recognize excerpts from several of my *Barbarella* columns. From what I can understand, Edgar is trying to say I am endangering my unborn child by drinking and smoking and doing pot and this pisses me off. I never said I smoked pot and I didn't, which is something Kelly specifically had to post on the *Barbarella* forums when the column came out and people started freaking.

Edgar needs to mind his own business. I write *NO THANKS* in big letters across the top of the first page of lawyer papers, put them back in their envelope, tape it up and write *RETURN TO SENDER* on the front and back.

I drop the envelope in a mailbox on my way to Kelly's. She wants to meet. She says she has a great idea for a column. I'm currently working on the one about navy blue being the color of mommies, but it seems a little dull compared to the one about pot and Cassie Acevedo's bombshell. I hope Kelly has something good.

"What is your due date again?" Kelly asks

"January fourth—why?"

"What about January first, 12:01 a.m.?"

"What about it?" Janet's wedding is on New Year's Eve. The invitation she sent me is tacked to my fridge and stares back at me every time I go in for a snack.

"How would you feel about having next year's San Francisco New Year's Baby?" Kelly is really excited about this, but I still don't understand. What the hell is a *New Year's Baby?* "You do know about the New Year's Baby, right?"

"Not really."

"Mason, come on, it's the first baby born in the new year—every city does it and it's covered by all of the papers and the TV stations. It would be great publicity if *you* were the one to have it—think of the coverage!"

"But I'm not due until the fourth and my doctor says that a lot of first babies are up to a week late," I say.

"It doesn't have to be. You *can* have the New Year's Baby. I even found an obstetrician who'll do it—some doctors get all uppity about this kind of thing, but she's great, completely agrees that women should be able to choose when their baby is born."

"But how?"

"Scheduled C-section. As long as you're at term, which you will be by December thirty-first, you can schedule the labor for that evening and then we keep our fingers crossed and hope you deliver shortly after midnight. You were planning to have a C-section anyway, right?"

I wasn't. My doctor said that they only do a C-section when the baby is too big or is in distress or in a weird position. She didn't say anything about being able to plan your due date, but this sounds great. I was terrified of getting all torn up *down there* anyway. I have an unusually large head and can only imagine what damage could be done if I pass that trait along to my child.

I inherited my large head from my father. I'd see him sometimes at school functions, there supporting his legitimate children. My mother insisted on giving me his last name and sending me to the same private high school his older kids attended. Alex was three years ahead of me, so he was easy enough to avoid, but Clara is only a year older and I'd see her at parties and at the school smoke doors. We dated the same guy in the same year when I was a junior. We attended the same schools for more than a decade, but she didn't speak to me once.

"Do you think my doctor would do it?" I ask Kelly.

"You can ask, but I'll bet she won't. Most obstetricians are living in the dark ages when it comes to this kind of thing. It's all natural labor, natural everything. They don't take into account that women like us are *busy*."

All the things Kelly is saying make sense. If I have the option without any big risks, why not? I think I've been seeing the wrong doctor. "And you have someone who will do it? On New Year's?"

"Yup. She's great—delivered Jeannie. Not a scheduled C-section—it *was* eight years ago, almost no one was doing it then—but every drug imaginable. She doesn't believe in pain. She's booked her New Year's Eve off already."

"She doesn't have somewhere else to be?"

"She'd rather be in the delivery room with you, and standing beside you when they take those first New Year's Baby pictures. Just make sure you mention her by name in any interviews you do. She's eating all the medical fees."

"I can do that."

"Good. I've set up an appointment for you to see her on Thursday. Her name is Jemima Greene—here's the address." Kelly hands me a card. "And I think you should get to writing about this straightaway, keep the momentum going."

"You mean piss more people off," I say.

"Exactly."

"What should I tell the doctor I've been seeing?"

"I don't know—nothing. Who cares? It's not like you have a contract with her. You've moved on."

★ ★ ★

I'm not doing any of this to piss people off, I'm doing it because it's fun and I want to raise awareness about women's choices. They can choose to have an abortion or not, they can choose to immunize their kids or not, there are a million different choices they can make, so why this one is such a big deal is beyond me. But it is important that I ask these questions and give women who are dedicated to having a progressive pregnancy a voice. Kelly came up with that one: *progressive pregnancy.*

After seeing Dr. Greene, I have no question that I'm doing the right thing and go home and write my column up in about twenty minutes. I send it to Kelly immediately. She likes things in at least five days early. It used to be three but she changed it to five. I don't mind that she makes changes to my copy. She's the editor and whatever she does always makes me look wittier or smarter.

I grab the mail and the phone and relax in front of the television. There are two messages from Ron. I talked to him this morning and promised I'd go to Sausalito tomorrow to scatter my mother's ashes—and the ashes of my haunted notebook, but he doesn't need to know about that. There's a message about some overdue DVDs and another from Pearl Lee. No matter how many times I tell her I'm not selling, she refuses to listen. The other day I found a short stack of newspaper clippings in an envelope she'd slipped under my door—all about the city's real estate market. Now she's calling about another Realtor. *Why don't you get a property assessment—it can't hurt,* she says. Finally, there's a message from Janet. Hearing her voice gives me a jolt—we haven't spoken in so long. She wants to talk, she's concerned, she still wants me to be her maid of honor. I save the message. We'll see.

I open the mail—mostly bills, nothing fun. But there is one

envelope with no return address and my name and address handwritten across the front. I get a paper cut slicing it open with my fingers and a spot of blood smears onto the letter. It's from Edgar—not his lawyer, but Edgar himself. And there are papers attached and a check. I do a double take when I see the amount: two hundred and fifty thousand. There has to be a catch.

I read the rest of the papers and learn that there is. He is willing to pay me a onetime sum and relinquish his parental rights completely. Accepting the money means I'm not permitted to contact him or any members of his family, I'm not allowed to write about him, refer to him or defame his character in conversation, personal or professional. It also means he's off the hook for child support, which I didn't want in the first place anyway. *Two hundred and fifty thousand.* All I have to do is sign and return the papers to his lawyer's office. He's thoughtfully included an envelope, already addressed and stamped.

I should probably have a lawyer of my own look over these documents, but fuck it—I've had enough of lawyers. I read the papers again. Nowhere can I see anything where he calls me an unfit mother or tries to force me to see a shrink. I sign and seal everything but the check up in the courtesy envelope.

When I toss the first handful of my mother's ashes toward the water, the wind blows half of them right back in my face. "Ugh!"

"Well, you did like to complain that Britt was always in your face," Ron says with a smile. How can he be happy? Shouldn't he be depressed and wearing black? And he looks different—better. He's shaved his disgusting mustache.

"Ha ha."

Ron points to a small alcove up ahead. "Let's try over

there—it's a bit more sheltered and if we face this way then I think it will work."

We take turns throwing the ashes. There are more than I'd have thought and they're chunky, heavy, not light and smooth like cigarette ashes or dust. When we're done it's just me and Ron and an empty gold urn. We don't speak as we walk back to the ferry. I don't know what to say.

Once we're on the water, the mood shifts and Ron gets chatty. "I read your column today," he says. "Very interesting. Bet you'll get a lot of response."

"I usually do," I say. I'm not trying to be arrogant, I'm simply stating a fact.

"I'll bet. I had no idea women can choose the time they have their baby. In my day it just happened when it happened. When my daughter was born it was 4 a.m. and my wife had been in labor for more than twenty-four hours. I suppose they don't let that kind of thing go on anymore."

"You read that *today?*" Ron has a daughter?

"Right before I came here—I have it on a feed so whenever something new of yours is posted it pops right up on my screen."

"I didn't think that piece would run until next week," I say, wishing the ferry would speed up so I can get home and call Kelly to see what's up. It's too loud out here on the water and I'm too tired and fat to move inside. Nine more weeks to go.

Ron wants to have a late lunch or coffee or hang out but I tell him I have to go to meet my editor. He just smiles and kisses me on the forehead. "Oh, you newspeople and your meetings. Promise we'll do it next week?"

"I promise," I say, and I mean it.

"I'm holding you to that—I'm treating myself to a month

in Hawaii starting mid-October, but I want to see you before I leave," Ron says.

"Okay," I say as I wave and get into a taxi. I give the driver my address in North Beach. I could go directly to Kelly's but if she's not there then I'm stuck trying to get another cab and in any case, I want to go home, put my feet up and eat dry, sugary cereals. I punch Kelly's number into my cell phone.

"Hey there," she says. "I was just about to call you."

"You put the column up early," I say.

"I really wanted to get it out there—get the buzz going. And it worked."

"What do you mean?" I ask.

"You're never going to believe who I just got off the line with—Carla Douglas."

"That woman from that morning show?"

"*National* morning show."

"What did she want?"

"You," says Kelly. "She's anchoring a new daily one-hour to air after *Good Morning, Great Day.* Sort of a roundtable, like *The View,* but all about motherhood. It's going be shot here since Carla wants to move back after having *her* baby. She'll be hosting, but she's looking for three more outspoken mothers to be on with her."

"What would I do?"

"Talk. Argue. Make television. She said she's been following your column, but when she read today's piece about scheduled C-sections she knew she had to have you. She has to meet with you first, of course, but I think the slot is yours if you want it."

"I want it," I say. Wow. This is it. This is *TV.*

RENO

All the other mommies on *Modern Mommy* hate me. We're taping mock shows every day this week so the producers can work out the bugs before we go on air for a two-week trial period during November ratings sweeps. There's Pat, the working mommy: she's a lawyer with two kids and two nannies; there's Rita, the stay-at-home wife mommy; there's Maggie, the twenty-three-year-old married mommy who's finishing college; and there's me. I guess I'm the cool mommy? Carla Douglas is nothing like she is on air. When the cameras are rolling she's all smiles and perk, but the minute we cut for a commercial she's barking orders at the staff and complaining that her coffee is too hot or too cold or that the lighting is harsh.

I think they hate me because I'm not married and I get to do what I want, and the ones that work talk to me like I don't work, but I do. Thinking of something *important* to write every week is not that easy *and* I'm overseeing the renovation of the apartment, which takes up an obscene amount of my time. That a camera crew from the show is coming to shoot a special segment with me about "the new urban nursery" doesn't do anything to ease relations between me and the other mommies. They're jealous because they're boring and when the camera crew comes to their houses they'll just see their babies screaming or catch them fighting with their husbands, or—if you're Pat, the two-nanny mommy—watch as she goes shopping or to the spa or whatever she does while other people raise her kids.

The nursery is pretty much finished; it's just the rest of the place that's a mess. Kelly has been helping me source the greatest vintage stuff. She takes me to shops I didn't know existed and sends me links to the best online stores. I'm not an all-pink girl like her, so I'm doing a black-and-white theme, along with one bright color in each room: in the kitchen it's red, the living room is purple, and the master bedroom is silver. The nursery's one bright color is pink—but a bright pink, shocking pink, none of that pastel crap. My old bedroom is now the nursery. I had my old bed temporarily moved into the giant walk-in closet in the master bedroom. As soon as the master bedroom is done, I'll start sleeping there, but not until the new bed arrives. The old one still smells like my mother's Shalimar perfume, no matter how many times I wash the sheets.

The coming and going of the workers is of course driving my next-door neighbor, Pearl Lee, crazy. Every day she finds something to complain about. She slips notes under the front door outlining her grievances or, if I'm having something delivered and the company's truck is parked in the No Parking zone in front of the building, she calls the police. She never confronts me directly and when I pass her in the hall I swear she actually recoils at the sight of my big belly, like *Rosemary's Baby* will come tumbling out.

I wish the baby *would* come out. My ankles are swollen and sore and I can't walk without a waddle. People smile at me on the street and in stores. Strangers want to touch my stomach. It's like I'm public property. Now I know how Angelina Jolie must feel. *She* should be a guest on *Modern Mommy*—I bet we'd really get along. I suppose I should get used to being stopped and pawed at and chatted up by random people. Being on television five days a week will undoubtedly put a stop to any private life I may have. But I guess I'm used to that. It certainly won't be as much of an adjustment for me as it will for some of the other mommies on the show.

Standing in the nursery amid the rows of pristine vintage dolls, all dressed in custom-made hot pink minidresses and gowns, I look at Aaron's painting, the one of me naked running through the sprinkler. I didn't bother sending it back to him after things between us ended and he didn't ask for it. If he did ask now, I wouldn't let him have it, not after that rude e-mail he sent me. I had one of the renovation guys hang it for me. It took forever to get it straight, and then I decided I wasn't sure I wanted it up at all, and I had him take it down. Now it's propped up against the wall.

It's an all right piece of art, I suppose, if I look at it objectively and try to forget it's me in the picture. My baby doesn't have to know that—she'll only know what I tell her. I call Tom the main renovation guy into the room and ask him to rehang it. I'm far too fat to be lifting anything.

I am fat, there's no question, but it's not a bad kind of fat. I'll worry about losing weight after the baby is born. Everyone says you lose tons of weight just by breast-feeding, but I'm not entirely sold on that idea. My breasts are saggy enough as it is—I don't need to speed up their slow-motion fall, and it's supposed to hurt like hell. If I choose not to breast-feed, it will make great fodder for my column and the show. I don't understand why women who don't breast-feed are so reviled. Somebody needs to stand up for them and say that formula is okay.

I walk from the nursery to the kitchen table that I'm using as a desk. It's an old one from the fifties, and red. I sit in the office chair I had recovered in red patent leather and tap away at my new Mac. I check my e-mail and find, as usual, a slew of messages from Kelly. Most are angry letters she's forwarded, but there are always a few complimentary ones, from women like me, who aren't timid little politically correct mice that do things just because everyone else says they should. They're smart and do what they want. Some of them write to me after every column, letting me know their thoughts and sometimes I write back.

There are also e-mails from Kelly about my latest column— and the revisions. She used to fix it up herself, but lately she's wanted me to do rewrites and *pay more attention to structure and grammar.* I don't see how that is my job—I'm not an editor— but she's been helping so much with the decorating I wouldn't feel right begrudging her this favor. We can talk about it after the baby is born. She's had a kid—surely she won't expect me to be able to do *everything.*

When the camera crew shows up, I push them through the foyer and up the hallway to the nursery. I don't need them filming the rest of the mess the apartment is in. I'm wearing my usual black uniform of a big, long men's sweater, leggings and my Docs. I have to wear shoes to contain my swollen feet. I even fell asleep with them on last night—the thought of struggling to pull them off was too much. Plus, there's a chance I may never be able to get them on again.

The crew sets up lights and I try to hide the fact that I'm feeling a bit cheated. I assumed there would be hair and makeup people like we have at the studio, but it's just a cameraman, a lighting guy, a sound tech and Rachel, one of the junior producers. She'll be asking me questions off camera that I'm supposed to reply to by repeating the topic of her question so it sounds unprompted. If she asks, "Where did that unusual painting come from?" I would have to say something like, "This unusual painting was a gift from the artist and I think it gives the room a fun, carefree feel." When they cut it together it will be like I'm just talking to the camera, showing the viewers around. That's how they do it on TV.

I was expecting Carla Douglas to do the interview, but I don't know why—she doesn't do much except yell at the staff and leave early. But they could have at least sent a senior producer. How am I to know whether this Rachel person has a clue what she's doing? She keeps asking every five seconds how much longer I'll be, and I keep telling her it'll be a few more minutes. I'm rushing to get my makeup and hair done since I apparently have to do everything myself.

When I'm ready, Rachel speeds me into the nursery and the camera goes on. She says we're running behind—she needs to be at Rita-the-stay-at-home-wife-mommy's place in forty minutes to shoot her at-home segment. But I'm sure it won't really matter if they're a bit late. It's not like Rita has a job to be at.

The questions go smoothly as I show the camera around the room, pointing out cool details and name-dropping the stores and sites I found some of my treasures at. I don't reveal the best ones, of course—I'm not finished decorating and I don't need the public competing with me for the best skull-print organic cotton receiving blankets or a rare, lavishly illustrated edition of a book of Russian folk tales.

Rachel asks me about my birthing plan and whether I'll be employing a nanny. I explain that I'm having a hospital delivery, a scheduled C-section and that I don't believe in hiring help to raise my child. I've started contacting agencies about people to clean and cook, but I leave this part out. Finally, Rachel asks me to talk about what I've learned from my own mother and what I hope my daughter will learn from me.

"My mother taught me— She taught me that I— Can we cut for a second?" I don't know what to say. This is supposed to be about me and my baby—and about decorating, not about Britt. But I am a professional; I can answer any question with grace and uncompromising honesty. "What I've learned from my mother is how *not* to raise a child. Now, this isn't something I mean in a negative way." Kelly reminds me constantly how I should speak my mind, but find ways to do it without sounding like a victim or bitter. I should sound strong and fully invested in my convictions—and *empowered.* I should always sound empowered. "My mother lived her life in the spotlight and consequently I did, too, but that wasn't my choice. I will give my daughter that choice."

Rachel exchanges looks with the crew. The lighting guy rolls his eyes and Rachel lets out a little laugh. The cameraman and boom guy won't look at me. Apparently, I am the only professional in the room.

SWAP

The *Modern Mommy* set is like a Starbucks—literally—except that it's on a soundstage. Starbucks is the show's sponsor and they've got a counter set up in the corner. The women in the audience order Frappuccino and Americanos before sitting at the tables set up on the stage. We have the biggest table, right in the middle, and unlike the others in the room, which are small and round, ours is huge and in the shape of a half-moon. The table faces the studio audience, which is separate from the selected audience that gets to sit up on the stage at the tables. Sometimes I wonder about the people who line up for tickets to these tapings. Who wants to sit in a studio audience to watch a group of women argue while the most attractive women of those who stood in line get to sit onstage and pretend to talk to each other so it looks like we're all gabbing away at a café?

We're the only ones who are mic'd and so the other women on the coffee shop set have to fake-talk. There's a junior producer who briefs them on how to do this before we start the taping. The ones who don't make the cut and are relegated to the cheap seats still get free coffee and a gift bag for coming so they shouldn't feel so bad. Plus, they're the ones who get to cheer and clap at the things they like and groan and boo whenever I talk about my scheduled C-section or having a drink.

On most days there is a smattering of applause for me and a few die-hard fans who cheer like mad when I'm introduced. Kelly says it's like being the bad guy on *Survivor* or one of those other elimination reality shows—there always has to be someone to love to hate. When I think of it that way, it's quite flattering.

After the taping in the morning, we meet with the producers and researchers for a debriefing: what worked, what didn't, that kind of thing. Then we move on to the rundown of the next day's show and discuss possible topics for upcoming shows, which I can't help but notice are often poached from my *Bad Mommy* columns. But today, our biggest concern is putting together the shows for our premiere week. We'll be in the studio to do same-day tapings so we can be current with news events, but we have to tape all of the segments for the *Her Shoes* series the producers are hoping will be what everyone tunes in to watch.

So for four days this week, we each have to spend a few hours in the life of one of our cohosts. We have to go to their house, wear the clothes they have chosen for us and hang out with their kids or their family or friends and do the things they normally do—all while the camera rolls, of course.

Yesterday, I had Pat, the lawyer working-mommy. I had to wear a business suit and go to an office. They didn't let me talk to her clients or anything, which was a bit disappointing— that would have been fun—but I did field about twenty calls from her two nannies and had to go home to check on the kids twice. The children—both girls—are four and six, are clearly little shit disturbers and were feigning illness just to get their "mommy" to come home. I don't know whether Pat forgot to tell them about the *Her Shoes* thing or if they were just being extra bratty for my benefit, but when I showed up at the house to see if they were okay, they started bawling. Then they called me mean when I told them to suck it up and told the older one's nanny to send her back to school. The four-year-old only goes half days, so she could stay home with the two nannies.

The second time I went back to the house was because the little one had shoved a marble up her nose and it wouldn't come out. We had to take her to emergency. It was ridiculous. We watched the edited footage after today's debrief. Everyone but Pat laughed and now she's not talking to me. Rita, the stay-at-home mommy, says it's because I rolled my eyes at her kids a lot, like I thought they were pulling some kind of scam.

"But they were," I said.

"Not exactly," explained Rita. "You have to understand that kids like to push boundaries."

I wasn't that thrilled when I had to watch Maggie, the college student, in my apartment, looking through my stuff and saying things like, "Mason doesn't know how lucky she is" and "Mason's got the cushiest life." My life is not *cushy;* it's hard, just like everyone else's. And I'm doing everything on my own—I don't have a husband, I'm not twenty-three with an elastic body that makes it impossible to believe she actually gave birth. Today, I spend the afternoon as Maggie, so we'll see who's lucky.

Maggie lives in a one-bedroom suite on the lower level of her parents' house with her husband and baby. It's cute and

Maggie's into all that DIY crafty stuff, so her simple crib is collaged with illustrations cut out of old children's books and the dishes are all fifties Pyrex diner-style plates and bowls. Almost every available wall space is filled with pictures of her family in ornate vintage frames she's painted candy colors. Her life seems cozy, not so bad at all.

Her hipster husband, Zeke, stops by and hands off the baby. He's wearing cords and has a beard. He runs down all the things I have to remember: feed her at one, nap until two-thirty, drop her off upstairs with Maggie's mom and be in class by three. Then I have to pick up the ingredients for dinner and get home by five-thirty to cook. Zeke will pick the baby up at five, so I don't need to worry about that. Great. I think I've got it. It's pretty straightforward.

"Oh, and there's one other thing I should tell you," Zeke says. "The baby's had a bit of an upset tummy today, so you might have to change her more than usual."

"Sure—not a problem," I say. Diapers don't scare me.

I change into my "Maggie" outfit: a hippie-dippie paisley skirt and a vintage sweater with deer on it that zips up the front. It makes my body look even more huge than it usually does these days, but it's better than suffering another day in that uncomfortable suit I had to wear to be "Pat." Another bonus of being Maggie is that I get to wear my Docs because she does, too. I make a mental note to thank Maggie for not being a girl who wears heels.

Everything goes along fine for the first while and I almost forget the cameras are filming my every move. Maggie's baby, Francie, is a cute little thing; she smiles and laughs when I pull faces and she barely cries. It's all going just fine until out of nowhere she starts to wail and squirm. She scrunches her tiny face. She looks like she's in pain. I pick up the phone, ready to dial my doctor and ask for emergency advice when the room is suddenly filled with the foulest smell.

I lay Francie on the changing table and open her diaper. She's still crying, but not as bad, and her face is no longer scrunchy and weird. I just about puke when I see what I'm dealing with. This isn't some easy-to-clean pile of baby-poo pellets, it's a full-on diarrhea explosion. How can all of this—*mess*—come from such a little person? And the smell—there is no describing the smell. I take a deep breath and hold it. I work as quickly as possible to remove the stinky diaper and wipe Francie clean. I get the diaper all the way off and fold it over before setting it on the edge of the changing table. I'll figure out how to dispose of it in a minute. First, I need to get the baby cleaned up, but she keeps kicking. She's laughing now; she wants to play. The only way to keep her still is to hold her legs with one hand and wipe her with the other. It takes four moist baby towels to do the job. I put them on top of the dirty diaper. What am I supposed to do with this stuff?

Getting Francie into a clean diaper is a challenge. She's like a worm: she won't stop moving. I finally manage to get it on her. It's not perfect, but it will do. I pick her up and she's all smiles. I bend down to set her on the floor so she can play, but my bulky sweater hits the dirty diaper and wipes and the next thing I know, the diaper lands facedown on my boot.

I scrubbed my boots the best I could and washed the laces in soapy water, but everything still smells of poo. I won't have a chance to deal with this properly until I get back from Maggie's class. She gave me a small tape recorder and asked me to take pictures of the whiteboards with my camera phone. It's a logic class. It might be interesting. I'm a logical person—I'd probably be good at it.

Walking through the campus, I notice the energy and purpose people walk with. Maybe I should go back to school, get a degree in something I'm good at—maybe psychology. I know a lot about people and their strange thoughts about things. And what about this logic class Maggie is taking? She made it sound like it was really hard, but that may be because she's not a *logical* thinker like me.

I'm feeling confident and want an unobstructed view to take pictures, so I take a seat in the front. Kids file in and set up their laptops and notebooks. A couple of the students have to be well into their thirties. I'd fit right in. Minus the exploding diapers, I kind of like Maggie's life.

Maggie could have warned me that logic is some kind of advanced math. She said it was a *philosophy* course, not a math course. I thought it would be all big questions and discussions about life and what's *logical* to do in situations. I wasn't expecting *math*. What does that have to do with philosophy anyway? I don't like Maggie's life anymore and I'm sure not looking forward to stepping into Rita's—it's probably all *Barney* cartoons and housework. Of course, we don't get to be Carla because she's too important. Her kids are teenagers and she's probably scared they'll give up all of her secrets. I don't want to be her anyway, or anyone else—my own life is just fine.

MAKEUP

It's Halloween, and one week before *Modern Mommy* hits the air for its two-week trial run. I saw a print ad for it yesterday and we screened the TV commercials at the studio yesterday. Each *Mommy* gets her own spot—well, her own spot shared with Carla. We shot mine in a grotty coffee spot in the Mission. Carla and I had to act like girlfriends and deliver our lines as if they were something we'd actually say.

Me (to waiter): I'll have a coffee—black.

Carla looks at me with mock disapproval.

Me: What?

Carla: Coffee while you're pregnant? Isn't that against the pregnancy rules?

Me (to camera): In my world, there are no rules.

Then my name appears on screen with the words THE REBEL at an angle in a red font that looks like a rubber stamp.

Cut to Carla, smiling and fake saying, "What kind of mommy are you? Find out this November on *Modern Mommy*."

Watching the commercial made me cringe, but thank-fully I'm not Maggie. She had to do her spot with Carla as she breast-fed her daughter on a chilly fall day in Golden Gate Park while a man stood behind them in creepy clown makeup and juggled balls that said "work," "school," "mar-riage" and "baby." I have no desire to be Maggie Johanssen, THE JUGGLER.

Pat, the lawyer with two nannies, is THE GO-GETTER and Rita, the stay-at-home mom, is THE HOUSEWIFE. Carla Douglas is just Carla, but I think she should be THE DIVA or THE BITCH. As the show's air date nears, she's getting worse.

To promote the show, we're required to make public ap-pearances and get people excited about watching. To that end, we're all attending a Halloween charity benefit party tonight. The party has a Hollywood theme and is at the Top of the Mark at the Mark Hopkins Hotel. The last time I was there I drank martinis with Janet and Seth. My mother was dead but I hadn't slept with Edgar and if someone had told me then that I'd still be in San Francisco seven months later, I would have laughed. If someone had told me then that I'd still be here and be pregnant with my married ex-stepbrother's baby, I would have called them insane. But here I am.

I'd rather not go tonight. Earlier today, the executive pro-ducer's assistant sent around an e-mail outlining our responsi-bilities. It said that we must arrive as a group and be prepared for photo ops and when talking to the press we must mention the name of the show, the network, date and time slot when-ever possible. We also must treat the event as though it were an official meet-and-greet, circulating and speaking with as many people as possible. And here's the worst part: we must come in costume, no exceptions.

I don't do costumes—I never have, except maybe when I

was five or something. And a *Hollywood* theme? It couldn't be worse. Kelly is coming over to help, but as far as I can tell, it's futile. I can either go as a pregnant movie star or film character or as a fat female actor and everyone knows there aren't many of those. Kelly suggested I get a bunch of Cabbage Patch Kids and attach them to me in various ways and say I'm Angelina Jolie. But as much as I love Angelina and think we'd be great friends, I don't think anyone will buy it.

"You don't think it's too much?" I ask Kelly. She's dressed as comedienne Margaret Cho, which is likely to be considered subversive by the crowd at this event. For a city famous for its radical thinkers and its counterculture, the charity circuit in San Francisco society can be a very stuffy, conservative scene, so I'm not sure about this costume Kelly has found for me.

"No way—it's great. You're supposed to be *The Rebel,* right?"

"Shut up." I hate *The Rebel* label almost as much as I hate costumes.

"You can't just go as someone boring—this is perfect."

"I don't know—" I turn to one side and then the other. The dress Kelly brought is sequined and spectacular—it's perfect— and it's very stretchy so it fits. She's also brought a wig and done my makeup. I have blue and green eye shadow up to my brows, false lashes and a ton of blush. My lips are outlined in black and filled in red.

"Do you have any better ideas?" Kelly asks.

I don't. And it's getting late—I am scheduled to meet the show's publicist, the other *Mommies* and Carla in a half hour. It would take me that long to wash the heavy makeup off. I let out a deep breath and take a sip of the wine Kelly has in her hand. The alcohol burns down my throat. It's an almost-unfamiliar sensation—I haven't had a drink in months. I haven't wanted to, but none of the *Barbarella* readers know that; they probably think I'm out getting pissed every night like a good *Bad Mommy* should. One of the *Modern Mommy* producers called me earlier today to discuss what she called a "delicate situation." Basically, they don't want me to drink tonight or be "under the influence of narcotics." TV people don't like their bad mommies to be *too* bad.

In the taxi, I pop a piece of gum into my mouth. The driver drops Kelly off in front of the Mark Hopkins. "See ya in a bit," she says. "You're going to blow their minds."

"Thanks," I say. The driver pulls out of the Mark Hopkins and cruises across the street to the Fairmont Hotel, where I'm meeting the *Modern Mommy* people. They've arranged for a limo to meet us there and drive us across the street to the Mark Hopkins. It's all a bit ridiculous, but that's the business and frankly, I'm grateful for any minutes I can spend off my feet. Kelly brought a pair of royal blue satin stilettos for me to wear, but there was no way. I'm wearing flats and if anyone wants to make a thing of it, they can go right ahead.

All of the women are there when I arrive except Maggie. Carla huffs as she paces back and forth in the lobby, and looks at her watch every time she turns to change direction. She stops dead when she sees me. "Good God, Mason," she says.

The others stare at me. "Who—" says Pat.

"What—" says Rita.

"You're Divine!" It's Maggie. Everyone was so stunned by my costume that nobody noticed her walk into the lobby.

"I don't know if *divine* is quite the right word, Maggie," says Carla.

"Nooo, not 'she looks divine,' she *is* Divine. As in the drag queen," says Maggie. The other women look perplexed, but Maggie is excited. "The one in all those John Waters movies!"

I have to give her some points—she did know who I was, plus she seems to know John Waters made Divine a star—and she seems to like the costume.

"Oh. My. God." I turn around to find Xavier, our very gay publicist. "You, Mason McDonald, have balls—turning up here, dressed like that. I love it! The press won't know *what* to do with you. Everybody ready?"

I'm not, but I nod anyway. I can handle this, I tell myself. I'm used to people not knowing what to do with me. It's just that usually I'm sitting behind a computer or in front of a camera, I'm not live-and-in-person and I'm definitely not dressed like a dead drag queen.

The party people seem frightened, but intrigued. As I make my way through the crowd, people point and laugh. Some say hello and a surprising number of them know who I'm supposed to be.

I find Kelly at the dessert table munching on a chocolate hazelnut tartlet and talking to someone dressed as John Waters, complete with black suit and pencil mustache. It's Seth. Seth? It takes a moment for it to register that there is something wrong with this picture. I'm not talking to Seth and Seth's not talking to me, but he's talking to Kelly, who I didn't know he knew.

"Hey, Mason," says Kelly. "You have to try one of these."

"They're *divine*," adds Seth. His voice is quiet and tentative. He smiles at me and I smile back. He hands me a tartlet. "How are you?"

"Good—really good," I say. "You?"

"All right. I got a gig scouting locations on a new film—it's only for the B-roll stuff, but still."

"That's great," I say. I've missed him.

"I've been reading your column."

"Yeah?"

"It's pretty funny—you sure are good at pissing people off."

"What can I say? It's a gift," I say jokingly, but Seth is distracted. His smile has disappeared and he's waving to someone. I turn my head to see whom, but then I wish I hadn't. It's Janet and she's walking quickly toward us. Her expression is stern. Victor is trailing behind. She comes straight up to me and I almost duck in fear that she'll start yelling. But instead she hugs me.

"Where have you been? Why haven't you returned my calls? I've been worried sick," she says.

"Sorry," I say. I haven't returned her calls, it's true, but she should know better than anyone that I'm terrible for that. I've wanted to call, but every time I'd psych myself up to do it, I'd chicken out. I didn't know what to say.

"We need to talk," she says. She's acting weird—nervous and cagey. She keeps looking around like she's scared. She takes my elbow and marches me away, leaving Seth and Kelly and Victor behind.

I'm so big and the room is so packed and Janet is walking so fast, dragging me behind her that inevitably, I bump into countless people on our way to who-knows-where. One man splashes his drink on his date as we storm by. He curses at me, but stops when he sees I'm pregnant. By the time we arrive at the ladies' room I'm out of breath.

"You need to get out of here," Janet says.

"What?"

"You need to go—I can drive you."

"What is going on?"

"They're here."

"Who?"

"Aaron and Edgar—and Edgar's wife."

"Oh." I lower myself onto the velvet-covered bench in the sitting area. It hadn't occurred to me that they might be here, or that Seth and Janet would be, either.

"You don't want to make a scene," Janet says.

"It's all been settled," I say. Aaron sent me a shitty e-mail, Edgar paid me, Candice is stupid for staying with him.

"Mason, these kinds of things are never settled."

"So I'm supposed to avoid them for the rest of my life?"

"Yes, you should."

"I have as much of a right to be here as they do."

"I know, but that's not what I'm saying."

"Then what *are* you saying?" I ask.

"Are you sure you want to make more of a spectacle of yourself than you already have?" I don't think she's talking about my costume. "I've read your column. I've seen those TV commercials—what the hell is going on with you?"

"Nothing. I'm fine," I say.

"I'm not so sure about that. You seem like you're, I don't know, doing all the things you swore you never would."

"Like what?"

"It just seems—"

"Spit it out, Janet." Her good manners and concern are grating.

"It's like you've turned into your mother."

I don't think, I don't speak. I just slap Janet—hard—once, across the face, before walking out of the washroom and through to the elevator that will take me to the lobby. I don't start to cry until I'm in a taxi, speeding toward home.

LIVE

Daytime parties don't seem authentic, but here we are in the studio, at 8 a.m., waiting for *Modern Mommy* to go live for the first time. We taped the audience portion of the show at six, giving the editors a chance to make any necessary tweaks or changes and get it up on the satellite, ready to air on the East Coast at eleven. Big screens have been rigged up all around us and there are waiters in tuxedos handing out complimentary champagne to production executives in suits. One of the screens shows the *Modern Mommy* website forum, so we can watch the comments about the show as they pop up in real time.

The Internet thing seems a bit lame. How many comments are they expecting? And do people really feel the need to respond to what they're watching on television second-by-second?

Kelly is my date. She's as excited as I would be if I could break through the wall of lethargy I've been slammed up against the past few days. I'm drained all day and at night I can't sleep enough. I wish I could drift into a deep slumber, like a hibernating bear, and be woken only when it's time to go to the hospital and have my baby. It's not a very practical dream, but it's a wonderful fantasy.

Carla makes a brief speech about how much the *Modern Mommy* experience has meant to her so far, and what great friends we've all become. "We may have different lives, different opinions, but we're bonded forever as colleagues, women, and most of all...mothers."

"Is she actually crying?" I whisper to Kelly.

"I think so."

The whole room is applauding. Carla should have been an actress, not a broadcaster. Xavier, the show's publicist, leads us in a countdown from ten. Flashes go off. Reporters make notes. "Three! Two! One!" Everyone is silent as the *Modern Mommy* theme song kicks in. It's an old top-forty song that I think is by Jewel.

One by one our faces pop up on the big screens, along with our assigned monikers. The crowd of suits cheer for each of us, and then we all settle into our seats to watch the broadcast.

At the end of the hour, the applause is decidedly less enthusiastic. I want to slink out of the studio, hide in a hovel, dye my hair back to black and change my name.

"It wasn't *that* bad," Kelly says. "The show just needs to be a bit more cohesive, find its audience."

"They *hated* me," I say, sinking farther into my seat.

"Not just you. And you're the easiest target. Don't let this get you down, Mason—it's only the first show."

"You saw the things people were saying." Apparently, people do feel the need to respond online to what they're watching on television second by second, with comments like: "What a disgusting woman," "She should be arrested," and "Mason McDonald is a retarded whore—just like her mother."

"Since when do you care what people say or think about you? There has been much worse on the *Barbarella* forums. Come on, it's fun—it's part of the game."

I'm not sure if this is a game I want to play anymore. "But this is TV," I say. My column is different. It has my name on it, but I could be anyone. I write in this bubble, and sure, people read it and say things, but somehow it doesn't seem real, not like this.

"Look at it this way—you're getting way more attention than the others, even more than Carla. *You're* the one they'll remember. They'll watch again tomorrow just to get riled up. People love to be outraged. *You're* the star. Don't back down now—if anything, amp it up, give them something to really talk about."

Kelly's right. I need to embrace my position. Isn't it better to get a negative reaction than no reaction at all? And I have all of the other *progressive* mommies out there to represent. Don't they deserve a voice?

The producers call an emergency meeting of all the *Modern Mommies*. There will be big changes to tomorrow's show; namely we each have to present a "news you can use" item. Before the emergency meeting, the producers held an emergency focus group. They determined that women want two things from a show like this: to identify with one of the co-hosts and to get a little useful tip, something that makes them believe the last hour they've spent watching wasn't a waste of their time. That's *the takeaway*, explains one of the producers. I'm assigned to work with Rachel, the junior producer, to come up with four *takeaway* ideas, one for each of the remaining shows this week.

Rachel doesn't laugh when I suggest fried chicken, cheeseburgers, tacos and a Japanese bento box as my contributions to the show. "Fried chicken—takeaway. Get it?"

"I get it," Rachel says in a flat voice. These TV people have no sense of humor. "Now, what were you thinking, Mason? Any useful tips?" She says this like it's an impossible idea that I might have any wisdom to impart.

"What about something about clothes?" I suggest.

"What about clothes?"

"I don't know—maybe something about alternative baby clothes?"

"Like what?"

"I bought some really cute baby shirts with skulls on them."

Rachel makes a face. "That's so old. We need things people don't know about already."

"Oh." How can skull baby shirts be old? I'd never seen them before. I rack my brain for ideas, but come up blank. It's hard to think under this kind of pressure and everyone knows that your mind isn't as sharp when you're pregnant.

"Let's look at this another way—what have you learned during your pregnancy?"

Mostly I've learned that people are really uptight, but I know that's not the kind of thing Rachel is looking for. She needs practical information. "That having a baby is really expensive?" I say tentatively.

"Okay—good. We could do a 'baby-on-budget' theme—we need four penny-pinching tips."

I don't know what to say. Once I had my inheritance check, I didn't pay much attention to price tags. But there was one thing. "I altered some vintage maternity dresses my mother kept and dyed them black."

"We can use that—a how-to segment. What else? We need three more."

"Can I think about it and e-mail you a list of ideas later?" I look at my watch. "I have to be at the doctor in twenty minutes." I don't, but no one—not even Rachel—is going to ask a pregnant woman to miss a doctor's appointment.

"Fine. But I'll need them tonight. Oh—and you're going to need to wear one of those dresses for tomorrow's show. I'll write up the segment and send it to you for changes."

"Sure, okay," I say. I have to go home. I need to find a dress that fits that I can alter and get to work on these ideas. It can't possibly be that hard.

I go through my mother's closet for the third time—it's the only part of the flat that hasn't yet been boxed up and stripped of any evidence that she once lived here. I don't know why I've put it off for so long—they're only clothes.

I start pulling hangers off the metal rods. I should make piles: clothes to keep and clothes to give away or sell. I spy a pink goddessy floor-length dress with marabou trim and drape it over a chair. This will be the get-rid-of pile, I decide, but almost immediately change my mind. The dress is so camp and over-the-top; maybe I could use it for a costume; maybe my daughter would like to have it. She'll need dress-up clothes.

After an hour, I realize I have no giveaway pile—just a lot of dresses piled high on a chair. I haven't even touched the drawers and boxes yet. And I still haven't found something I can wear tomorrow.

I'm hoping I'll have better luck with the boxes. I grab two off the high shelf that runs all the way around the giant closet, above the racks of dresses—they're heavier than I thought they'd be and I almost lose my balance and fall off the short stepladder. There—that's something I've learned during pregnancy: your balance is screwed up. It's true, but it's probably not news-anyone-can-use, so I'll have to keep thinking.

The first two boxes are filled with antique bedding my mother must have collected during her "French country" decorating phase. I'm extra careful as I bring down more boxes and only lift them one at a time. I go through six more and find sweaters, handbags and the most wonderful vintage silk scarves—but nothing that helps me for tomorrow's taping.

I sift through boxes of accessories and old mail-order catalogs I'm not sure why she kept. I find costume jewelry and a handful of porno tapes on Betamax. I'm hoping there are no sex toys in the next box when I open the lid. *Oh my God*. I can't believe what I'm seeing.

My mother not only saved her dresses, but mine, as well. About a week before my birthday every year, we'd go shopping and I'd pick out a dress. There are more dresses in the next box. Twelve in total, one for every year we did it—I stopped wanting birthday dresses when I turned thirteen. I hold each one up and examine it. It's a nice tradition. I think I'll do that with my little girl.

When I pick the last dress up out of the box I notice a scrapbook. It's one of those old paper kinds with blank newsprint pages and a photograph of flowers on the cover. Inside, my mother pasted all of the columns she wrote while she was pregnant with me. I skim a few and am surprised to find myself smiling and laughing at some of the passages. They're light and quite funny and she actually gives some decent advice.

This is what I could talk about on the show, I decide. I could do something on advice being passed down from generation to generation. It's not exactly radical, but it could work, I think, and the idea of trying to come up with something that will shock and outrage people is too exhausting. I have to e-mail Rachel and let her know the vintage dress segment won't work.

Everyone loves my idea and I think Carla and the other *Mommies* are jealous. One of the producers said it was "sentimental, but edgy." They're calling it *alt.mom*. I wonder what people have to study in college to come up with these names.

I'm sitting alone at a table on the Starbucks café set, leafing through my mother's scrapbook. On the floor director's cue, I look up at the camera, like I didn't know it was there, and read a short excerpt from one of my mother's columns. I wanted to do the one about not buying expensive new shoes while you're pregnant because your feet are probably swollen and the shoes won't fit the same after the baby is born. I wish I had read this before I bought those shoes at Nordstrom. But the producers wanted a more personal topic and, after looking through my mother's columns, I chose the one about losing friends.

So I read the passage about my mother and her friend, Rose, and how their relationship was impacted by my mother having a baby. I remember Rose but never knew any of this. It makes me think of Janet and Seth and that afternoon I spent with D.D. I talk about feeling judged and hurt and I forget about the script and ramble on until the floor director is waving her arms wildly in an effort to get me to stop. I do, when I feel the tears coming on.

I compose myself during the commercial break and join the other *Mommies* at the big table. They all congratulate me—even Carla—and though I'm heavy and sweaty under the lights, I feel lighter than I have in months.

After the show, we gather around Rachel's computer to see the reaction of the East Coast viewers. It's better than yesterday, but not much. I'm confident that my segment will change that.

I'm nervous as I watch the online comments roll in as the segment airs. The first few are negative, but there are always going to be those people who hate everything, I tell myself. But they just keep coming, each one worse than the one before it, many of them bordering on cruel. "Mason McDonald doesn't deserve friends," "I wouldn't want to be her friend, either," "Some women should be sterilized." It doesn't get any better. They hate it—they hate me.

I'm not sad and I don't want to cry, but I'm angry as I sit through the postshow meeting. Then I have to endure a painful session with Rachel, trying to script another segment that everyone will undoubtedly despise. I just agree with everything Rachel says and it's over quickly. I'm too distracted by my anger to really care what she puts in the script. I'll say whatever she wants. I skulk off to the green room to lie down before heading home for the day. I try out one of the visualization exercises I learned at The Window seminar, but I can't shake thoughts of maiming and torturing every single person who has nothing better to do than make brutal, anonymous comments about me on the Internet.

My mind fights with itself: as much as I try to visualize only positive, wonderful things, all I can see is faceless people calling me names while I gun them down with a semiautomatic.

My revenge fantasy is interrupted by an announcement on the speaker system that there's a meeting on the set—all talent and crew are to report there immediately. It's another emergency meeting. What are they going to get us to do or change this time? I wonder.

We are asked to sit in the first rows of the studio audience seats. Carla Douglas stands beside the executive producer. She's crying and this time I think they're real tears. I brace myself for the latest focus group news, but it doesn't come. There will be no changes to the show. There will be no show at all: we've been yanked off the air after only two episodes; *Modern Mommy* has been canceled.

GUEST

I've told everyone I'm away, that I've gone back to Canada to get my things. I sent an e-mail the day we got canceled—to Kelly, to the renovation guys who were thankfully almost done, to my doctor, to Seth and even to Janet. I didn't mean to hit her that night at the Mark Hopkins, but I'm quite sure she meant what she said. The door buzzer goes and the phone rings, but I don't answer. When I need food, I wait until dark and slip down to the corner store two blocks up. I don't want to go to the one that's actually around the corner just in case of—I don't know what.

It's been two weeks since the *Modern Mommy* disaster and I still don't want to speak to or see anyone. I won't turn on the TV or check my e-mail, or even go online at all. I'm afraid I'll see something: the story of me slapping my best friend, gossip about the show's cancellation, more trash talk about me on thousands of blogs. I want to be left alone with my baby. She's moving around constantly, but who can blame her? It must be tough to find a comfortable position in there.

I've packed up my mother's clothes and moved my own into the walk-in closet. Before Halloween, my new bed arrived and one of the renovation guys took away my old one. He said it was in really good shape and he would pay me a hundred bucks for it. I let him have it for free.

I want to be alone and memorize the breathing techniques outlined in the one pregnancy book I have—the practical one that Kelly said was the only one I'd need. I'm starting to wonder if she was right about that, or if I should be reading something, doing something, fixing any damage I may have already done. The drinks and the occasional cigarettes, it was never that much but the book says that most of the defects and bad things develop in a baby in the first weeks after conception when barely anybody even knows they're pregnant.

I alternate between sitting in my sleek, European rocking chair, which doesn't look a thing like a rocking chair but a piece of abstract sculpture, and my wonderful new bed. Without television or the Internet, I listen to my old records and cassettes. I read my old journals and wonder what it will be like when my girl is a teenager, whether she'll be grumpy, moody and miserable—another me—or one of those happy, helpful, cheerful kids like the ones you see on TV. I think I'd prefer another me.

I skim the spines of all the books in the apartment, checking out the authors, looking for ideas for names. I start a list, but keep crossing out anything I've written down—none seem quite right. I want a classic name, not a hippie name like Rainbow or Solstice. I don't want something made-up or strangely spelled. I know what I don't want, but have no idea what I do.

I'm almost through another stack of books filled with names I don't like when I hear a noise at the front door. I turn the music off and listen, still and scared in my new bed. Sure enough, there's the sound of the door clicking shut and the sound of a shoe dropping onto the foyer tiles—and then another. I wasn't aware that intruders took their shoes off before robbing a place or raping someone. God, no one would want to rape a pregnant woman, would they?

My heart beats faster. This is it; this is how it ends, with me raped and murdered, the crime the focus of a future TV newsmagazine special. I wrap my arms around my belly—the baby is moving, having a great time, oblivious to the danger. I squint, hoping to catch something—movement or a shadow—but the lights in the hallway are off. It's pitch-black. I can't see out but he can see in. I hear footsteps and my breath stops. I have to remind myself to take air in and let it out again. It sounds so loud, I'm sure he can hear me. I close my eyes and pray. I'm not sure I believe in God, but it certainly can't hurt. The footsteps get closer. I shut my eyes tighter. He's here, I can feel his presence, he's watching, he's—

"Mason! My God, you gave me a start—I was sure there was no one here." I open my eyes and see Ron standing in the doorway of the bedroom, clutching his chest. He's tanned from his Hawaiian vacation. He looks healthy and relaxed.

"Ron! I thought you were—never mind."

He walks over and sits on the edge of the bed. He sets down a small, gift-wrapped package and rests a hand on my belly. "She's really moving in there," he says.

"Tell me about it."

"I heard you were out of town, so I thought I'd come by and drop off this package your friend Janet gave to me this afternoon. She rang me up several times and left messages while I was away—she's very concerned about you. She said you'd taken off to Canada and that no one has heard from you."

"I needed some space," I say.

"It's okay," Ron says. "Oh, she asked me to leave this here for you, but since you're alive and well and in San Francisco, here you go." He hands me the gift-wrapped package.

There's a note. It reads:

Wherever your life takes you, whatever you choose to do, please remember that I'm always with you, and the baby, too.

If the fashion thing doesn't work out, Janet could get a job writing for Hallmark. Underneath her little rhyme, she's written, "For baby girl McDonald. Love, Auntie Janet." I unwrap the gift and find a velvet box. Inside is a perfect strand of pearls.

Ron won't leave. He's brought over a bunch of his things and he's sleeping on the sofa. He cooks proper meals for me and helps me practice my breathing for labor. He rents old movies for me to watch and doesn't answer the phone or the door. He wants to stay with me through Christmas, until the baby comes and for a couple weeks after. He says I'll need the help and I'm afraid he could be right. He doesn't ask me what I'm going to do with my life now that *Modern Mommy* is canceled and a joke and I've probably burned any bridges I'd built with Kelly and the magazine.

I flinch when I think of Kelly, so I try not to. I try not to think about Seth or Edgar or Aaron or that awful party, either. I think about Janet every time I look at the velvet box with the perfect pearls that's sitting on my bedside table. There have been a few times I've come close to calling, but couldn't finish dialing. What do you say to someone whom you've slapped and ignored, but who still sends you presents and makes up corny rhymes?

I try to concentrate exclusively on old movies and preparing for the baby. When something else creeps into my head—a twinge, a flashback to the Halloween party, to fucking Edgar, to the way things ended with Aaron—I turn up Katharine Hepburn or Joan Crawford's voice or go over my labor positions for the umpteenth time. Having a scheduled C-section does not eliminate the labor process, according to my doctor. I'll be getting an epidural; there will still be pain.

"I'm thinking about naming her Brittany," I say.

"Really?" asks Ron.

"You don't like it?"

"No, it's lovely—I'm just surprised." He takes a bite of the Brie-stuffed chicken breasts he's prepared for tonight's non-Christmas, Christmas dinner. I don't feel much like celebrating anything, but Ron is a very good cook.

"My mother was just plain 'Britt,' not 'Brittany,' so it's not the same," I say. I don't want him getting any funny ideas.

"It's lovely, Mason. It's a pretty name."

I like Brittany. It's just a nice name—pretty, like Ron says. I wonder what she'll look like, if she'll look at all like me or like Edgar, if she'll be tall like him or more short and round like me. She'll have blue eyes, I'll bet, since both Edgar and I do. The baby—Brittany—kicks hard and low. I gasp and double over. It's never felt like that before.

"Are you okay, Mason?" Ron asks.

The sharp pain fades, and slowly, I sit up again. "I'm fine—she's just acting out."

"Probably getting restless."

"Two more weeks to go," I say.

We continue our meal and Ron tells me stories about my mother that make it hard not to miss her. I wish she'd been more like she was with Ron with me. He makes her sound fun—and funny—and generous and loving. It's hard for me to believe she was the same person I knew.

"Ow! Fuck!" It's that low, sharp pain again. I grit my teeth until it subsides. I take another bite of chicken before I realize I'm sitting in a warm puddle. I stand up and look at the chair—it's wet. I touch the back of my big black dress—it's wet. I know what it is, but it can't be. It's too early, I'm not ready. Ron is already up, scurrying around, collecting things. I stand stunned and wet beside the kitchen table.

"Where's the number for your doctor?' Ron asks.

"Her card is in my wallet in my purse."

"I'll get it," Ron says.

"Agh!" The pain strikes again. I hang on to the back of the chair and bend forward, trying to exhale as much air as I can. I need to get out of these clothes.

Between contractions I change into another loose dress. I sit on the toilet to pee and feel something coming out of my body, something big. I'm opening up. I stand up as quickly as I can—the baby is coming! I can't have her drop headfirst into the toilet. But it's too late, it's coming out, it's coming! I scream for Ron, but he can't get into the room—I've locked the door. "Get a bobby pin from beside my bed!" I yell. I'm terrified. The cramps keep coming, faster now, and then: plop. Something falls out of me and splashes into the toilet bowl. I look down. Ew. That's not a baby. I don't know *what* that is. I look closer. I think it's a "mucous plug." I read about them in my book, but there wasn't a picture—that thing is gross, I can't believe it came out of me. I flush it down just as another contraction comes on. I open the door and it hits Ron in the head—he's been trying to jimmy the lock. "Ouch!" he says.

"I'm so, so sorry." I am, but we need to get to the hospital.

★ ★ ★

My doctor comes into my room. She's calm and smiling. She snaps on a pair of vinyl gloves. "Let's see what we've got here," she says as she lowers her head between my legs. The nurses wait for instruction. There's an anesthesiologist here waiting for the go-ahead to stick me with an epidural and stop this fucking pain. Ron is holding my hand. He tells me I can squeeze as hard as I want and I do.

"It's crowning," my doctor says. "Forget the C-section. No time for an epidural—it's coming fast."

I want my drugs.

"Okay, Mason, I'm going to start asking you to push. But I don't want you to until I say so and stop when I tell you. Push—now."

I bear down and push. The sound that comes out of my mouth is more a growl than a scream.

"All right, stop," says my doctor.

I want my drugs. I want my New Year's Baby.

"Good—you're doing great. Now, again—push…and stop. One more time and I think we'll have it. Come on, Mason, push—one more time—push really hard."

This time I scream and so does the baby. The doctor holds her up for me to see while the nurses gather round, towels and blankets ready.

"It's a boy!" one of them says.

I wipe my eyes. I must have been crying through the pain. I don't remember. Nothing seems real. I look at my baby, all covered in red goo. She's right—that's a penis. It's a boy.

CEREMONY

"What if he's not warm enough?"

"Look at him, Mason. He's got his sleepers, his fleece, his blanket—he's fine," Ron says.

I peer into the stroller. He looks so *small*. Ron's right—he's got plenty of layers and the only part of him that's visible is his big round face. It's December 31, but according to the weather channel, it's not very cold out. Maybe he's too *warm*.

"If he gets too hot, how will I know?"

"He'll let us know, Mason. Now, relax, we're only going across the Bay."

I haven't taken him out yet—not very far, anyhow. He's been home for two weeks, but this is the first time I'll have taken him farther than the corner store and even that was terrifying—those snuggly sling things aren't that comfortable and I was scared the whole time that he'd fall out. The stroller seems like a better idea—more sturdy.

I double- and triple-check that the wheel brakes work. We're going on the ferry—I don't need him rolling off into the water if I lose control of the stroller. I don't know why I would lose control of the stroller, but it could happen.

Thankfully, many of the clothes I bought for "Brittany" were in solid colors that aren't gender specific, like red and green and black and white, so Brett isn't dressed like a girl. The nursery is still hot pink, though. Ron said he'd paint it for me, but I'm afraid that the fumes could cause brain damage. So it's pink, at least for now. I can't believe I yelled at my doctor like that after he was born. He was supposed to be a girl. She was a girl—how could my doctor have failed to tell me she was really a boy? When I had an ultrasound, the technician said it *looked* like a girl but she couldn't be sure because of the position the baby was in when we did the test. If it *looked* like a girl, it had to be a girl. What else could it be?

I have a baby boy. He pees on me when I change his diaper and the other day Ron had to stop me from calling 911 when I discovered that the baby's balls had disappeared up inside him. Ron said this is normal, but it looked anything but.

I don't know what to do with a boy. He can't really play or do much of anything yet, and I'm not sure who he is. Sometimes he'll just stare at me like he knows everything I've ever done or said, all my secrets and the things I wish never happened. Ron says he's an old soul. I think that maybe there's something wrong with Brett's eyes even though they were checked and the doctor says he's healthy, fine in every way. Brett could be playing mind games with me. Men are like that but I didn't know they could start so young.

He likes to be tickled and it's funny to watch him squirm and squeal. We sit in my bed and watch old movies together. Well, I watch and he falls asleep or cries halfway through, hungry or wet. He's not what I expected, but I can't shake the feeling that I'm exactly who he was waiting for. It freaks me out and makes me want to smoke, though so far I've resisted the urge.

I sit in the backseat of Ron's car with Brett. He hasn't been in a car since I brought him home from the hospital. I was shocked that they discharged me the next morning. He was three weeks early—shouldn't there be tests? Shouldn't he be hooked up to a machine that helps him breathe? But, no, he's healthy and totally fine. "He was just impatient," was the explanation I got from my doctor, which isn't much of an explanation at all.

In Sausalito, Ron and I stand at the spot overlooking the Bay where we scattered my mother's ashes. I take Brett out of his stroller and hold him against my chest, his head resting on my shoulder. The wind is strong and it looks like it might storm later. We don't talk; we just stand with our backs to the wind, watching the birds, waiting for someone who's not going to come.

We walk away from the pier and to a café. There's a line of empty strollers outside. I line mine up and brace myself for the scene inside. There are moms, dads, kids, babies—the noise assaults me as soon as we walk in. I cover Brett's ears; I don't want him to cry. But he's curious, no longer sleepy. The way he looks at other babies is weirder than the way he looks at me. It's as though he recognizes them. There's this unspoken acknowledgment that's hard to explain—they know their own kind.

"See, it's not so bad," Ron says. He's going back to his apartment in a couple of days and I think he wants to make sure I don't turn into some sort of shut-in, too scared to take my baby outside.

"I guess," I say. I want to relax, but the crying and the

shrieking and the kids running between tables is too much. I need to smoke. I want to drink.

Ron scans the room. "Not really your scene, huh?"

I shake my head. "Not really."

"Let's go then—we'll find somewhere else. What about that little place your mother was always on about—that sushi place."

"In the Japantown Mall—on the annex side."

"That's the one," Ron says, then suddenly looks sad. "We never did get there together." He claps his hands together once and a smile returns to his face. "Let's do it then."

"But what about Brett?"

"Kids *are* allowed in most places, Mason."

Brett throws up on me in the restaurant just as our food arrives. My appetite is gone and so, I think, is Ron's. He politely asks the waiter if he could pack the sushi up for takeout—and bring me a cloth. I know I have one somewhere in this diaper bag, along with every other baby necessity and accessory imaginable. I spent Christmas Day shopping online, but I still can't bear the thought of checking my e-mail. I think I might cancel my account and make a whole new address so everything waiting for me in the old one will simply disappear.

People rush past us as we make our way back to Ron's car. It's late in the afternoon and everyone is putting the last touches on their New Year's Eve plans. New Year's parties are always a letdown—not that I was planning to go to one. Ron bought a bottle of champagne so we'll stay in and drink that and watch teen pop stars on TV lip-synch their hits in Times Square.

Some of these rushing people may well be rushing to Janet's wedding. I wrote her a letter after I got the pearls but it's in my purse, somewhere at the bottom, waiting for a stamp I haven't bought. I wonder what her dress looks like and who's there. My voice mail box is long maxed out so she couldn't leave a message even if she wanted to. Ron says I need to start answering the phone and the door again, get into a routine.

The church Janet's wedding is at isn't far from here. "I think I'll meet you back at the apartment," I say. "I'm going to take Brett for a walk before it rains."

"That sounds like a great idea, Mason. You have your phone?"

I nod.

"Good. Call if you need me to pick you up."

I push the stroller up a short hill and down another. Forget breast-feeding, all a woman has to do to lose her baby weight is walk around San Francisco. It's exhausting. I think I'll buy a car.

I stop about half a block from the church. People are filing in. There are lots of women in hats. A black Town Car pulls up in front and I watch as Seth helps Janet out of the backseat. Even from here I can see that her dress is gorgeous: it's long and slim like her, with tiny straps. She looks like a forties movie star. I watch her walk up the steps with Seth at her side and her mother behind her and vanish into the church.

I start pushing the stroller toward the church. I should be there. I wait for the light to change at the corner directly across the street. A young woman also pushing a stroller pulls up beside me. "How old is he?"

It takes me a moment to realize what she's talking about. "Two weeks," I say.

"Oh, just a little guy! Mine's eighteen months," she says. Christ, woman, just say *a year and a half.*

"That's great," I say and force a smile. When is this god-damn light going to change?

"Wait a minute—do I know you from somewhere? Have we met before?"

I study her face. "I don't think so."

"I know," she says, her eyes narrowing. "You're *that woman*."

"What woman?" I ask. The light changes. The woman with the stroller cuts ahead of me.

"I feel sorry for your child," she says as she passes me.

I open my mouth, but nothing comes out. Who the hell does this bitch think she is? I speed up my pace and then we're neck and neck. "Fuck you," I say and break into a jog. I need to get in the church before the ceremony starts.

When we reach the steps an usher in a black tuxedo lifts the stroller to the top while I run up with Brett in my arms. I leave the stroller where it is and dash inside. Who would have the nerve to steal a baby stroller from the entrance of a church?

I squeeze into a pew at the back just in time to see Janet appear at the head of the aisle, her arm linked through Seth's. Brett makes a gurgling noise and I'm afraid he's going to puke again, but he doesn't. Janet and Seth both turn toward me, a look of shock on their faces. Janet mouths "Oh my God" and blows me a kiss. The wedding march starts and Janet is gone, moving slowly up the aisle to join Victor. From here he doesn't look as old and gross as he usually does. Maybe he's had some work.

Brett starts bawling the second the priest starts to speak. Everyone turns to look. I am mortified, one of *those* people: the ones I used to think were bad parents because they couldn't control their kids in public. Now I know that a baby will cry when it cries. But it's not right to let him wail through Janet's ceremony—that's something my mother would do. I find the thought of her sitting in a church, holding me as baby and letting me cry at her friend's wedding strangely comforting, and a little smile creeps onto my face. She really didn't care what anyone thought. But I'm not her. I scoop Brett and my giant diaper bag up and dart into the hallway. I follow the signs that lead to the washroom. There, I run a bottle filled with formula under hot water until it's lukewarm. I stick the plastic nipple in Brett's mouth and he's happy.

I can't bring myself to go back inside. Everyone will stare. This is Janet's day, not mine. But I *will* call her or buy a stamp for that letter.

I push Brett along the downtown streets. It takes forever before we hit North Beach. I stop at the corner store to buy stamps, but walk out with stamps, potato chips, red licorice and a pack of Marlboro Lights. And as I turn up our street, Madonna's "Like a Prayer" pops into my head out of nowhere—maybe it has something to do with having just been in a church. I take my phone out of my jacket pocket and smile, quietly humming along to the song in my head. I dial Kelly's number. I wonder if she'd let me write for her again? There's so much to say.

★ ★ ★ ★ ★

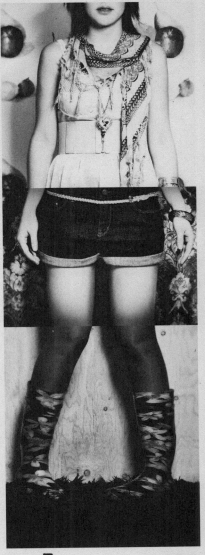

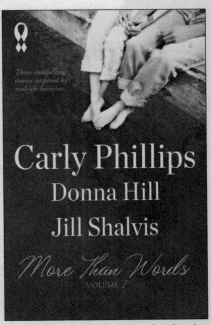